SOUND OF A DISTANT HORN

Sound of a Distant Horn

by SVEN STOLPE
translated by George Lamb

SHEED & WARD-NEW YORK

Sound of a Distant Horn was originally published in Sweden under the title *Lätt, snabb och öm.*

CONTENTS

SOUND OF A DISTANT HORN

PART ONE

All-in Wrestling

CHAPTER ONE

The creaking of the revolving door always got on his nerves: it usually made him jump. But today he hardly heard it. As he entered, there came from the bar wave upon wave of shouting and laughter, and on the right, in front of the desk where Madame was showing off her massive, silk-sheathed breasts, a wild scene met his gaze: arms were swinging, bodies lunging hither and thither, and in the midst of them a shapeless something seemed to move.

Nobody had noticed him, and he had to touch the thick arm of the blonde barmaid—who as usual had only two buttons on her blouse instead of three—before he could get his double Fernet Branca and whisky. He felt giddy and light in the head and his nerves throbbed. Almost before he had clambered up on to the bar-stool he had gulped down half his drink. His face contorted, and tears came into his eyes. A smell of human flesh and sweat assailed him, and he heard the other barmaid—the one who was supposed to have done away with her baby—say in her hoarse voice,

"Sharp, eh? Just like medicine!"

He could barely shake his head. In any case she was right: the burning pain in his gullet and on his tongue contained a mixture of tastes reminding him of herbal medicines and chemists' shops.

3

All at once the weight lifted, the band across his forehead disappeared, and his senses began to operate again. He was free. The evening's prospects were not at all bad.

There was a sudden crash of metal; a moment's silence; a woman's shriek; and then the mumbling of a deep masculine voice.

Now he could contemplate the situation.

With his billowing old cape swinging violently from side to side with the fury of his movements, the one-legged man retreated towards the exit. Kansdorf was not sure whether he had actually seen the incident or merely divined what had happened: the crash had come from his crutch, which after a string of hoarse curses and drunken insults he had smashed down on the bar counter. The landlord had shoved his belt up over his paunch and, roused by the angry exclamations of the barmaid, now came round past the till. He was afraid for what had happened and he was in a bad mood; his short arms sawed across his flopping body in the general direction of the one-legged man, who was now stumbling around emitting incomprehensible obscenities. The three women hung greedily over the counter: Kansdorf let his eyes move with satisfaction over the fantastic hideousness of their appearance—the scrubbed and shining silk, the frowsy flesh, the moist eyes under the unkempt masses of hair with their traces of careless tinting. . . .

Had the scene had a meaning?

What had happened?

Why *should* it have had any meaning?

His ear was conscious of a flood of accusations and excuses, interspersed with shouts of laughter—he immediately forgot them. Someone had paid, or not paid, or someone had been insulted or not insulted. What did it matter, anyway? Probably it was only an argument about the main item in the all-in wrestling, which he was going on to see. One would throw the other. Or the other would throw the one.

4

He turned round a little on his high stool and swallowed what was left of the Fernet Branca. This time the effect was so strong that rattling iron curtains descended around him on all four sides with a deafening noise, and his throat burned.

He sat still behind the four iron curtains which had been pulled down in front of him with such a crash; he sank his head on his hands and the outside world ebbed away.

In the bar opposite the sports' stadium, or in church in the morning during the stillness of Mass—it made no difference. The clanging curtains had fallen, he was alone, and beyond the intervening metal counter one-legged men and fat-paunched publicans, barmaids with voluptuous bosoms and the whole verminous human race could writhe in its dance of death as much as it liked—he paid no attention to it, his eyes were fixed elsewhere.

What did he see when he looked into himself?

It always began in the same way, with vague unco-ordinated associations dancing away over a stretch of foaming bottle-green water. To go deeper one had to get *under* the waves of thoughts, which were certainly not himself, for they spilled in from the outside and followed their own logic, which was not his. If only he could dive down and get below all this tumult! But when he did manage to silence the voices and drive away the disturbing words, images, thoughts, then at last he found underneath—mere greenness, death, a gently heaving emptiness. That was his essential self—this emptiness, this sense of need! And that was what someone was supposed to want to redeem! Could emptiness and nothingness be redeemed?

How long he sat there with his head in his hands he did not know. But when he looked up everybody was streaming through the groaning, complaining, revolving door.

The girl with the silk bosom was standing in front of him with her hand on her hip.

5

"Another double Fernet, right? You've got time. The main bout won't be on yet."

He was just about to nod agreement when he remembered something. Part of the attraction of the wrestling was Cretin Charlie, who crept round with the tray of brandies between the bouts so as to befuddle the befuddled crowd still further. He did not want to miss a single detail of the drama. Without answering he pulled a few greasy notes out of his pocket, stuffed a handful of potato crisps into his mouth and slid down off his seat. The Fernet Branca, as so often before, had given him new life. It smoothed throat and stomach, it killed pain and the sense of need, it dissipated weariness and disgust. Now he was ready. He felt in the right mood to enjoy the great drama, the human Mass, to the full.

As he pushed his way out through the revolving door he heard within him the words of the psalm:

"Therefore do I make my face as hard as flint."

"Quite so," he said aloud and stepped onto the stairs leading out.

The moon was sailing behind ragged, scurrying clouds, and in the strong wind the Eiffel Tower sailed through space too. Hardly any stars, as always in Paris. The street that ran from the bar to the stadium was full of people streaming to the entrances and being helpfully directed and halted by the agile hands of policemen.

He let the crowd carry him forward. It was some time before he got through the barrier. In the vast corridors were hordes of people, noise, laughter. Stained brick walls, grotesquely horrible—hell must look like this. The faint stink of urine and a foul smell of sweat: the human aroma.

At last he was up in the hall. He stood there blinking and leaned against the railing. An endless sea of heads under clouds of smoke, with the spotlights playing above. A surge of shrieks and excited shouts—angry, menacing waves that roared forward and broke shrill and white. In the middle of the hall the brightly lit stage, the altar, where the beasts of sacrifice struggled. There, in the far distance, he saw one powerful body hurled over its opponent's head and land on the canvas.

There was a thundering surge of hatred and jubilation.

Slowly he made his way to his seat. Past experience helped him: he knew the best place for seeing. Not right up against the ring but a little distance away, on the same level as the altar. There sat the connoisseurs, the temple's faithful, never-failing patrons, the friends of the human sacrifice. It pleased him to see them there again: the one who had at some time been beaten up, with his artificial nose and his one blinking eye, now in a trance, moaning with excitement; the little dark girl, stroking her boy friend's hand; the boy friend's remarkably low forehead, his uncouth jaws biting on his handkerchief, his pounding excitement; the tall, fair, melancholy man from the travel agency, whose face never moved, but who never missed a single Mass. . . .

He leaned forward and looked along the next eight seats. They were all there: no one was missing. His sort and their sort. Human beings.

He had still not given the arena a glance. He was never much interested in the early, unimportant bouts. He went on looking out over the sea of human beings. He could see everything perfectly clearly, and yet at the same time he felt a buzzing, dizzy feeling. He would soon be having another attack. Even now he would have liked to tip forward like a penknife and close his eyes. But he mastered the feeling.

He felt a stab of pain in his leg. One always had to be prepared for that in the sports' stadium. The human animal's faithful followers.

The bout had ended. A roar went up in a soaring column, and as suddenly sank into a subdued mumble of voices. And

look, here came Charlie with his tray of brandies! *"Une fine!*
Une fine à l'eau!" The tray was rapidly plundered. The little
bottles of Martell passed from hand to hand. At the last
moment he had the good fortune to get one for himself. Of
course it was not essential, but it was part of the proceedings,
one of the rites of this human Mass. He unscrewed the top
and raised the narrow bottle to his mouth. After the Fernet
Branca, the Martell seemed mild. Hs tongue told him at once:
adulterated, watered down. Naturally. How could one expect
anything genuine here?

"This place is the temple of mankind. There are not
many things I like on the earth or in this city, but I do like
the savageness of all-in wrestling rings. 'All-in': has anyone
ever thought of a better way of describing human life? Doesn't
it circumscribe the whole sphere of our human beliefs? No
holds barred. The whole gamut of savagery, cruelty, horror.
Life and truth as though in one single drop under the micro-
scope."

As he looked out again over the sea of human heads he
seemed to see the arc lamps under the roof swaying, as though
still vibrating from the movement of the powerful bodies in
the arena. The altar was still empty. The crowd still waiting
—with empty, hungry eyes. Waiting for the truth, the human
gospel.

Oh, all the low foreheads, the apelike skulls with expressions
almost of piety on their faces, all these wretched, oppressed
human beings living their own lives in dirt and comfortless-
ness and yet taking fire here as though in religious worship
before the Holy One! And this Holiness was the truth—
revealed in blinding white light in the arena: the mystery
of man. The hideous bodies and facial expressions, the belly
grips and the stamping underfoot, the twisting of the arms
and merciless pain until one of the contestants either gave
in, absolutely "all in," or had his shoulders pressed down three

8

times on the canvas. He usually brought his glasses—they were his mother's little pair of opera glasses!—with him, so that he could carefully study the looks on the faces of victor and vanquished at the moment of victory. He was not so much interested in the loser: it was simply a case of black hatred and grinning pain. But the winner! The pride, the joy in his face!

Why on earth did he come here so regularly, drinking his brandy after each bout, smoking one cigarette after another, unknown and alone in the vast temple crowd? Was he a sadist? Was he ill?

Now!

Suddenly the two contestants were in the ring, an excited roar all around them.

He took out his little mother-of-pearl glasses and focused them, saw first the rows of people by the ringside, leaning forward, gesticulating, clapping their hands; the thick rope ran through his field of vision and then he saw the face of one of the contestants. No, this was simply another of the preliminary bouts, there would still be some time before the champions appeared. An exchange of greetings. A show of serious instructions and warnings. The fight began.

Two ponderous human lumps crouched forward, arms swinging, circled round each other and tried to make the first contact. The first ten minutes were only a mock battle. Throws were not counted during this period. The crowd knew it, nevertheless they were absolutely engrossed.

A glance at the programme informed him that one was the former French champion, the other, the challenger, the new champion of the English navy. The Frenchman was a shaggy café proprietor from Marseilles, bald-headed, openmouthed. But the Englishman. . . .

Kansdorf started. The Englishman was young, graceful, slender. When he got his face into the field of vision his astonishment increased. An open, almost beautiful face under fair curly hair. A tanned body. True blue eyes; dependable, courageous.

He settled himself in his seat. This match might turn out to have a meaning he had never expected. He instinctively sided with the fair young fellow and against the greased and oily ape. And just as instinctively he knew that he would be defeated. Why? Because it was a law that beauty and chivalry always went down before savagery and brutality. Because all-in wrestling was a true symbol of human life.

During the first ten minutes nothing of importance happened; only the usual skirmishing and leg twisting. The Frenchman had a highly individual way of kicking his opponent, like a horse, disdainfully, from quite unexpected positions. From the young Englishman's reactions it was obvious that the kicks hurt. He himself apparently didn't use such methods.

Kansdorf's interest continued to increase. All-in wrestling delighted him as a symbol. Here the symbol was unusually easy to explain. The youth was spirit. The ape was body.

Poor spirit!

The Englishman had tenaciously worked his way round towards a dangerous hold. He forced the Frenchman's legs open cross-wise and pressed his shoulders back. But the next moment his head was caught between the café-keeper's thighs. With his hands propped on the canvas behind his back, and his young opponent caught in the vice of his thigh muscles, the café proprietor lay panting. The Englishman too paused for breath. Then he made a desperate effort to break away. The café proprietor's legs shut like iron and beat his opponent's head on the canvas again and again like a hammer, till he lay still. Tremendous applause.

The young Englishman's beautiful defeated body had been brought low. The hairy ape grinned, satisfied.

A new struggle to get free—with the same result: again the fair head beat like a smith's hammer against the canvas.

Kansdorf felt his pulses beating faster and faster. His excitement was a mixture of anguish and a kind of triumph. Anguish, because the fair-headed young fellow was done for, triumph because he was still trying, because the law was proving valid in all circumstances.

Only when he got a push from the spectator sitting right behind him, almost fell forward and then just managed to keep his balance, did he realize that he had risen in his seat. He did not turn round; of course the man behind was quite right. One does not stand up and hide a great mystery with one's own insignificant person.

He looked around. Thousands of staring faces, most of them utterly transported. In front of him, a little to one side, sat a young woman, obviously in ecstasy. As a woman she must have seen that down there a young human being was fighting an ape, nevertheless she was holding on convulsively to her companion's arm and emitting loud excited shrieks which she tried in vain to stifle. He looked in the opposite direction—rows of inhuman figures with their coat collars unbuttoned, grinning faces, all full of triumphant delight over the victory by their brother gorilla. Oh, this collective lust to see the light, the fair-haired, the chivalrous, humiliated and brought low!

He knew that there would be no point in *speaking* to the fair-haired youth. He would probably turn out to be as uncouth as the café proprietor. But as a symbol he could only be understood in one way. It was the humiliation of this symbol that called forth these resounding shouts of delight.

Then something new occurred. With a mighty lunge that for a moment left him standing on his head, the Englishman forced himself out of the hold. But it was soon clear that the café proprietor had let him get free on purpose. One could see it on his face, which wore a look of quiet, watchful triumph. He knew that the fearful pressure and the banging of the head on the ground had done their work. The next moment, the young Englishman swayed slightly, and tried to get out of the hold, and the ape had swung his opponent over his head and thrown him onto the canvas. Resounding jubilation from all the thousands in their rows of seats. With trembling hands Kansdorf tried to catch the café proprietor's face in his glasses: there was brutal triumph there, the joy of victory. Again the tanned body was swung into the air and hurled resistlessly to the ground. The third time it could no longer stand up properly before it was raised aloft again, and again hurled down. And a fourth time—a fifth. . . .

The hall was one vast uproar. The lights swung to and fro, the dust danced in the spotlights, an intense smell of sweat and dirt arose. The café-keeper, taking his time about it, went up to the tanned figure, which tried to avoid him, seized it in a hold, and without difficulty pressed its shoulders down on the canvas.

Kansdorf lowered his glasses. The fight was over.

But he raised them once again. The opponents were shaking hands. The winner was received with a roar of acclamation. The loser was whistled at derisively. He did not look up. His face was a picture of misery. Leaning on a trainer he went out.

"Une fine! Une fine à l'eau!"

Charlie came shuffling along, his tray was empty, he made a desperate effort to defend his property and keep a check on his takings, but in vain. He was despoiled of all he had in a twinkling.

Kansdorf stood up. A quarter of an hour's interval before the main fight. He moved towards the exit. In the corridor he was jostled along by the stream of human beings, dazed by their smell of sweat, dirt and garlic. Slowly he was sucked towards the exit. This, precisely this, he thought, is human life: hemmed in in one long, terrible corridor, squeezed into a single stream on which the single individual is in every respect utterly dependent, slowly impelled from a senseless beginning to an equally senseless end. "He gave thanks that it had been granted him to live his life on earth as a human being." Thanks, O Thou beneficent Creator! We worship Thee, we glorify Thee, we thank Thee for Thy wonders. . . .

He went into the massive Gents'. A stinking stable, with the echo of coarse voices and hundreds of men relieving themselves. Again he stood in a queue, a number, simply one more human being. He passed water, felt his body paining him and closed his eyes.

"They shall be seized by dreadful fear . . . doing penance . . . and groan in anguish of spirit . . ."

Someone turned a stiff, bull-like neck and stared goggle-eyed at this man murmuring incomprehensibly to himself. Crazy? Drunk? A bottle of Martell was sticking out of his breast pocket.

He stood motionless, as though struck lame. *Was* this reality? *The* reality? The actual, true condition of human living? Or was it a frightful dream, a horrible illusion? He was not well, he was not meant for this existence: it required qualities which he did not possess. His own working tools were too fine and fragile: they became useless as soon as he tried to apply them to the harsh reality. He could take refuge in a spectator's seat of torpid cynicism, that was all. But that was not living.

He fastened his buttons and went slowly towards the exit, got pushed by the revolving door, banged his head against the tiled wall, heard laughter, got up, sluiced his hand, which had got dirty, dried it on his handkerchief, put the handkerchief to his nose, and smelt a faint whiff of scent, which he breathed in deeply. . . .

Immediately a surge of memories arose. He did not actually

13

close his eyes; nevertheless he took nothing in as he wandered back along the long corridors of the slaughterhouse to his seat. He was far away, in Sweden. He was young, and Dagny was walking by his side. It was her scent that gently assailed him. He had still not dared to touch her. He was trying to be soulful and deep; she was listening, friendly. Like all who are in love he groped around her in his desire, trying to find the way in, the point of contact, where their two tendernesses could meet. He could not find it. The smell of her came, barely perceptible, to him, almost as though it were her breathing; he inhaled it eagerly, as though to draw her very being into himself. . . . Sweet was the memory. But in a moment it had changed to pain. His face contorted into a grimace. He should never have allowed his thoughts to rush on so. They led inevitably, irrevocably, to pain.

When he got back to his seat Charlie was standing there grinning.

"I kept one back," he said, and pulled a bottle of Martell out of his pocket. "I know you always like to have one before the big match, monsieur. Thank you. It's just starting!"

Kansdorf paid automatically, put the bottle in his pocket and sat down.

The contestants were already standing in the arena. Their names came bellowing through a loudspeaker—the Dane, Martinson, the European champion, and Willard Dalton, the challenger, champion of Ireland.

During the first, introductory, ten minutes his eyes registered the changing scenes without his being able to remember afterwards anything that had happened. Then, however, life came into the fight. He did not notice this half so much in the whirl of movement on the actual canvas as in the behaviour of the crowd. Behind him he suddenly heard a kind of hiccuping noise; he felt he had to turn round to find out whether it signified laughter or tears. He found himself looking into a distorted painted female face; it might have been quite pretty in repose but now looked absolutely horrible because the make-up did not coincide with the new features: a grinning artificial visage on which tears had dug channels in the make-up. A man was gripping her fiercely round the shoulders.

"Now this is the real thing," said Kansdorf again and again, biting his lips.

Then he turned back to the ring. The resounding yells in the vast hall showed that something had happened. The European champion, Martinson, was lying with his left arm tightly locked in a frightful hold; his forehead was being pressed against the mat and he seemed unable to do anything about it. The Irishman was giving everything. Balancing on his splayed legs, he was putting all his strength into the job of wrenching his opponent's arm off.

When Kansdorf had the good fortune to catch Martinson's bald head in the glasses he could see the sweat on his forehead and the contortions of pain on his face.

This could end badly.

But Martinson knew his holds. After a few minutes he had succeeded in lifting his body up; inch by inch he forced his feet nearer to each other, threw himself on his head and using the entire weight of his enormous body tore himself free.

A storm of jubilation.

The next moment, however, the unexpected happened. The Irishman went into the attack again, and although Martinson tried to cover his injured arm he was once again caught in exactly the same hold: again the two were on the ground and the atrocities recommenced.

Through the glasses he could see the Irishman's look of savage triumph. His range was certainly not as great as his opponent's, but with this one grip he might perhaps hold on to the European champion until he gave in.

The hall thundered. Was it possible? Could Martinson, the greatest living expert, be about to be beaten by a crudely endowed novice with only one stranglehold, even if it was a frightful one? Things looked bad for Martinson. Even if he got free, his strength would be considerably reduced, for his arm was already damaged.

He lay for a long time with his forehead on the mat, resting. His arm hurt, but he felt in no danger of his opponent's extending his hold and throwing him. And suddenly, after a perfect sequence of heaves, tugs and holds, the old campaigner was free again.

Before the Irishman could get up he found his own head between the Dane's muscular thighs. Now the result was a foregone conclusion.

Again Kansdorf focused his glasses on Martinson's face. Either he was a perfect actor, or he was still suffering severe pain. Could his left arm really have been hurt?

Kansdorf had been watching this part of the fight with an almost scientific calm. He had taken a gulp out of the new bottle. Suddenly he felt the intoxication coming over him. And in a twinkling the arena had vanished and another scene was before his eyes, an insect film he had once seen which had kept him awake the whole night; a film of murder, cruelty, torn-off heads, torture, cold-blooded sadism, so life-like, so devilish, that it should have been shown in all the schools to put a final end to the myth that behind creation there stands a Creator whose nature is essentially Love. . . .

Hard, fearsome insects. All-in wrestlers. And yet their behaviour was idyllic compared with the pain that one human being could cause another, or which could drive two human beings, both full of love and tenderness, remorselessly against each other.

16

He saw the Irishman, quite unexpectedly, free himself. These leg holds were never ultimately successful. And the next moment Martinson's injured arm was again locked in an iron grip, and the Irishman had straddled his legs on the canvas and was pulling a helpless Martinson along with him.

Te hominem!—"You, O man!" A chorus arose, from the mouths of jubilant trumpets and the deeper trombones. The hero had been beaten: sing praises, O world!

Pange, lingua, gloriosi lauream certaminis![1]

This was not simply a hellish human Mass. It was more than that. Through Kansdorf's feverish brain surged a stream of images—giantly magnified insects, with eyes like prisms, tearing each other's heads off, German sadists pushing hollow-eyed Jewish children into seething mass graves, Chinese philosophers with sly smiles on their faces enjoying through half-closed eyes their victims' slow deaths, a fawn shot by hunters sinking down bleeding and being fastened onto by a persistent bloodhound, Irma Grese with her white teeth and blonde hair using half-naked, half-starved Polish Jewesses for target practice: the whole ring of the world for age after age pursuing the same everlasting round of senseless cruelties. . . .

He saw Martinson tear himself free, but was no longer in a condition to follow the fight. He slumped forward and laid his head on his hands, his elbows resting on his knees. Down came the iron curtains with a rattle, and he himself sank, hounded and oppressed by pains and aches in the head, down into a black stream. The Psalms had said it all:

"Many calves have surrounded me: fat bulls have besieged me.

"They have opened their mouths against me, as a lion ravening and roaring.

[1] "Sing, my tongue, the glorious battle,
Sing the victor's crown of bay."

"I am poured out like water: and all my bones are scattered.

"My heart is become like wax, melting in the midst of my being."

Kansdorf came back to life outside the stadium. He discovered that Charlie had helped him out. His overcoat was dirty, likewise his trousers. Had he fallen down? He saw Charlie's toothless cretin-mouth move, but could not understand what he said. He managed to pull a few notes out of his pocket and held them out to him. They fell on the ground; Charlie was down in a flash.

"Do you want a taxi, monsieur?"

"No, thank you; I'll walk. I'll soon be better."

"Your bottle fell out of your coat and got broken. Will you have another one?"

He was holding out a fresh bottle of Martell to him, all ready.

"No, thank you; not tonight. Thank you, Charlie."

He stood there swaying, and then said, hoarsely,

"Tell me, Charlie—"

Charlie looked up expectantly.

"All this—," he motioned vaguely towards the stadium, "is it—is it really *us*—who have made it all?"

Charlie's bird's eyes blinked.

"Us? How do you mean? Which us?"

"I mean—we men—actually us?"

Charlie shook his head.

"Who else could it be?" he said. "Are you joking?"

"No, not at all. But it seems so unbelievable. Mustn't it have been someone else?"

"But who, monsieur? Who do you mean?"

"Him, of course—him, the devil!"

Charlie stood there in amazement, still blinking.

Then he pulled himself together.

18

"Are you quite sure you won't have a taxi, monsieur?"

"No, I'm going to walk. Tell me, who won in there?"

"Oh, Martinson, of course."

"It looked bad for him, though! How did he get on about his arm?"

"Oh, pure play-acting, monsieur! All part of the plan. It's the same thing in all these fights: Martinson could have won in the eleventh minute. But he gets more money if he acts as though he has to suffer a bit. He knows what he's up to. That Irishman is an absolute novice compared with the Dane!"

"I know, but it looked dangerous. I thought his left arm was going to be wrenched off. Didn't you see, Charlie, how he went down quite helpless when he got himself free?"

Charlie laughed his soundless Chinaman's laugh.

"Oh yes, I saw that. Of course I saw it. Monsieur, you've been here so often and yet you still let yourself get taken in! That was all bluff! An all-in fighter doesn't bother about holds like that at all! He could have thrown the Irishman on the deck any moment he liked with that left arm of his, he could knock him flat with his right arm tied behind his back, he's a terror, that Martinson, there's no one in the whole world he couldn't down. Once he had a tough Negro against him, Hugh Jackson, who was kicking out at his liver and heart and kidneys all the time—like a mad horse. He managed to land a few times. This got Martinson mad. Before the fixed time arrived he had nearly killed that black man! He lost hundreds of thousands of francs for not sticking to his contract. But he was mad, you see. He doesn't like being kicked. And after all, you can understand it."

He nodded and went off.

The Seine embankment was empty, and there was still frost in the air. No smoke was coming from any of the many chimneys. Paris was freezing. Kansdorf gradually sobered up.

19

He wandered slowly off, but instead of going over the bridge to the left bank, where he lived, he turned the other way.

His brain was active, but as though in a kind of vacuum. He could no longer see any images or think any thoughts; all he was conscious of was dull pain.

He was brought back to himself by a sudden screeching of brakes behind him: he was out in the middle of the road, half way down the Champs Elysées near the Clemenceau memorial. The taxi-driver stopped by him, cursing. He was obviously a Russian.

"Are you free?" asked Kansdorf.

"That depends," answered the taxi-driver. "Which way?"

What should he say? He suddenly remembered that the Sacré Coeur was the only church in Paris that was open at night, and then only for men.

"To the Sacré Coeur," he said.

The Russian scowled.

"Impossible. I have to go home. The petrol is all—"

The usual excuses.

"I'll pay double," Kansdorf said calmly.

His head swam, the alcohol was still working.

"Double night rate," said the other, eyeing him carefully.

"All right."

It was outrageous, it meant that the journey might cost up to eight hundred francs. But it couldn't be helped. He got in. The padding in the upholstery gave way, the whole car was a wreck; it shook and jolted and kept banging his sick body until he nearly fell through to the floor.

As the car worked its way up past the Trinité to the entertainment area, whose streets were as usual swarming with the melancholy figures of vice, he closed his eyes, and a cool vision stole across his brain. He couldn't tell where it came from. There was the plash of waves, a smell of lilac, and young but somehow bodiless women, all foaming around him

20

like some cool and gentle natural element. He did not dare move, but held his feelings in check religiously: he must not ruin moments of such sweetness. His brain was too tired to imagine anything. There were no sweet sounds: it was a scent, a breath, but of no very special kind, something light, cool. Was this the soul's—his soul's—true home? Was there a way back to it?

He was awakened by the braking of the car and—making a wry face—found himself back in the real world.

His tired brain sought eagerly to recapture the vanished scene. Gone. All through his life he had had these momentary flashes that suggested something different, something truer, but he had never been able to hold on to them.

As he got out in front of the Sacré Coeur and paid his fare, he felt cold drizzling rain spattering on his forehead.

The car slid away. Paris had disappeared in the mist at the bottom of the hill. Not a single light was to be seen. It was cold.

Moving slowly, he climbed up to the church. When Marshal Foch came back to Paris from the Front he used to spend a whole night in the Sacré Coeur; so he had heard.

The main door was locked, but he managed to find the right way in. The gigantic church, which he had never liked, lay in darkness; he saw candles round a statue of Our Lady and went towards it. He fell on his knees and put his hands together.

When he looked into himself he saw as usual an endlessly heaving, shimmering, green void. He was nothing, he was a void.

How long he stayed there he did not know, but his knees were giving him agony; he felt dead-tired. He looked up, the candles were guttering out. He had a feeling that he was the only person in the church. Shivering with cold, he looked up into the vaulting, which lost itself in the darkness. He felt alone, as though under the open sky, in icy cold. It was as still as the grave. In front of him, to one side, he could see the crucifix, directly ahead, Our Lady. Not a breath, not the slightest suggestion of warmth. Was he bewitched? Yet it was here that he was supposed to find the one thing of any value, the only Truth: other people found it, why couldn't he too? He had found it once, when he became a Catholic. But something seemed to have happened to it.

He got up and took a few paces forward, stumbled over a chair and fell. The legs of the chair screeched on the stone floor before the chair fell over; he thought he heard a cry of terror, a call for help, echo through the vast church.

He hadn't the strength to get up. He had fallen on his right arm and it hurt. He slowly turned round onto his back. The floor was ice-cold.

Then, after a sudden flicker, the last candle went out. He lay unmoving, from time to time shaken by shudders of cold. The roof above him disappeared, he was lying alone on the cold dead ball of the earth, around him were revolving other worlds, he was dead like the stone and the earth, he was being rolled around in an endless, meaningless process—and he would only be able to share in it and perceive it for a little while longer.

Why, why? he wanted to ask; but all he could do was to groan. He sank into nothingness and was no more.

CHAPTER TWO

Father Perezcaballero, the Dominican friar from the monastery of Sainte Croix, allowed himself to be borne forward into the Métro by the stream of human beings.

He was carrying a small suitcase and had to shorten his naturally long strides to keep in step with the crowd. From time to time he tried to get his thoughts to follow a continuous sequence, but without success. He felt outside impressions forcing their way into his mind, rather like the light from a lamp coming into the compartments of a roaring train. He would catch hold of some thread of thought or other, but no sooner had he made the first logical connection than everything became confused. He scowled. He hated being driven or influenced. He wanted to be all will and controlled activity, not a prey to vague thoughts and feelings.

To free himself, he concentrated on a single thought. How in fact did one manage to turn the unco-ordinated stream of consciousness, chaotic as it was, into an ordered train of ideas? And how was it that there were people of an intellectual kind—the English in particular—who were quite content to let their conversation follow their changing moods, without the slightest sense of shame and without making the slightest attempt to control or guide it? It was almost impossible to have an argument with an English Dominican! Being a Frenchman, Father Perezcaballero felt very sure of himself. Occasionally, however, he would ask himself whether there might not be some secret in all this which escaped him. Could there be *something* in his English friends' distrust of ideas and iron logic? Was it conceivable that by giving free rein to their imaginations they achieved something truer and more direct than he himself was capable of?

He passed through the barrier and again lost his train of thought. It popped up again just before the train came in, and he decided to take it up later at the first opportunity. He would try to deal with the illogical on the basis of logic! Now he became aware of a sweetish odour of oil and sweat; he was hustled into a packed compartment, his case was pushed behind his back, and he could smell garlic mounting up from a driver in a leather coat. Not that this aroused any sense of distaste in him. He was in Paris. He was at home.

He got out at his Métro station, and from there it was only two minutes to the monastery. He would be just in time for breakfast. He had done his job, and he felt pleased with himself and relaxed. A few days before he had set out with a clear plan of campaign in his head, he had been conscious of his own gifts and seen his object clearly before him. The prospect of having to go out into the world had excited him —much though he loved the monastery, the liturgy, the anonymous, tough work for souls. There had been a strong wind blowing that morning, the Prior had given him his blessing, he had felt as though he had been endowed with wings. And God had been with him.

He went through the door, joined the others going into the refectory and took his accustomed seat. He sat down as he had done a thousand times before. Near him was the novice who was saying the prayers. As usual, he was stumbling over the Latin: here and there a smile flickered over a monk's face. He discovered that the food, which he usually never noticed, was not so good as it was out in the world. He had to smile at himself.

Slowly a memory came into his mind.

One morning recently he had had a few hours to spare and had decided to go and see an old friend of his, Jules Lebrun, who had for a brief moment in his early teens wanted to be a priest, but had gone on to study medicine instead and was now a well-known Parisian doctor. Lebrun had sent him a copy of an article he had written about their old school and had added an invitation: would he not call and see him some time? Perezcaballero had been on the point of accepting the invitation more than once, not really because he had any special feeling for Lebrun but because—well, because. . . .

So he went to his friend's surgery. But there he was informed that the doctor was ill. Perhaps he would like to go and see him at his home? Yes, Dr. Lebrun only had a slight cold.

So he went to his friend's house. Lebrun lived in a quiet street in the Saint-Sulpice district, in a modernized old-fashioned, low-roofed house. On the stairs he met a school-boy who looked as though he might be his friend's son. And the image of Lebrun's wife came before his eyes—the fair-haired, frank-faced Ilse Lemat, who had made such a strong impression on him in his student days. Had she forgotten him? She had been the immediate cause of his decision to become a priest. Nobody knew that now—and nobody needed to know. There had been other, deeper reasons, anyway. He had realized his vocation very early.

Father Perezcaballero was thirty-five years old and an uncommonly fine-looking man. He was a Basque: people who heard him preach were amused and delighted by the way he rolled his r's. He had caused quite a stir when he was still very young with an article in the *Revue Thomiste* which had shown unusual talent. "A new St. Thomas" was the whisper.

He seemed destined for a scholarly career, in a scholarly Order. And undoubtedly he had amassed great scholarship. In his desk in the Sainte Croix library lay a number of works still in manuscript. But after his first article he had published nothing. At first people were surprised that he seemed to have faded away. On the other hand, they knew that the Dominicans always take their time. He would make a come-back one day. If he was asked about this—as he would be occasionally by some inquisitive lady with intellectual inter-ests—he would answer with a modest half-smile that his work was of the quiet, retiring kind and that there were much better heads in his Order. He started on big works but never completed them: at the last moment he could never stifle the doubt—was it quite perfect, should it be allowed to ripen a little more? Years passed, and he published nothing.

It was for this reason that he had felt so delighted when the Prior had singled him out for other, more difficult tasks. He was undoubtedly the monastery's best preacher and singer. Difficult and involved matters had been entrusted to him and he had dealt with them to the Prior's highest satisfaction. Not least on the recent journey. He could indeed be thankful that God was prepared to use him as His instrument! Per-haps his literary work would begin now too? Perhaps he would now really feel the wind filling his sails? There must indeed be quite a different kind of work waiting for him than mere continued residence in the monastery, however much he liked it there. He was made for battles, for danger, for difficult, complicated labours in the service of the Church.

Father Perezcaballero had a face that reminded many people of St. Dominic himself—a noble profile, dark eyes with a steady, almost majestic expression in them, and a sensuously modelled mouth in striking contrast with the powerful lines of the chin and the expression on the face, which suggested will power and determination. When his eyes moved they did not do so slowly and gradually but with a sudden jerk—one could tell from the rapid change in his look when he came upon a new idea, which he would then shoot down upon like an eagle. This look frightened many people, others found it enchanting. When he was listening, on the other hand, a characteristic slow change could be perceived in his face: suddenly a shadow would fall over his countenance and somehow deepen—one couldn't quite tell how—until in the end the expression was one of sadness, melancholy even. And just as slowly the shadows would clear and the face become firm and resolute again.

He had an unusually deep bass voice, resonant under the vaulting; and he accompanied his words with a choice variety of gestures. In the course of a Lenten sermon in Notre Dame which had become famous—he had been asked to give it as being the most popular preacher of the year—he had not allowed his arms to fall below shoulder level for a single second for fifteen whole minutes. He could deliver simple geographical names—Alexandria, Constantinople, Jerusalem, Cairo, Babylon—in such a way that those who heard him imagined they were listening to great poetry. People said that his personality, combined with his oratorical skill, was so compelling that he could have moved an audience to tears simply by reading a page from a directory. Once he had preached when he had had a very bad cold. When he had to sneeze he did this so artistically that everyone was fascinated. Never before had a white pocket-handkerchief been pulled out with such practised refinement, unfolded—with *one* hand —used, and put away. More than one young priest tried after that to blow his nose as spiritually as Father Perezcaballero did.

The door opened. It was she: Ilse Lemat!
Strange that her husband should have sent him his piece

of writing all those weeks ago with such a friendly note. They had hardly seen each other since their student days and the time of the—conflict. Did the friendly request to come and see him mean that everything had been forgotten, that no bitterness remained? Perhaps. Why should there still be any smart, anyway? Lebrun had in fact won the girl—got his own way. He, Perezcaballero, had retired, offered himself up as a sacrifice. . . .

"How do you do, Ilse. . . . You still remember me, I hope?"

She blushed under her fair hair as deeply as when she had been a girl. Had she always been so short? Or had he grown bigger? He could see that she had aged, but not to any striking extent—she had kept her blonde charm. But her face—though he failed to see any wrinkles—bore the marks of grim experiences. With the practised look of a confessor, he gazed into the once-loved countenance.

They exchanged a few casual remarks. They lived in the same town. She had seen him once or twice. Had also been to Vespers at the monastery. But of course he knew—her husband didn't think much of religion. And so things were as they were. . . .

Was Dr. Lebrun—was Jules—at home?

Yes, he had been slightly ill, nothing dangerous. Perezcaballero need have no fear about coming in. She would go and tell him.

As she moved past him towards the library door he noticed that the years had been very kind to her figure; which surprised him, because she had tended towards plumpness. Perhaps she had fought a systematic battle against growing old. The walls of the hall were hung with engravings and prints—valuable ones, so far as he could judge. Even in the lobby he had seen some Renaissance chairs and pictures that showed that his old school friend possessed both money and

taste. He had had taste as a student, of course; although . . .
yes. . . .

Dr. Lebrun was sitting in an armchair, and had a book
lying in front of him on a small movable reading table, which
he now pushed away.

He gave the impression of being carved out of dark wood.
He looked as though he had been hammered together by
the blows of fate, and made massive and unshakable. He could
never move his head without moving his shoulders too—he
had possessed this characteristic even when he was a student.
The result of some accident. But before his body moved his
eyes came into play: they slid round first, then the whole
massive figure followed—the eyes were the advance guard,
the lookout men, then the whole weight of the army itself
was pulled round, and the heavy artillery could begin to fire.
He did not laugh very often, certainly not more than once a
day. But when he did, it could be most unpleasantly affecting
to anyone who did not know him. He would open his mouth
in an expression almost of suffering, as though he had
suddenly felt a sharp shoot of pain, raise his short arms,
which reminded one of flippers, in a half-protective gesture
in front of his chest, and shriek his laughter out, his eyes
immobile, his mouth stiff—a short shriek, as of someone in
dire need, which would stop again at once. Then he would
slowly close his mouth.

Perezcaballero came in.

"Forgive me for coming along and disturbing you," he
said, "but Ilse tells me that you are not so very ill. And I
felt I had to thank you for that splendid little book of yours
about our school. It has given me a great deal of pleasure—
awakened many memories. And for your kind invitation. . . .
And so, you see, I've come along!"

"You are welcome," said Dr. Lebrun. "I am very pleased
to see you again."

Perezcaballero had not changed. It was remarkable that he had been able to preserve his self-satisfaction for so long. People usually lost it in the course of time. But the fact was undeniable—his deportment, like that of a king or future cardinal, his way of raising his head and at the same time closing his eyes before he turned to the person speaking and politely listened: the whole studied pose signified self-confidence and consciousness of power. Had he really been so successful that he could afford to nourish such feelings? Hadn't he ever learned to do without an audience?

Dr. Lebrun's hand closed tightly on the arm of his chair. No, he must control himself. One day he would have it out with this fellow. He knew why he had come. Not to see an old friend. Not to say thank you for a book which he naturally considered badly written and badly printed. But to show off his power, to look him over, to see what had become of him. . . .

"You rather suprise me, Perezcaballero," he said, to escape from the circle of his thoughts.

"How do you mean?" asked the other with a smile and a slight movement of the hand—oh, he had already become a real drawing-room friar, one of those Dominicans who love to shine! It could be seen in every detail of every pose. But he was aesthetically beautiful, that had to be admitted; he was master of the style, there was nothing ridiculous about him.

"I remembered you as physically weaker than you are. Clearly it would not be so easy to get the better of you."

"No, that would hardly suit the work we have to do."

Lebrun nodded.

"I know. I know the Dominicans. You are not enclosed, you go around converting the children of the world—as you have come to me today, to get me to believe in the existence of God, and my own sinfulness. Isn't that so?"

Father Perezcaballero shook his head.

"Do you think that that was my intention?"

"Of course. But you needn't bother. I am quite sure of the existence of God on my own account."

Perezcaballero's eyes bored into Lebrun's. Was he shamming?

"You are sure of the existence of God?"

"Of course. Surely you don't think that I ever fell for any atheistic nonsense, even for a moment, do you? I am a doctor. My business—just like yours—is with souls. I can see a divine battle—and another battle—taking place in them. But I believe that the other power is the stronger."

Perezcaballero still could not tell whether Lebrun was playing or not. He had felt sure that his friend did not possess an ounce of faith. Had not Ilse just suggested something of the sort?

"I am glad that you too take the power of God into account," he said.

"God should feel flattered," he was tempted to add. But he restrained himself. His face was polite, even friendly.

The conversation had continued. Occasionally it had touched on controversial topics, but on the whole it had kept to the surface. Perezcaballero had shown no disinclination to discuss the decisive event, that he had surrendered Ilse Lemat to Lebrun. He had swallowed the fact that he had been rejected, he said. Certainly it had hurt—for a while. But it had not been long before he had realized God's intention in putting him to this test. His vocation had been awakened. One did not always come to God along the superior, aristocratic ways one would have chosen for oneself. Lebrun had given him a penetrating look. Did he believe him? Half an hour later they had parted, with a vague promise to meet again soon.

Perezcaballero's thoughts forsook Jules Lebrun and his house. In their place there appeared before his eyes a true-life scene which had taken place many years before. He had been a student. Still not twenty years old.

Ilse Lemat had come into his lodgings. She had been crying, he could see that. Why had she come? Things were at an end between them. She had already made it quite clear that she preferred Lebrun. He had accepted the fact, thrown himself into his work, tried to forget her. Now here she was standing before him again.

"Can you forgive me?" she said softly.

He felt a wave of feeling rise up in him—she whom he had loved now looked so submissive, so weary! And he knew that he could revive her with a few words.

"Forgive? Forgive what?" he said, conscious of how unsure his voice was.

She still did not look up.

"But you know—with Jules Lebrun."

He stood up.

"I have no rights over you. I could only forgive you if I thought I had any claim on you. But you are not mine, you never were. You are free. You can do what you like—even if what you do may hurt me. Other things that you have done have made me happy—"

She looked up and smiled. In her smile was submissiveness and anxiety, shame and wonder—and, at the same time, a faint consciousness of victory.

She moved forward and stood before him, her arms hanging limply by her sides.

"Come," she said, "that is not true. You know that we belong to each other; and I know it too. I went with Jules because my pride had been wounded. I didn't think you—"

"You were quite right," he said softly.

"But it was no good! It was madness from the beginning.

There was no future in it. And now I want to ask you whether you think that we can forget all about it and—begin again? Oh, I know that sounds childish, but how do you want me to put it?"

He took her in his arms, perhaps he kissed her too.

Of course they could forget all about it. Of course they belonged to each other! His only feeling was one of great joy! He became magnanimous, said that it had really all been his fault, entirely his fault, and that he had been waiting for her all the time, could not live without her—and all the other things people say in such circumstances. As he went on and on, talking so eagerly, he failed to notice that she was sitting there quite pale and solemn. He only remembered that later.

The scene grew more and more romantic. They laughed, rather overemphatically, he gave her tea, they began, a little nervously, to discuss their future, and finally the thought came to him, "Now the moment has come to seal this, the most important decision you have ever taken in your life, by taking her. Now, at this very moment, on this sunny afternoon, she must become yours!"

He said it to her.

She thought for a moment. Then she smiled, closed her eyes, her face turned serious, and she nodded agreement.

He was in the seventh heaven. He did not feel desire so much as affection, almost awe. Now, after all the follies and mistakes, the consecration had come. Now his real life was beginning.

For a long time he lay by her side, without taking her. Her eyes closed under his caresses. Transported, she said, in a hesitant voice which he was to go on hearing afterwards for a long, long time:

"How wonderful that you can forgive me—that you don't mind about it."

"Why shouldn't I be able to forgive you?" he answered.

33

"What does it matter if some other man has been out with you? We love each other, don't we?"

She laughed happily, she was far away, as unsuspecting, as little mistrusting, as he. Just a little while, and they would be one.

"Oh, how good you are," she said. "Of course it doesn't mean anything. It was only the body. I was never really involved. But I wish I had come to you first."

He started when he heard these words, with his head on her breast and her body clasped close to his. He heard her, and he didn't hear her. Only after a while did her meaning become clear. He lay there transfixed, still holding her tightly. She suspected nothing.

"Take me," she said softly.

He still lay still.

"Only the body," she had said. "I was never really involved."

Had she—*given herself* to that fellow? Had she—?

Suddenly the truth was clear to him. He jumped up. She too sat up, with a slight cry, crossing her arms as though to protect herself.

"What is that you said? Tell me, what do you mean?"

He never knew what he said then, but they were probably not exactly well-chosen words. It had never occurred to him that she might be *that* kind of person, that she could have done anything like *that*—with someone else!

She was sitting huddled up against the wall, covering herself with the sheet with one hand and propping herself up on the bed with the other.

"But—" she said, "what is it? What do you mean? You said you could—forgive me? I don't understand you."

He couldn't understand himself. He couldn't understand his own blindness, his simple-mindedness. What he had heroically imagined himself to have forgiven was that she had

34

accepted one or two invitations to go out with Lebrun, had perhaps been kissed by him, had. . . .

That was what he had forgiven, with such regal high-mindedness! His high-mindedness had moved even himself. He was human, he had a heart. Upon the noble resources of his life her life, her weak life and his strong life, should now be built up. It was up to him, to build for both of them. If she did wrong, he would forgive her, raise her up anew. And he would work on her image throughout the years, to turn her into a human being, to infuse a soul into this beautiful, weak vessel of blood and muscle.

In a fit of sentiment he had even decided to crown this nobility by agreeing to join his body to hers.

He threw his clothes on and left the room.

A week later Jules Lebrun and Ilse Lemat became engaged.

Breakfast was over. The friars got up. He was to give the Prior a report after the meal.

CHAPTER THREE

With slow steps Clothilde climbed up the two flights of stairs in the house at 7, Rue du Bac, where she had now been in service with Edvard Kansdorf for three years.

Her work was not particularly arduous. He did not mind what he ate, even though he could at times be very generous in his praise. Flowers especially he never noticed—he was colour-blind—and so long as his books were left in peace he seemed to be content.

He had practically no visitors. Occasionally he might be sought out by a passing Swede, whom he generally did his best to avoid. Otherwise, he read and wrote. And he had to look after his health.

She opened up and went into the little drawing room, opened the window and looked out. It was cold, but seemed likely to be a clear day. In the house, not a sound. Monsieur was sleeping well—that was unusual; he was usually up early.

She turned back into the hall, put down the bread and milk that she had bought on the way, and went into the kitchen. She began to get his breakfast ready. While the water was heating up for the coffee, she cut off the one third of the butter which she was in the habit of appropriating for her own use. That she should take as much bread as she needed went without saying: she could always tell herself that it was old and hard and would not have been good for him.

Clothilde was the widow of a caretaker who had drunk himself to death. She now preferred to work for Kansdorf and another young fellow. She wanted if possible not to be in a house with women in it, men were more considerate. Kansdorf had once caught her when she was packing up what was left of a joint, two bottles of his best wine and a number of other things. He had come back unexpectedly after staying for only a quarter of an hour in the Bibliothèque Mazarin: he had forgotten something. He had noticed the theft at once, but had said nothing. It was not a very nice thing to do, of course, but if he was to make a fuss about it she might very easily go. She had her relatives from Pau staying with her: he could easily afford to let her have a little something out of the good meals she cooked for him. And of course he did let her have it.

Clothilde went to early Mass every morning: occasionally she was troubled by feelings of guilt—in the confessional she could talk about them: that she had said unkind things about a neighbour, had had bad thoughts, and so on. But it never occurred to her that she might be doing anything wrong when she stole from her employer. Clothilde was an exceptionally decent, friendly, believing soul, ready to make the greatest sacrifices. She stole, and intended to go on stealing. She was French.

The coffee was ready, she put the milk, marmalade and butter on the tray, pushed the door open with her foot, put the tray down in the drawing room and knocked on the bedroom door.

"Monsieur Kansdorf!"

No answer. She tried again. The same result. She opened the door. The bed was undisturbed. He had not been home all night.

She made a face and carried the tray out again. She should really have taken the trouble to find out first. Then she would have saved herself double work.

She waited an hour.

Then she began to get uneasy. This was not at all like Monsieur Kansdorf. He might occasionally, though seldom, lie in a little longer, but he hardly ever stayed out the whole night. In the earlier days there might have been some brief "adventure"—either at home or elsewhere: Clothilde had been able to tell this by various signs. She was always delighted when such a thing happened, too. He needed it so much, it could do him nothing but good—so long as he didn't go and get married and make himself thoroughly miserable. But later such occurrences had grown rarer and rarer. Of course, he was so ill. He had cancer—at least, that was what the doctor thought. And everyone knew how that ended.

She went down to see the concierge. He was sweeping the street at the front door and had the wet stump of a dead cigarette hanging from his lower lip. No, he didn't know anything about it. Monsieur was simply out enjoying himself —could there be anything more natural?

No, no. . . . Clothilde was wondering whether she might take advantage of the moment to go and buy a piece of meat: then she would be able to take quite a decent bit for herself tomorrow. . . . She was standing there in two minds looking down the street, which was full of the noise of hooting and shouting, when suddenly a taxi swerved in towards the door of the house. She saw at once that Monsieur Kansdorf was in the taxi, and by his side was—a policeman.

She was so terrified that she ran back through the front door. The police? There was no power she had a greater respect for. Monsieur Kansdorf did sometimes get visits from the police—he said that it was only because he was a foreigner;

and the policemen always went away quite happy, with brandy in their stomachs and a cigar in their mouths. But all the same, it was rather upsetting. And now he had been arrested! If only she had been able to buy that meat! She was hardly likely to get the chance again.

From her position, half in hiding, she saw Kansdorf get out of the car. His coat was dirty, he himself was unshaven; he looked dreadful. The policeman, however, was kindness itself, and spoke to him most courteously; he seemed to be saying that he was glad to have been of assistance, that he hoped the gentleman would get better, and that the best thing would be to get a doctor along as soon as possible. Kansdorf paid the taxi fare and slipped the policeman a note. There didn't seem to be any danger after all. She could come out of hiding without more ado. Perhaps she would be able to get that meat after all! Should she risk taking a bottle of his best red wine too? He was certainly not supposed to drink so much: the doctor had said so.

She was just about to go up to him when, not having noticed her, he turned the other way and went into the café.

She went after him, however.

"Your breakfast is ready, monsieur," she said in a voice half scolding and half anxious.

He did not look at her.

"Thanks, I'm coming," he said.

And to the proprietor, fat Jean Marie, who had popped up in the opening that led down to the cellar and was drying his hands on his apron, astonished to be receiving such an early visit:

"Good morning, Jean Marie," he said. "I'm rather early. I haven't slept. I must have a Fernet Branca as a pick-me-up."

Jean Marie mumbled something, but obeyed. He was a Communist, a very unusual thing for a café proprietor to be: Kansdorf was in the habit of twitting him about the contrast between his bourgeois occupation and his Communistic ideas.

"A double?" he muttered between his teeth.

"Single," answered Kansdorf.

He had managed to buy a box of Sandol tablets containing phenedrine and caffeine at a chemist's and had soon recovered from the horrors of the previous night. Now just a Fernet Branca and he would be in a fit state to face Clothilde and all the other storms of life. And be able to forget all his memories. To remember nothing at all.

He gulped down half the apéritif and felt the poison spreading out from his throat and stomach, bringing stimulation and spreading life along a thousand different channels. He would have liked to have had an opponent on his own level present, and worked him up into a towering rage. The only person in the bar, however, was the fat, rich Communist, Jean Marie.

"How's Monsieur Thorez?" he asked, and noticed that his voice was still not quite clear. "When is he coming to power?"

Jean Marie looked furiously up from the floor, which he was working on with a piece of rag tied around an old broom.

"When the country learns sense! And all the bloodsuckers are hanging up on the lamp-posts!" he said.

"Except for the café owners, of course," said Kansdorf.

He heard a growl but received no answer. He had got *one* blow in.

As a matter of fact he really liked Jean Marie, even though he did curse all governments. He remembered his wife, Jeannette, a round, friendly woman, who had died the previous year. She had been the typical devoted wife, motherly, earthy, utterly selfless, with no power of decision of her own, living entirely for her quarrelsome menfolk. He himself could not abide that kind of woman. In his earlier days whenever he had happened to find himself next to such a person at a party he had always hastened to mention that he never

40

danced, on principle. He could never bring himself to lay his hand on those swelling, effervescing forms. . . .

Suddenly deep within him, there was the sound of the horn—it was faint, but so clear that he started up and listened intently. Who was it, playing in his heart? Who was able to release events there which he himself did not understand or appreciate? He tried to see through the trees and branches and penetrate to the cool, unreachable something that lay beyond, but it had already gone again. All he could sense was a faint scent in his soul and a light breeze fanning his forehead.

He took a sip at his glass.

Remarkable. Could a dead tree go on sending up sap?

He now perceived that Jean Marie must have said something in reply to his last remark—and some considerable time ago. But he had no idea what it was.

"You are not listening to me, monsieur," said the bar-keeper irritably. "I have to listen to everything anyone cares to say to me, but *they* won't listen to me! I'm too simple-minded for them, of course! But just wait, one day—!"

"But I am listening," Kansdorf lied. "I've heard every word. But perhaps I haven't understood the whole thing properly."

The proprietor had finished the wiping up and was now dragging the basket chairs out from under the tables. Then he came up to the Swede and planted himself in front of him, hands on hips.

"So, monsieur, you believe that Jeannette is still alive, eh?" he said, in an angry and at the same time pleading tone of voice.

Aha, so here we are, back with religion again, thought Kansdorf.

He often during their dice and chess games talked to Jean Marie about religion. It amused him to watch an unadulterated atheist giving way to transports of unashamed bitterness.

Jeannette, the gentle, twining, swelling, friendly consort, had gone around slowly being eaten away. He had noticed a kind of agony in her eyes: why, why should such things be? It was just the same sort of thing as when their daughter Jacqueline had got herself a child without getting a husband to go with it—and when their son Jean Paul had been arrested by the Germans. Jean Marie cursed and spat out imprecations, cursed and drank; but when he came out of the room where Jeannette had finally had to take to her bed tears were running into his moustache.

"Oh, if only I could get hold of him, if only I could have him here for a moment!" he had once growled. Jeannette had grown so tired by then that she had not even been able to expostulate. Her tongue was so eaten away that she could in fact hardly speak at all. But Kansdorf knew whom he meant, whom he was threatening. The Communist, the massive café proprietor, was threatening God Almighty, the Creator and Sustainer of all things, the Person responsible for the fact that his wife was being eaten away by cancer, the Person whose existence he did not believe in. He wanted so very badly to have just one go at His Lordship and knock Him flat, as his fathers had slaughtered the aristocrats during the Revolution!

Kansdorf looked into his angry-dog, dissatisfied, ugly human face. He had no desire to fight any more; he had grown over-excited and was anxious for peace.

He propped his elbows up on the counter, which was still not dry.

"Yes," he said, "to me it's a certainty that she is alive, exists."

Jean Marie snorted with rage so fiercely that it brought tears to his eyes.

"Yes. On the other hand, it doesn't seem to me to be quite so certain that *you* are alive, Jean Marie—that one can be

42

justified in saying that *you* exist. All I can see in you is mere dull, heavy matter. That is not simply doomed to die; it *is* dead, already. Your Jeannette, however, was and is a spirit; she is alive, she possesses eternal life."

What ghastly nonsense was this he was saying? Who had developed this knack of speaking with his tongue? Who was it, blowing on the horn in his heart? Who had bewitched his brain? Was it the Fernet Branca? He certainly admired the person who had introduced it—not only for the drink's sake but because of its attractive, ingenious label: "To be taken every hour. If ineffective, to be taken oftener." What a jolly sense of humour, what a cheerful benefactor! But it didn't explain why he should be sitting here spouting the exact opposite of what he had seen proved up to the hilt in the sports' stadium and the Sacré Coeur: that everything was death and emptiness.

Jean Marie stared fixedly at the Swede; twice he had felt like giving him a sock on the jaw, but had restrained himself. He began, to Kansdorf's delight, to spit out a curse peculiar to the south of France, but then broke off, brushed the counter with a mighty sweep of the arm, which made the Swede pull his elbows away quickly so as not to be hurled off his stool, and then, with a sad look in his eyes, burst into noisy laughter: it was almost like a shriek of pain and misery.

"She's alive?" he cried. "Exists? Has eternal life? You don't believe it yourself!"

The laughter ceased. He bit into his moustache and suddenly raised his clenched fists threateningly against the Swede —not angrily however, in sheer despair, more as a gesture against the Lord God Himself. Then he disappeared down the hatch. Kansdorf heard him moving about amongst his barrels and bottles. Today was drawing-off day, he remembered. The barrels had just arrived.

Kansdorf remained in his seat. Then he drained his glass

and put a hundred francs on the counter. He suddenly saw right into himself. What he had said was right, except that he had not been speaking about the café-keeper Jean Marie but about himself. It was *he* who was made of lifeless matter. (In this matter, however, something was active, someone was calling—again it sounded, like the echo of a mysteriously distant horn.) Yes, the soft, gentle Jeannette was alive: he knew that. He could prove it beyond any possibility of doubt. There *was* another existence. This one on earth was a world of shadows in which the spirit was supposed to develop. But obviously one could resist this process and cling instead more tightly to the clay, *become* clay and grow stiff and die. Some, the more flexible, more vital ones, received eternal life, found their way out of the dream, the appearance.

Suddenly the pain came and bent him double. Thanks for the respite, which was now over. He had foreseen it. It was only a matter of hours.

He groaned and pressed his forehead hard against the cold metal of the table top. Still bent double he stumbled out of the café and to the door. The concierge stared after him and shook his head.

Slowly he forced himself up the steps. When he was half way up Clothilde came to meet him, the fat, thieving, good-hearted soul that she was—she had been afraid of some catastrophe. Now she hauled him up, muttered comforting, motherly words, got him to the bed, unbuttoned his collar, and hurried to the telephone and called the doctor.

Then she brought him his pills: she knew what he needed. With an effort he swallowed them down and fell back.

The pain increased, but his brain remained as clear and hard as ringing crystal.

And deep down within the crystal sounded the horn, and with longing, caressing eyes he saw, far within, between the trunks of trees, a light, slim, tantalizing figure disappear.

CHAPTER FOUR

The Prior of the Sainte Croix monastery received Father
Perezcaballero after breakfast in the chapter room. The Prior
was freshly shaved and looked perhaps a little paler than
usual; the W-shaped furrow of gloomy thoughts on his forehead stood out more clearly. Had something happened in the
monastery while he had been away?

Perezcaballero had no chance to ask any questions, however.

"How do you do! Well?"

The Prior bent forward, as though determined not to miss
a word. No more questions. Not a word about the journey, or
about his health. That was a good sign too. Perezcaballero
had felt a certain discomfort since breakfast—in his subconscious he was still thinking of that meeting with Lebrun.
What an idea had that been, to look him up!

"I went straight to Father Guillon," he said. "He was just
the same as usual. He made no attempt to explain the affair.
I gave him about two minutes. Then I saw that he would
never broach such a ticklish question off his own bat. So I
did so myself."

"How?"

The Prior sat motionless, gazing fixedly out of the window.
He looked dreadfully tired.

"I don't know whether I did it the right way—"

45

The Prior made a gesture of impatience.

"I told him more or less what we had noticed here amongst ourselves—what we had heard about the differences between him and Father Gentile, and with the Jesuits. I told him that we have a report that says that our mission work is in danger as a result of these differences. I asked him whether he would agree that the statements were more or less true."

"And he said?"

"Simply said he hadn't done anything wrong: said his conscience was clear before God. I went on and pointed out that during the last six months the whole work has come to a standstill, that there are no conversions coming along, that two former converts have lapsed and another two look like doing the same—obviously as the result of something connected with him. I urged him to realize that I was only trying to help him in his work. I asked him not to hesitate to confide in an old friend if he had anything weighing on his mind."

"Good."

"He was silent for a while. I noticed that he had gone thinner and was aware of a kind of anguish in him. 'I have nothing to hide,' he said. 'I cannot regret something that I haven't done. You know quite well that our work can stagnate for long periods: God wills it so—to show us how powerless we are by ourselves—' "

"In itself, true enough. Go on!"

"I got nothing out of this conversation at all. I went and prayed with him in the chapel and thought I noticed his hands trembling in a way that I don't remember seeing before."

"Trembling hands, interesting. He used to suffer from that years ago, when he was a young man. I remember it quite clearly. It was connected in those days with a personal crisis too. Go on!"

Father Perezcaballero coughed. Now the Prior was in for a

46

surprise. Now he would recognize his tactical ability. The job had been incredibly difficult. He had pulled it off.

"When I arrived, I knew one or two things, of course. And I knew that I shouldn't discover anything further by talking to the other priests. But I should never have got to the bottom of the matter if I hadn't been helped by God. A young woman came to me to confession. I had not been listening to her for long before I realized that she was mixed up in some way with Father Guillon. She asked if she could have a private talk with me the following day, and naturally I didn't say no."

As a matter of fact Perezcaballero was not quite sure that the interview was her own unaided idea. He had guided the conversation in such a way that the young woman had found herself asking if she could see him next day. A rapid wrinkling of the forehead showed that Perezcaballero was not unaware of a slight rearrangement of emphasis.

She had been a radiant figure. A delicate profile, lively eyes, the animation of her features! And what a beautiful figure! And yet her real charm lay elsewhere: in the contrast between the gravity of her eyes, and the richness of her mouth. She seemed to stand between two worlds. She had glimpsed the kingdom of God, but her physical being, unbeknown to herself, was turned towards the earth. A very satisfactory instrument for earthly love, made for the whole gamut of passion, with a hint of submissiveness around the often only half-closed, slightly moist lips; at the same time, however, a sense of perplexity, a fumbling striving into another world. . . .

"I was guided by God," said Father Perezcaballero, conscious of a slight warmth in his cheeks as he said this. "I had not to ask any questions. The talk turned to Father Guillon quite of its own accord."

Not quite so easily, as a matter of fact. He had had to work very hard before he had managed to get her to speak her mind, as it had seemed, quite spontaneously.

"I said that I knew about the crisis that Father Guillon was going through and could see that he was in need of assistance. The time had come to help to get him back to normal. Perhaps she could help me?"

In reality he had suspected almost at once that there were connections between Father Guillon and this young woman that were not absolutely all they should be. What had betrayed this to him? A certain fleeting sense of restlessness behind her outward indifference when he brought the conversation round to Father Guillon. He had tried to approach the matter again in an utterly different way, but she was very much on her guard, watchful and alert. She had escaped him in a flash. He tried again with a direct question, phrased however in such a manner that it could easily be given another meaning if it turned out to be a wrong move. She had answered with perfect equanimity: there was nothing left for him to do but to get out of the situation as tactfully and plausibly as he could.

"Well?" asked the Prior. "What did this young woman have to tell?"

"At first, nothing at all," answered Father Perezcaballero. He could feel himself turning red as he thought of his visit to Father Guillon. Why did he always find this man so disturbing? Possibly because he had published so many books of scholarship, whilst he himself—? He stifled this dangerous thought.

"We talked for quite a long time," he said, "before I happened to come upon a clue. She talked to me about all Father Guillon's admirable works, which was in itself quite edifying. She also mentioned amongst other things that he performed a wide range of charitable work—for instance, he had helped a whole family she knew to get on its feet again. The thought suddenly came to me that there was something hidden behind this."

"Why? Nothing could be more natural!"

"So it might appear, certainly. But I wondered where the money came from. I decided to make a very thorough investigation into these—domestic connections. I couldn't in fact discover anything else."

That was true. He had done his utmost to convince himself that Father Guillon was responsible for the dissensions and conflicts, but had found no proof. He had had to admit frankly that these dissensions centred upon quite different things. And in reality he was not by any means certain that the mission had in fact declined to anything like the extent that it seemed to have done from a distance. It rather looked as though Guillon's adversaries had been exaggerating, if not actually lying. Then, however, late in the afternoon he had happened to come across a deed of gift.

"Then I discovered something rather serious," he said. "An old lady had left a large sum of money as a bequest. I made a copy of her deed of gift. It leaves no room for doubt: she expresses the wish that the whole of the interest shall be devoted to the chapel and its upkeep. But when I looked into the matter I found that Father Guillon had been using the money for the upkeep of the family the girl had mentioned: a family that one almost feels obliged to describe as Marxist. I looked the family up, and it was quite true. They had had their rent paid, and a number of other things. In itself the whole business was quite moving. What surprised me, however, was the fact that the family was still anti-Christian in outlook and that Father Guillon had obviously not made the slightest attempt to convert them."

"Remarkable," murmured the Prior. "Most remarkable."

Perezcaballero had brought this matter up in the course of a conversation with Father Guillon. The latter had replied, quite calmly, that he regarded any sort of missionary activity amongst people who did not enjoy the most rudimentary material security as a waste of time. He had to provide the security first, he said; then he could talk about Christ. All too often the Church had gone about it the opposite way—and the result was the working masses' distrust of Christian charity.

Father Guillon had defended his point of view with great acuteness. During the conversation Perezcaballero had been strengthened in his dislike of this inflexible man. He was unable to prove that there was anything wrong about his relationship with the young woman, though he felt sure there was. The only thing he could fasten on was the fact that the terms of the bequest had been set aside—that the money had not been put to its rightful use. He swooped onto this academic point like a vulture. Father Guillon admitted at once that strictly speaking that had been wrong. He had, however, acted from the best motives. He had known the late benefactress and was sure that she would have approved of what he had done.

"It was all most provoking," said Perezcaballero. "He has developed a kind of family assistance work to a high degree— mainly with the help of gifts that are at his disposal and which there can be no doubt that he has the right to use as he thinks fit. I went on to the point that the nub of the problem lay in the fact that he was neglecting his religious duties in favour of a social duty. He defended himself by saying that one had to satisfy the stomach before one could bring comfort to the soul. This could have the most remarkable consequences, of course. It was this that had brought him into conflict with his brothers. But he held firmly to his conviction. He wanted first of all to raise the level of the whole district, economically."

In the end the conversation had become really heated,

50

mainly through Perezcaballero's fault. It had not been so easy for him to prove that Father Guillon was materially in the wrong. The only thing that he had been able to go back to again and again was the infringement of the terms of the bequest. That was a serious matter. He had been surprised, however, that it should have been able to rouse such a storm within him.

"You think, then," said the Prior, getting up, "that the reason for the difficulties and dissensions lies in the fact that Father Guillon has neglected his religious duty in favour of a social one and that he has ignored the terms of the deed of gift?"

"Yes," answered Father Perezcaballero. "That is the heart of the matter. It was not easy to see through to it."

"Right," answered the Prior. "We will talk about the rest later. The matter of the girl must be followed up. I am—as usual—pleased with you. I know no one I can rely on more. But you know that already. Besides, I have certain plans with regard to your future."

Perezcaballero remained behind, alone. Now was his chance. He knew that there was talk of founding a new priory.

He felt an inner excitement, and interpreted it as just pride and well-earned satisfaction.

It is true, of course, thought Father Perezcaballero, that God often chooses the strangest people as His instruments, and does not measure things by human standards. Nevertheless, He obviously has a certain predilection for the gifted people, the people with will and judgment and the power to act. Despite everything, thought Father Perezcaballero, it is ultimately the really gifted people who guide the Church and decide her destinies with a firm hand.

With an almost imperceptible smile on his face, Father Perezcaballero mounted the stairs to the library.

CHAPTER FIVE

"Put your clothes on," said Dr. Lebrun shortly, and walked to the window.

Kansdorf obeyed. He liked Lebrun; he had come into his hands by chance and stayed with him ever since. Lebrun had a good reputation as a cancer specialist. He had written articles on the subject that were frequently quoted. Even Swedish doctors were interested in what he said. The fact that Kansdorf had remained with him for three years had depended mainly, however, on something quite different: Lebrun attracted him as a human being. He was a determinist, an exponent of "realism." His early religion he had shed completely. He was the mortal enemy of all mysticism. And he was a "character"—not to say mad. It was he who had first taken Kansdorf along to the sports' stadium.

Lebrun lit himself a cigarette by the window.

"Has your attendant spirit anything with any strength in it?" he asked. "I have had a cold. Alcohol is no use for a cold. But for that very reason—"

Kansdorf rang. Clothilde came in with a questioning look on her face, and seeming rather ill at ease.

"Give the doctor—what will you have?"

"Well, what is there? Brandy? Whisky?"

"Both."

"Whisky, then. Half a tumbler! Go on, hurry up with it, Clothilde!"

Clothilde hurried out. She always looked at Dr. Lebrun apprehensively, almost spellbound. She was so fascinated by him that she never properly heard what he said.

Kansdorf slowly dressed. As he stood in front of the mirror tying his tie, Lebrun said:

"Yes, you'll die, all right."

Kansdorf carefully buttoned his waistcoat.

"Thank you so much."

He put his jacket on.

"And what about you?" he asked drily. "Will you live for ever?"

Clothilde came in with the glass of whisky on a tray. Lebrun took it without looking at her. Just as she was about to disappear through the door he said, without looking after her:

"Clothilde!"

She stood still, as though she had been struck.

"Yes, monsieur?"

"Herr Kansdorf says that it's quite dreadful the way you steal. Is that so?"

Kansdorf had never mentioned the matter to Lebrun.

"Clothilde," Kansdorf said, "I assure you that I have never suggested any such thing, even by a single word!"

Clothilde had turned as red as a beetroot.

"Well, it doesn't matter *how* I know about it," said Lebrun, looking out of the window. "But it's quite true, isn't it?"

"It—it is definitely not true," stammered Clothilde.

"Thieving *and* lying, that's a bit too much," Lebrun observed calmly. "Now, it's ultimately all the same to me whether you steal or not, Clothilde, for as a matter of fact Herr Kansdorf will soon be dead—"

"What's that you say?" cried Clothilde.

"What's that I say? That he will soon be *dead,* that's what I say! Soon! Then you can steal from someone else. That's none

53

of my business. But one good thing, you will undoubtedly go straight to hell for it!"

The poor woman had had to put both hands behind her back and support herself against the door-post.

"I hope that—I hope not," she stammered. "God is good— and there is a Redeemer—the Redeemer of mankind—"

Lebrun had walked up to her and stood, whisky glass in hand, in front of her.

"It's a shame, when you are otherwise such a decent woman!" he said. "You have many good points, Clothilde. You're a good cook, you're tidy. But you're a thief and a liar. That's bound to mean the everlasting fire in the end."

"It's not true," cried Clothilde.

"Ask your confessor, then!" said Lebrun amiably. "Ask him how anyone can manage to avoid eternal damnation when they have behaved as you have all their life. *I* don't see how they can."

Clothilde threw her hands up to her face and rushed out of the room. From the kitchen came the sound of sobbing.

For a moment there was silence.

"A doctor and a friend to man," said Kansdorf softly.

"Yes," answered Lebrun. "A friend to man too!"

"A remarkable way of showing it!"

"Just wait. I have no intention of leaving her in peace."

"How did you know?"

"In the first place, all housekeepers steal. In the second, I saw as she came in that she had a conscience about something or other. Can a woman as ugly as that have a conscience about anything else? Hardly. For a woman like that there's only one sin, and that's stealing. So she must have been stealing. Besides, I've seen her coming out of here more than once with parcels."

"People only carry stolen things in parcels then?" said Kansdorf.

"No; but they don't carry ordinary things in the same way as they carry stolen ones, when they are so apprehensive and deceitful! In any case you *know* quite well that I'm right."

"Of course you're right. And you can do whatever you like! But please don't take her life *before* you take mine! I'm lucky to have her. Petty thieving has never seemed to me to be such a great sin."

Lebrun had drunk all his whisky. He was standing in front of the mirror contemplating himself: square scowling face, blinking eyes, black moustache, short neck, massive great paunch.

"A quite unusually ugly fellow I am," he said, quietly summing up what he saw.

Kansdorf had lain down on the couch.

"Yes," he said, "no one can deny that. It's remarkable that you don't go out of business."

Lebrun's face did not change.

"And yet women like me," he said. "Remarkable."

He went up to Kansdorf on the couch.

"In about six months you will be dead," he said. "In case you want to know. The radium treatment is no longer any good."

"Thanks," said Kansdorf.

"The amusing thing is, however, that you will not be dying of your complaint."

"Really?"

"You will be dying quite simply because you want to die. Oh, I don't blame you. There's much to suggest that you are quite right."

Kansdorf lay quiet. He enjoyed having the truth served up to him like this.

"Do you know," he said, somewhat muzzy in the head from the effect of the drugs he had been given by Lebrun, "during

55

the last few hours I have been hearing a remarkable thing inside me."

"Really? What?"

"A horn. And then I see a kind of Walter Scott landscape —or rather sense it, a park or something of the kind, with what looks like a woman, disappearing. An hermaphrodite, I think. I find her refreshing."

Lebrun nodded.

"It all fits in," he said.

"What fits in?"

Lebrun folded his arms.

"Your death wish is a result of your attitude to life. Your attitude to life is a result of your attitude to women, especially your dead wife, whom you have never managed to get away from. Your—tragic—attitude to your wife is the result of secret homosexual tendencies which you will not admit. But which you hide under that kind of symbol. Deny it, do! Nothing shows what you really are better than your arguments against it."

Kansdorf was unable to laugh.

"You doctors are fools," he said. "If a man *does* commit a homosexual act, then he is a homosexual. If he doesn't do any such thing, if he will have absolutely nothing to do with it, then he is showing a dislike of homosexuality which gives him away and he is *really* a homosexual! Thanks, I know all about that kind of argument!"

"And nevertheless you know quite well that between this androgynous figure that keeps popping up in your subconscious and your death wish, there is a connection!"

He is astute, thought Kansdorf. Cynical and astute. In a certain sense he is quite right. There *is* indeed some connection of the sort. But I don't know what sort.

"Perhaps," he said. "I don't deny that. But how do you explain the fact that a man like me, who at one time or an-

56

other has experienced every kind of vice, and had all sorts of erotic experiences, should never once have felt attracted towards men or boys? I can't even go into the public baths, because the men's bodies simply disgust me. How do you explain that?"

"Because you're a homosexual," Lebrun answered calmly. "Do you imagine that a normal man is repelled by the ugliness—notice that: the ugliness!—of the masculine body? He never even notices it. *You* notice it. And detest it. Why? Because you like young men's bodies to be beautiful!"

"I've nothing against it at all," said Kansdorf. "I have no moral prejudices. I know homosexuals who are exceptionally cultured people. But unfortunately, it won't do. I have never been attracted to young men! Only to women, always."

"That's what nearly all the people of your type say. May I ask you one thing, however: which sort of women do you prefer? The feminine or the un-feminine? I have seen your picture of your wife and heard you talk about her type. I saw you once a couple of years ago with a certain young lady. Now and again we have been to the Bal Tabarin or the Folies Bergères or in cafés together. It has always amused me to see the kind of women you looked at."

"Namely?"

"The slim, boyish—androgynous ones!"

"You mean, the young ones! They're not usually so fat, you know."

"Don't try to get out of it! You know as well as I do how things stand. As a matter of fact you've known it for a long time."

No, thought Kansdorf, only from today. No longer. He is right, the devil. But I never realized it.

"Thanks," he said. "You're a goodhearted chap. If you want some more whisky, just ring! But don't do Clothilde in, please. I need her."

"No thanks, no whisky," said Lebrun.

"How will I die?" asked Kansdorf. "Pain—and so on?"

"Frightful pain," answered Lebrun. "Absolute torture. But I shall be here at the right time, to look after you. I suppose you will allow me to put an end to you and so save you a little pain, a little while before you would pass over in any case?"

"Thanks, my dear chap," said Kansdorf. "If it would please you, then. . . ."

"The pleasure is entirely yours," answered Dr. Lebrun. "In the meantime you must go on with your diet, take your pills, get in touch with me as soon as things get really bad, go for your radium treatment as usual—"

"Why that?" asked Kansdorf.

Lebrun smiled briefly.

"I don't know," he answered. "It isn't the slightest use. Of course I could do away with you at once. If you feel like coming to see me one evening, we might discuss the matter. But you must pay me first, so that I don't have any lawsuits with your inheritors."

"Thanks, that's very decent of you," said Kansdorf. The doctor was joking. "Perhaps I will come."

"Just as you like. It's cheaper if you come to me. But I am quite ready to come to you here if you prefer it."

Lebrun picked up his hat and coat.

"Do you still go on seeing all those priests and churches and so on? What were you doing in the Sacré Coeur?"

Kansdorf did not reply to the latter question.

"Yes, I see quite a lot of churches. Not priests."

"Every man to his taste," said Lebrun. "But why should anyone waste their time on things like that? You're not a believer."

Kansdorf raised himself up on his elbows. He was very pale, but the pain had stopped.

"Yes, I am," he said. "It's odd. I really do believe—that I

believe. I go up and down, of course. Sometimes more, sometimes less. For a while after my conversion, it was very real. Then I lost hold, rather. And now I'm believing again."

For the first time Lebrun's face showed signs of some sort of feeling.

"Interesting," he said. "And *what* do you believe you believe? If you feel like answering the question."

"To begin with, I don't believe that you exist," said Kansdorf.

"Thanks," answered Lebrun.

"And then I believe that there is some Power at work around me. It has given me signs of itself once or twice. Not lately. Lately, it has grown tired of me. I can't grumble at that."

Lebrun looked out of the window. Snow was beginning to mingle with the rain. In the room it was already almost dark.

"A really *good* power?" he said. "For my part I don't know, for certain, any other good power than—myself. But I don't suppose it was me you were thinking of?"

"No, it was not exactly you," answered Kansdorf. "I was speaking of a Power that really exists, that strives and suffers."

"And why do you believe in it, eh?"

Kansdorf hesitated.

"I should like to live a little while longer, to be able to answer that question," he said. "At the moment I can't. I realize that I know the truth, reality. But I don't know *how* I know it. I simply do not know which organs one grasps true reality with. Which organs lead one astray into the world of appearances, on the other hand, I know quite well. I long so much to get out of this world of appearances for a little while, though! If such a thing were possible."

Lebrun's mouth betrayed no emotion.

"You have no other symptoms of softening of the brain," he said. "It is therefore really odd to hear you talking such nonsense. Somehow it always upsets me when talented people say silly things. I for my part never do. On principle."

He went to the door.

"Farewell then," he said. "Do exactly as you like! I'll come if you want me."

"Thanks, you old devil," said Kansdorf.

Without turning his head he heard him shut the door and then the hall door banged twice. Anyway, he had at least left Clothilde in peace.

Kansdorf was growing drowsy. His thoughts were dull, hazy, sporadic.

Homosexual, he thought. No, thank you. Not interested in the least.

He lay there quietly, his right cheek on the pillow. As he was practically deaf in the left ear, he was almost isolated. He listened.

But now he could no longer hear the horn sounding within him. He lay perfectly still, but no cool androgynous figure came forward, no breath fanned his forehead.

When Clothilde came softly in—tear-stained, handkerchief in hand—he was asleep. With such a peaceful expression on his face that he might just have had good news.

Clothilde studied his expression. Thank goodness, she thought, it is not so serious after all. He has got over it again all right.

She went into the bedroom for a blanket and spread it over him. *He* could never have said anything so nasty about her. Nor could he believe such a thing; such a rotten lie, that she—

She stifled the thought, and tears came into her eyes. That wicked doctor was always upsetting people! Should a doctor do that? Hell? Was there such a place, then?

She put the light out and stood motionless.

Was there *really* such a place? Might she, perhaps . . .?

She stifled a sob, and with beating heart went out.

Now she would never have another moment of peace in her whole life. She no longer *wanted* to steal.

She closed the door as softly as she could and went into the kitchen. There lay the parcel. Surely he didn't begrudge it her? He was so decent. And it really was a fact that he should not drink wine. So perhaps she might. . . .

She bent down and pulled a bottle out, found that it was one of the cheaper kinds, put it back with a sob and took out another one. This time it was the right one.

She felt her courage reviving. Nasty men's talk! One had to be a little human.

She could buy the meat on the way home. Monsieur Kansdorf certainly wouldn't want her any more today. She would come in a bit earlier in the morning.

She got her coat and went down the stairs. She went into the butcher's and bought a piece of lamb on Kansdorf's account. She had some onions at home.

When she came out and passed the bar counter, she felt a cool breath on her neck and turned round. Through the open door she saw Dr. Lebrun, sitting at the bar. He raised his glass and drank to her.

She was almost paralyzed with fear. The expensive wine bottle slipped from her hand and fell on the pavement with a crash. The wine splashed on to her shoes and stockings.

When she got up again she heard a loud burst of laughter.

Seated on his bar stool, Lebrun was shrieking with laughter, arms raised, his face rigid, his eyes expressionless.

She hurried away.

CHAPTER SIX

Clothilde had not arrived when Kansdorf got up.

After a few hours on the couch he had wakened up, gone into his bedroom and undressed. By about six o'clock he had had his sleep out. When he opened the window he saw that it was going to be a cold clear day. In the room it was icy. The central heating had not been functioning all through the winter—there was enough coal in the house, but it had been bought up by the richer residents at fantastic black-market prices and consumed in their private stoves, whilst the concierge lied and said that he had not received his ration. Kansdorf had often wondered whether he shouldn't get himself a few sacks too; but he had refrained on principle. Instead, he used logs, which of course were sold damp so that they weighed more. He would have liked to murder the man who secured his honourable living, at a time when Paris shivered and froze, by pouring water over his timber yard every night so as to increase the weight of his wood and hence its price. *Le bon citoyen*. In a cellar, whistling to himself. With his splendid watering-can.

Quite often, however, there were not even logs to burn; one had to be content with firewood—on the outside of which, against the wire, there were in fact a few real pieces of wood, but which contained nothing inside but thin sticks that burned away in a minute. It was pointless trying to make a fire before one went out.

He dressed, put on his warmest woollen cardigan and wrapped a scarf round his neck under his short fur coat. He couldn't feel any pain. He wouldn't die!

He was already dead, of course.

He went slowly down the stairs, keeping his left hand on the banister except when he came to the dangerous points where it was broken: then he lifted it up and felt his way down with the stick in his right hand. He was in his forties but had all the mannerisms of old age. Grotesque.

When he got into the Rue du Bac he felt the cold, which was sharper than he had imagined indoors. Now the question was—which church? He could do with a little walk to get warm. He avoided the big churches in the mornings. He would rather listen to early Mass in one of the smaller ones. He suddenly remembered the little chapel in the Rue des Saints Pères which was attended by drivers and housemaids —no doubt Clothilde herself went there occasionally; he might meet her.

He went out onto the embankment. The Seine was wrapped in mist, he could hardly see a hundred yards ahead of him. The town had not wakened up yet. Was it imagination, or could he really hear the faint rumble of the Métro under his feet?

Why, for year after year, did he keep going to early Mass? Lebrun could not find words bad enough for him. And yet he was unable to give it up. Did he get anything out of it? No. Or only occasionally. It too was a kind of death. A ritual, performed clumsily by unskilled hands, but nevertheless a lovely old ritual. Perhaps it had once possessed a real content. Perhaps it *had* a content now—for others. Not for him. And yet he always went to it. With a definite hope in his mind? What had he to hope for?

He passed the closed bookstalls. The black leather coverings on the lids glinted frostily in the damp air. He looked down the steps. The cold made him shiver and he pulled his fur collar up. A rat ran over his feet and leaped down onto the lower embankment.

There is hardly a single reason, he thought, for carrying on with an existence like mine. I am absolutely empty. If we human beings were to be weighed in the scales of morality, mine would go down with a bump. The only thing of any value that I can discover in myself is one tiny portion that has not absolutely lost all sense of honour. I possess a portion of decency—or desire for decency—but that is absolutely all. But why should such a portion of decency—the one remaining fragment of a shining mirror—still persist? That fragment should break too, of course. Obviously!

He stopped, raised his head, and took a deep breath. Was it not anomalous that he could never think a thought without immediately thinking of its opposite? He knew quite well that the thought that had just gone through his head by no means represented the whole of his experience. What *did* he believe in, then?

He moved on, put his hands behind his back, and let his stick trail after him.

I *know*, he thought, that my life has had certain consequences, probably dreadful ones. But when I look through this thought, I discover another one beyond it. That is not the only thing I know. I also *know* that there *is* a possibility, a freedom: it is quite simply true that there is Someone following us who wants to redeem us. I have experienced this more than once, especially that time—I shall never forget it—in the cinema. . . .

If he were to write that story down, he thought, no one would believe it. Or perhaps they would: they would believe what he said, perhaps they would agree that he had really experienced the thing, subjectively. And it would be quite a simple matter to analyze what he had experienced scientifically. It would then turn out to be illusion—like everything else.

Now that is certainly not true, he went on. But how can I ever prove it when I do not even know what my own criterion of truth is? All of a sudden I *know* that I am in the truth, I cannot doubt anything so self-evident; but I cannot say that I *recognize* or *understand* the reality—I am far from being able to do that. I am in fact so blind that I cannot even tell *how* I perceive something to be true. And the philosophers can't help me.

I have on one or two occasions opened a door—or rather, on one or two occasions a door has opened in front of me. But *how* did it open?

Perhaps that question helps to explain it.

When I open a door, I do not know what exactly the muscles of my hand do, whether my hand had to feel around for the door knob or found it at once, whether my fingers made any mistakes in their various movements or not—I do not even know which hand I used to open the door. But the fact is that I *did* open it, the door *was* opened, I really can *see* through it! I can't doubt the fact that I have opened the door simply because I can't give an exhaustive account of *how* I opened it!

A lorry roared past him through the puddles: the dirty water went through his trousers and he felt his feet go cold. But he went on standing there without being really conscious of it. He was looking into himself.

After a sleepless night—he had been reading Heidegger— he had come here once before. Yes, it had been at this very corner. There had been almost exactly the same dirty grey light lying over Paris, with a kind of mist threatening snow— he had hardly been able to make out the Louvre on the opposite bank. Then something had happened to him which he had never told anyone about except Lebrun, and which

Lebrun had at once found a psychological, medical explanation for. He had suddenly been taken out of the prison, he had all at once been outside time and space.

Of course he himself had raised all the objections he could think of. He knew all the current psychological explanations: St. Bridget's revelations, for instance, were partly prompted by sexual dissatisfaction and partly the result of unsuitable food, a learned positivist had explained to him at his home in Sweden. Only gradually had the conviction taken root in his mind that these isolated experiences were the only thing that signified any real truth and content in his life. Everything else was dream, imagination—irrelevant.

He had been taken out of time and space. His body had no doubt wandered on along the Seine embankment just as it was doing now—perhaps he had got out of the way of passers-by, for hadn't it been a collision that had wakened him up? Perhaps he had seen the bookstalls in front of him and looked through a volume or two here and there quite mechanically. Of all that he knew nothing. The last thing he could remember was the mist over the Seine, and an idea in his mind whose content was something like this:

"Here reality ends; the mist swirls towards me, perhaps it is behind me too, just as it is in front of me. Soon it will envelop me completely."

Thereafter memory vanished. Later, on considering and comparing one thing with another, he had decided that he could assume that he had been snatched away into reality for forty-five minutes: when he came back to his senses he was standing freezing right out on the Ile St. Louis, Charles du Bos's enchanted isle, that was so like a ship sailing away down the Seine—in the middle of Paris.

There he had awakened with such a violent pain, such an intense sense of disgust, that he thought he was going to suffocate. He was back. Everything was as before. There

66

wasn't a liberation. Everything would begin again just as before!

He walked on. Another experience came into his mind. As a boy he had once taken too deep a dive and been seized by dread—his face had landed in the mud at the bottom and he had thought he would never get to the surface again. But then the water had begun to turn lighter: in the end he was able to raise his head up over the mirror of water and he saw the sun, and the green banks, and he was able to fill his lungs with air again. . . .

The relief he had felt on that occasion had been great and wonderful, but it had been nothing compared with the experience when he had been snatched up out of time and space on the banks of the Seine! This latter experience had given him no concrete images, nothing at all in the way of felt experience, no invasion of consciousness—and no sense of struggle. But there had been light, warmth, power, wholeness. . . .

But even these words were meaningless; they only reflected the feeble ideas of our own world of shadows. Whereas he had experienced the true reality. Perhaps he could put the thing better negatively: it was a condition in which he himself was blotted out and yet lived more intensely than he had ever lived before; a condition in which he was aware of no limitations as against others and yet filled with power and happiness; a condition in which nothing happened, nothing moved, and yet everything seemed to exist in a state of satisfaction and fulfillment.

What nonsense! It would be foolish to try to get anyone else to appreciate such experiences. It would seem just as foolish if he said that these brief periods were the only things of any value in his life. It was better to keep quiet. He had no need to intrude them on anyone. No one needed to know about his fantasies. Let the rest, the healthy types, go on believing that reality meant taxes and sausages, lechery and newspaper gossip, he would not try to stop them. If they didn't freeze in the world of shadows, all the better for them.

But he himself shivered with cold in this real world of theirs, so that his teeth chattered.

He had turned round and come back to the corner where the embankment meets the Rue des Saints Pères. It was only a few steps to the chapel. He went in.

The priest had just begun. Kansdorf genuflected and took a seat as usual in a corner. A few dozen figures were crouching on their knees in front of him. It was damp, freezing cold, and as quiet as the grave.

He propped his head on his hands. Either this was all a swindle—a two-thousand-year-old swindle—or it was the truth. *If it was* a swindle, *if* mankind had been deceived in this way about the Power which they themselves regarded as their Lord and God, then there was no reason to go on living. But if it *was* the truth, if a transubstantiation, a miracle, really was to take place in a few minutes, then there was only one thing on earth that had any meaning, and that was to cleave to this divine Body and never let it go again. . . .

He looked down in despair into the void, the greenness, that was his soul. And his consciousness disappeared in colourless grief, as had happened so often during all these years. He was a beggar, whom nobody noticed, nobody bothered about.

He heard the scraping of chairs and feet as the time approached for the communion. He got up, his knees hurt, he moved forward. Senseless, senseless: he was indeed dead.

But just as he was kneeling down at the altar rail he heard the faint sound of the horn, and he felt as though a light, cool hand was touching him. He did not dare to look up; he did not dare to surrender to an illusion. But the sound went on, and when the priest stood before him he opened his mouth and received the transubstantiated bread. Now the miracle should have happened, it was supposed to be going on in him now. He did not feel any different, but he knew that that was quite beside the point: the Church did not concern herself with subjective views and experiences. As he went back to his seat, his hands folded in front of him and his eyes half-closed, he thought:

The greatest miracle in the world is perhaps taking place in me; and I have no perception of it.

And yet he was aware of the faint sound of the horn—first swelling up and then dying right away, as a promise, a distant summons. Was it possible that he too might one day . . . ?

He looked up at the terrible crucifix. And although he was revolted by its ugliness he was able to formulate the thought:

You were not in a state to feel anything at that moment! You didn't have any kind of subjective experience either! And yet it was all true!

With the little group of housemaids, housewives and drivers he went slowly out into the street.

Wet snow was beginning to fall. He remembered that he had a hole in the sole of one of his shoes.

Like a sinking boat with a faulty engine he struggled homewards through the snow.

Clothilde came in with his breakfast at once, just when he had taken his shoes off and put his big warm slippers on.

"Coffee is bad for me," he said. "You give me coffee! I must only eat bread if it is toasted: you bring me untoasted bread! Marmalade is not good for my liver: you give me marmalade!"

"But monsieur—" said Clothilde anxiously.

"Have you ever seen a corpse, Clothilde, eating things a corpse ought not to eat? That is what I am. You know what my wish is, don't you? That you will pray for me at my grave."

She stared at him, shook her head, and disappeared into the kitchen sobbing.

It was that horrible Dr. Lebrun who was responsible for all this. Monsieur was always queer after the doctor had been to see him. Was he too going to start talking about stealing? If he did, he would get his answer. She had had time to think about the matter and knew what she would say! He only had to come to her.

But she was frightened nevertheless, and as she sank down in her chair a few tears fell on to her ample bosom. Why did people hurt her? Why couldn't they be nice to her—as she was to them? There was no justice on the earth. . . .

CHAPTER SEVEN

"Dom Dusolier looks like a donkey," a girl had once said with a titter behind his back.

Usually he gave the impression that he was not taking the outside world in at all, but on this occasion he had pricked up his ears.

"Not like a donkey," he had said, turning to the blushing girl. "Like a horse, perhaps. A tired old horse. Whereas you look like a sweet little baby squirrel, my child!"

He had looked at her without a trace of bitterness on his face, and the girl, overcome by his forbearance, had burst into tears. The next day she had come and asked him to forgive her.

"But what for?" he had said.

"For what I said yesterday," she whispered.

"I can't remember what that was," he answered. "If you *really* want to make me angry, my child, then you must do something to yourself which you know to be sin! But you won't do any such thing, of course."

He really did look like a horse. His face was rather long, and he had horse's teeth—what was more, one was missing; at times he made clumsy attempts to hide the fact. His hair had fallen out prematurely; one of his ears stuck out more than the other, and it was red and looked absolutely frozen. He stuttered a little and his head tended to fall to one side. He could hardly ever speak except in the most stumbling sort of sentences: when he talked to anyone it always sounded as though he was trying to get him to help him to find the right words because he was unable to discover them for himself.

In choir he was the cantor's headache. The cantor had often been seen to raise his book threateningly in his direction, whereupon Dom Dusolier had at once dried up. How often he had fallen upon his knees to do penance for a wrong note, no one could say. And then, of course, he looked after the collections. No one knew why. Anyone else would have collected far, far more than bald-pated Dom Dusolier with his clumsy walk and lopsided horse's head.

Some children came to him for confession, but mainly it was the very old or the very simple. He had a kind of quiet humour, but this was only very rarely allowed to peep out.

One one occasion a plump, good-looking, middle-aged, upper-middle-class woman who came to confession and told him that she had a weakness for the pleasures of the palate and went too often to the best eating places.

"Where do you find these wonderful places, madame?" Dom Dusolier had thereupon asked, very humbly, without a change of expression. As a matter of fact he never laughed if he could help it. For a quite definite reason. He didn't dare to.

As a matter of fact he had once seen the devil.

It had been in Rome. At that time he had been going through a strange, highly productive period, during which he had written long books on theology which never got published. His teachers had very soon forbidden him to go on. In one of these works he had tried to prove that even evil was really an outpouring of God's love, as part of creation: nothing, he maintained, would ever get done if it were not for the difference between good and evil—and man was called upon to do things.

He had finished the chapter in a burst of tremendous en-

72

thusiasm. The last few pages were written so quickly that he was never afterwards able to decipher them. As a matter of fact this was a great stroke of luck, for if his superior had been able to read his writing he would have found that they contained a sort of defence of the devil as a true servant of God.

Just as he had thrown his pen down, and was stretching his arms out and yawning with a feeling of tremendous relief and release, he saw the devil.

The Evil One, whose existence he had queried, was standing there before his very eyes. He had described the affair, vividly, to the Abbot, but to no one else. He had sunk down, terrified, onto his knees, and made the sign of the cross over the figure. He couldn't remember any of the words used in exorcism. He had sunk down until his forehead touched the floor. When the Evil One disappeared, he had felt a sudden contortion in his face. He had gone up to the mirror, and there he had discovered that his mouth had been pulled to one side in a frightful leer.

The leer did in fact disappear after a few days, but it had returned when he got excited and particularly when he wanted to laugh. He had therefore never dared to laugh again. Sometimes he had forgotten this—when he felt free and relaxed, when he was talking to his children and the sun was shining and he could feel that their souls were in his hands. He might then be induced to tell some story about his younger days—he was a fisherman's son from Brittany. But he never did this after one terrible time: just as he was about to laugh over his own memories, and the girls were tittering like a flock of twittering birds, he had heard them suddenly go silent and seen them staring at him, horror-struck. His face had contorted into a frightful leer, his mouth twisting up to the right, and showing all his teeth; all the muscles in his face were quivering.

Since then he had tried to hide these attacks or to anticipate

73

them: he either did his best to make it look as though he wanted to wet his upper lip with the tip of his tongue, or else he put the palm of his hand up in front of his mouth and pretended to rub the end of his nose. But everybody knew what was the matter with him, and all kinds of conjectures were put forward as to the cause. The nastiest people tried to make out that a girl had once tried to kiss him—and he had never got over the shock of it. Others said that he had once been watching a horse that had suddenly bared its teeth in the same sort of leer—and ever since then he had had to follow suit. But no one knew the real cause of it except the Father Abbot of the monastery—the fact that Dom Dusolier had once dared to deny that the devil had devilish characteristics. To his death he would have to bear this ineradicable sign as a continuous reminder of his error.

His sense of balance was lacking in one particular respect: he could never kneel down properly and gracefully before the altar, but kept stumbling and then had to put one hand on the floor to support himself. He chose the simplest jobs for himself, he loved washing up, and sweeping floors. But the Abbot insisted on giving him difficult, important duties to perform: more than one of the brothers had wondered at the fact that their superior so often gave the most gifted people in the monastery the simplest jobs and yet made Dom Dusolier appear in public and preach. The Abbot himself usually answered these queries as follows:

"It's quite simple. We serve such a mighty Lord that it is quite sufficient to send out the weakest amongst us, the, humanly speaking, most defective ones. The main point is that God does not measure things by our human standards. . . ."

This did not prevent Dom Dusolier from very often being a total failure. He knew that himself. He realized quite well that he was absolutely lost whenever he dared to rely on his own common sense. He had long since given up the attempt to deal with anything off his own bat.

He mortified himself.

He always obeyed, but he would deliver himself and the affair concerned into higher hands. Then he would find himself saying things that he did not understand: a voice not his own would suddenly speak out of him. At first this had astonished and frightened him. Now he was old and used to it: he never felt quite sure of himself until this happened, until God Himself uttered incomprehensible words through his mouth. He knew from experience how these words could pierce the toughest obstacles, destroying them and bringing the truth to light.

When he had told the Dominican Father Perezcaballero— whom he admired and loved, and whose voice he always found so fascinating—before he went away, that there was some flaw in his faith, that had been, from the human point of view, the purest nonsense. How had he, the least important monk in his monastery, with nothing to offer but a devilish leer and never particularly clever about the subtleties of theology, had the temerity to criticize anyone as complicated and experienced and wise as Father Perezcaballero? But he hadn't really said these things himself: they had been said through his mouth.

So when Father Perezcaballero came in, Dom Dusolier felt a great sense of emptiness and anxiety. If anybody had asked him at that moment why he had said those revealing and accusing words he would not have been able to give the slightest explanation. He was more impressed—indeed oppressed— than ever by his friend's splendidly chiselled features, by his clear voice, which occasionally swelled out in a controlled but moving bass, by his impressive and expressive gestures—even by the melancholy that overshadowed his face.

For a while Father Perezcaballero sat there in silence. Then he lowered his eyes into Dom Dusolier's, which at once looked away. Dom Dusolier was afraid, absolutely afraid. Why had he uttered those unfortunate words? However had he had the temerity? Now a new humiliation was awaiting him. At that very moment he felt his lips open and the spasm came. At the last moment he managed to hide his quivering, afflicted, distorted, gaping mouth with his hand.

Father Perezcaballero, who had noticed what had happened, did not lower his eyes as he usually did, out of pity so as not to upset his friend, but kept on looking straight at him. And he thought:

You have faith, poor chap, I know. I know that it was people like you that Our Lord gathered around Him. What would He have said to me?

The conversation got under way haltingly. Father Perezcaballero was obliged to talk himself, for Dom Dusolier remained silent.

At first he talked about ordinary things, then suddenly he remembered Dr. Lebrun. Without knowing what it might lead to, he mentioned that he had been to see him.

Dom Dusolier did not always find it easy to follow Father Perezcaballero. In this case he listened for a while without understanding: the sound of the words reached his ear all right but that was as far as they went. Finally he shook his horse's head vigorously—his blue eyes had meanwhile been taking on an increasingly washed-out look—and he succeeded in catching the general drift. And without quite understanding why he was doing it, he asked, in a surprisingly firm voice:

"*Why* did you go and see him?"

Father Perezcaballero looked at him in surprise.

"I don't know. He had asked me to—quite a long time ago. And then I didn't want him to imagine that I looked down on him."

"That is the apparent motive. But there's another one hidden away behind it. Why did you really go and see him?"

76

"I don't know."

"Had you thought of going to see him before you left the monastery?"

"No. No, I think not. I had indeed been thinking of him, but I had no fixed plan. I had a few hours to spare because a library I wanted to go to happened to be closed. And as I chanced to be in the neighbourhood—"

Father Dusolier nodded.

"You are getting nearer the truth. Think it over a bit more! You have—off and on—always been thinking about him. You have felt drawn towards him. Why?"

Father Perezcaballero:

"I don't know."

"And you have never wondered about such an important matter? Don't you see, then, that there *must* be some reason for it? And that your very uncertainty shows that you don't want to know what it is?"

Father Perezcaballero raised his face, there was a suggestion of a haughty smile on it, which however suddenly froze. Perhaps—perhaps this old fellow with the horse's head was right? He propped his head on his left hand and reflected.

Right inside—right deep down—he knew that it was not to help him. That was certain. Curiosity? Hardly! Ilse?

He looked up. Dom Dusolier was sitting there with his eyes closed, as though asleep.

"I think I was impelled towards him because I wanted to feel superior to him," he said softly.

Dom Dusolier nodded, his eyes still closed.

"Right. That's what I suspected. *Why* did you want to feel superior? Because you really considered yourself inferior. What did you feel inferior to him *about?*"

He opened his eyes and directed a watery gaze past his friend.

"Or to put it better: in what respect *are* you inferior to him? *In what respect have you failed?*"

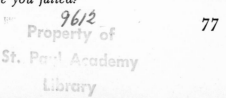
77

Father Perezcaballero's eagle eyes scrutinized every inch of his friend's face. He could feel something breaking up, opening up, inside himself—could feel that he was coming near to some kind of boil, a private, well-hidden, painful boil. But what was it?

"I don't know," he answered for the third time. And went on: "You know the way I act, my theatrical manner, the way I like serving God in a way that is aesthetically pleasing. I have often confessed to you about it."

Dom Dusolier shook his head.

"Yes, yes. A child can see that. . . . God simply smiles at it. In any case there's no greater sin in serving Him with beauty and style as you do than clumsily and ridiculously as I do. We are all the same poor human beings. But, my dear fellow, in your innermost being there is something that is in ruins. *You have no faith!*"

Father Perezcaballero was prepared for this. He had been told it more than once before.

"Then I don't know what faith is," he said. "I'm sure I live entirely by faith!"

"Are you quite certain of that?" asked Dom Dusolier in a friendly, almost childishly kind and gentle voice. "You perform all the acts of charity: the disciplined, the aesthetic, the sacrificial. You never arrive late, like me. You never sing the wrong note. I know that you keep yourself under the strictest self-control. You go to confession, and you pray. In a way, however, you used to *live* more than you do now. Now I don't know you anything like so well, I only know what you do. . . . And what you do has somehow become too—smooth. You seem—forgive me—to be encased in a sort of stainless steel. Do you understand what I mean?"

He laid his hand on his friend's shoulder.

"Do you ever cry?"

78

And before Perezcaballero could answer, he went on, quite unmoved:

"You see—you can't even cry any more."

Father Perezcaballero got up. He was very pale: a tremor ran over his face. His eyes were burning as he looked away over his friend's shoulder.

"I don't know whether you're right," he said. "But this much is certain: a cardinal sin is involved. I am in a way empty. But on the other hand—"

Dom Dusolier had also risen. He was not smiling, but his eyes were glowing, softly, emptily, like a child's.

"No," he said, "don't bother about any 'other hand'! We must pray, my dear fellow."

CHAPTER EIGHT

Kansdorf was sitting at his desk.

It was early morning, and Paris had not yet awakened to the February cold.

Could there be any more freezing place than an unheated Paris house? For a long time he had knelt at the hearth trying to make a fire, but the sticks were too damp and he used up one newspaper after another. In the end it began to burn, but miserably, without giving out any heat. In spite of the ban on using electricity for heating he had gone out and got his electric fire and put it under the desk. He didn't feel up to getting dressed until it was a little warmer. He could feel rheumatic pains in his back: the sheets had been damp the previous evening. He pulled his fur coat on over his dressing gown and turned the cuffs down over his fingers.

He was studying the state of his finances. For he was to die. As a matter of fact it had come just at the right time, for his money would not have lasted for more than two years anyway. But supposing Dr. Lebrun talked him into spending some of his money now, and then got him better? In the old days he had managed to get along on the odd article or translation. With the interest on his capital this had given him quite a decent income. But now he was no longer fit to work.

The paper fell from his hand and he saw his wife before

him, as she had looked when she had died. He gave a faint groan.

She had been taken ill quite suddenly—twelve years ago now. He had never taken her symptoms seriously. Nor had she. Pains, vomiting—they had gone on every day. She had held on bravely, doctored herself a little: he used to hear her lying awake in her room at night, sometimes whimpering softly. He would get up to her again and again. Shouldn't he call the doctor? Yes—tomorrow, perhaps.

And the morning came when he had to call him. The doctor made a brief examination of the boyishly slender body —it looked just as it had done when he had married her— and then called for an ambulance. An immediate operation was necessary.

He had still not taken the matter at all seriously. He had gone with her to the hospital, taken her flowers and fruit and papers, asked her if she wanted a radio. . . .

They didn't operate. It would be best, they said, to wait until the director returned. In any case they wanted to keep her under observation.

The well-preserved body had such powers of resistance, the woman herself had such patience—they were bound to pull through! He felt no anxiety, even though it was strange living alone in the house. Several times a day he went along to the hospital, and rang up still oftener. He was annoyed by the repeated information that they would have to wait for the director to come before they could do anything, and perhaps he made one or two rather thoughtless remarks. . . .

The director returned and the time came for the operation. But it was cancelled. For by now it had become too late.

Dagny could no longer eat. She grew thinner and thinner. Day after day he sat by her side, much to the annoyance of the doctors and nurses. He saw specialists. He tried right to the very last moment to keep Dagny cheerful. Finally he realized that the game was up.

At night he walked round and round the hospital, unable to sleep. He tried to pray—simply to find out where he had gone wrong. Early in the mornings he would call in at some workman's café, and in smelly surroundings drink bad coffee and eat sticky pastry tasting of oil.

On one of these mornings he came across a man walking slowly along in front of him with his hands behind his back. He hurried after him, seeming to recognize the shape of the shoulders and the way the head was bent slightly forward. As he came up with him the man turned his head. It was indeed the person he had thought—Erik, Dagny's first husband. Kansdorf wanted to take to his heels, but it was too late. For two whole years he had battled against this man before he had succeeded in driving him out of the field. Erik had resisted to the end. He knew that Dagny did not love him, but despite that he would not consider a separation. He was prepared to give her all the freedom she wanted if only she would consent to stay with him as his wife. Kansdorf had been to see him, explained that he was behaving despicably in refusing to give up a woman who loved someone else, shown him that he was only acting from jealousy and that he could not possibly love a woman if all he did was to cause her suffering. He had seen Erik burst into tears; it had been rather painful. But before he had left him he had managed to extract a promise from him. And Erik had kept it: he had given Dagny her freedom.

Kansdorf had realized later that Erik was in many respects an unusual person—gentle, sensitive, uncertain in health and rather peculiar in manner, but very good-natured. The only harsh words he ever heard him speak were:

"Watch out! One day you will suffer just as much as I'm suffering now!"

Perhaps he would suffer just as much. But not in the same way. With Dagny he had lived a life of pure happiness for their few brief years together.

Now he had to say hello to the man. He felt a certain embarrassment. So did Erik. Two men who loved the same woman stood there in the chilly darkness under a street lamp and raised their hats to each other. It was comic and undignified. But how could it be otherwise? There was bound to be something strange about their conversation. Perhaps they could now stop hating each other. For there was no longer anything to come between them except that they loved the same woman and she was doomed to die.

Kansdorf had already let him know how matters stood, and that there was no hope. Erik himself had rung up once or twice—he referred to it now, with a shy look from under his fair curly hair, which still looked soft and youthful.

Side by side in the light drizzle, they walked silently along.

"Do you still love her?" Kansdorf suddenly asked. "Don't answer if you'd rather not."

"Yes," answered Erik, "more than ever."

"Do you hate me?"

"No," he answered. "Why should I? You hurt me, and there was a time when I couldn't sleep because of you. But wounds heal. One realizes after a time that the whole of life is simply a wound—a sort of idiocy. You have found that too, I imagine?"

I? thought Kansdorf. No, not I. I have been happy. But now, now. . . .

"Yes," he answered. "I have found that too"

Erik held out his hand to him, and Kansdorf, confused and moved, pressed it. This was a man he had gravely injured. It was the first time that he had ever done such a thing. He remembered how brutally he had behaved, and was just about to say something about it when Erik, divining his intention, said softly:

"You needn't tell me anything. Love is a sort of being possessed. If we had to take full responsibility for what we do when love takes hold of us, we should none of us count for much."

There was nothing to add. They parted.

A few more days went by before Dagny finally died. During the last week she hardly ate a thing: her body was poisoned through and through. Her face was exhausted and unrecognizable, her hair lank and lustreless, she lay there with her mouth open, her breath rattling in her throat. He sat at her side for hour after hour, oppressed by the sense of his utter helplessness. He did not even know whether she could recognize him. But when he happened to leave the room he could see a change come over her face. So she knew that he was there; she missed him.

He was able to hear her last word. He had put his ear almost on her mouth and clearly heard the word:

"Forgive—"

He did not understand that. He had nothing to forgive her for. He knew that everything was clear and open between them. She had never kept anything from him.

During her last hours she was unconscious. She died one morning before he could get to her. When he arrived he was not allowed into her room. Beyond the door he could hear the noisy conversation of the nurses busy with her body. When he was at last allowed in, her chin was bound up. He fell on his knees. When he touched her forehead, it was already chilly. Her face had none of that peace of the dead of which he had read so much, but rather a look of struggle and suffering. He was filled with dread as he gazed into the countenance he had loved.

The next year had been hard. He had devoted his entire life to the memory of the dead woman. He had her portrait painted from the best photographs he had of her, her room remained exactly as it was, he gave none of her things away. When his friends warned him against this worship of the dead, he saw them no more. He became more and more of a recluse.

Two years later an event occurred which was to have a decisive effect on his life. Dagny had a sister who worked as a nurse in the north of Sweden. She died in a skiing accident and he had to travel up and see to her affairs. It didn't take long. Amongst other things he came across a few bundles of letters, wondered what to do with them, noticed his wife's handwriting on some of them and decided to keep them. He put them away unopened in what had been Dagny's desk. He kept them a whole year without reading them. One evening, when he had nothing else to do, he came across them again. This time he read them.

They contained an account of a love affair.

That was nine years ago, he realized, and the pain was still with him. He got up and began to wander round the cold, smoke-laden room. Wouldn't Clothilde be coming in soon with his breakfast? No, it was still too early.

He sat down again and took the letters out of the desk drawer—in all those years he had never been able to destroy them.

In one of the first he read:

. . . The most dreadful thing is that I think I love him. Edvard knows nothing about it, he is as attentive and dear a husband to me as ever, and you know how much he means to me. He suspects nothing, and that is a good thing. I have truly tried my very utmost to fight against it, but it is of no avail. . . . I never thought that anything like this could come into my life, but clearly I was mistaken. I have taken fire like a seven-teen-year-old. . . .

He stopped reading, remembering how dreadful he had felt. Who was the man? One of his friends? He had read on, feverishly. In a letter written some months later he came across this:

. . . It is an absolute mystery to me how such a thing could come to pass. You ask what is so special about him. I don't know how to explain it. It is not the physical side, though that does come into it. He is so wonderfully quick; he goes past me with a smile, a few words—and only afterwards do I really understand what he meant. He is always ahead of me, even though I am not exactly slow, as you know! You cannot imagine how he speaks—I have never heard anything like it. He talks fast, and yet he always puts a certain emphasis or implication or just the slightest hint into what he says—and this quite overpowers me. He can tell me that he cares for me without a single word—he can say it by an almost imperceptible tone of voice, by raising his eyebrows, by a movement of his finger. . . . You know what a splendid person Edvard is—even-tempered, kindly, reliable, sensible—everything you can think of. But he talks *with his words;* he has, so to speak, no radiance. . . . Nor have I of course. . . . *But he*—what kind of mystery envelops him? He has never written me a letter, he has never told me that he loves me, we have almost never been alone together, and on the few occasions when we have we have only exchanged quite meaningless words. But that makes no difference. He lives intensely, he has a kind of mind that I have never come across in other men, he is serious in a way that can absolutely shatter me, and his laugh is so un-forced. . . . Men are often so stolid and heavy. . . . And so down-to-earth. Edvard is not, as a matter of fact; he is in his way a complicated person, and he has eyes. But he hasn't noticed a thing! Sparks fly from the other man to me—and nobody notices. Oh, my whole life has gained a new content, a new dimension, since I came to know him! Yet nothing will happen. I shall never do anything to destroy our marriage. It will cost me suffering, I know.

The first time Kansdorf had read this letter he had been seized by despair. He had no idea whom she was speaking of. There was no one amongst his friends who could possibly be considered. He had felt such a rocklike certainty that everything between Dagny and himself had been clear and above board. Yet she had gone on living with him for year after year, keeping this dreadful secret to herself, and he had never even faintly suspected it! He had had complete trust in her—and she had responded by not giving him the slightest idea what was in her mind.

He read the letter over and over again, trying to get to the bottom of it, with the image of some exceptional but quite unrecognizable man before his eyes. What had happened between them? Was it quite certain that Dagny had told her sister everything in her letters?

In one of the later letters occurred this:

. . . No, you don't understand me. There is nothing directly or remotely sexual or anything of that kind in all this. I never think of him in that way. But he is . . . well, like poetry, like wonderful poetry. Do you know?—like a quotation that goes on ringing in one's ears and keeps on coming back, giving colour to every experience and depth to all the surrounding world. Perhaps that sounds silly, but I can only compare his power over me with the power possessed by the greatest lyric poets, Shelley for instance or Olaf Bull. He lives in the atmosphere I breathe, he is so close to me that I seem to have him under my skin, seem to be united to him—and yet, despite all this, sensuality plays no part in it. My heart is beginning to beat at the same rate as his, I am coming to see things with his eyes, soon I shall be judging everybody by his standards. He is the most winged creature you can imagine—and yet full of ardour—and in his ardour so considerate, almost reverential . . . can you understand that? He seems to have uncovered something in me that no one else has ever found, he never mentions it, to me, but his whole being suggests respect, care, consideration. . . . Oh; how I love his lightness, his fineness, his consideration—how stolid most men are, how down-to-earth, and how they love to reduce everything to simple formulas! But as for the merely hinted at, the complicated, the difficult-to-express. . . . And all this is to be found in one man, you understand, who is, it is true, slender and youthful, but is still a normal human being with a resounding deep voice and strong hands! It is all quite enchanting. And you will understand what it is like when I go on feeling all this in the company of Edvard —who is so loyal and faithful and affectionate to me, who would never deceive me, whom I respect and with whom I mean to stay, who depends on me with a most touching love and always will. . . . But in spite of all this he is inevitably an absolute stranger to the entire world in which the other moves as though in his element—*lightly, swiftly, tenderly. . . .*

He had read this letter ten times at least. It contained nothing that was not absolutely true. What was said about himself, for instance—it was if anything too flattering a picture. But the fantastic thing, the unbearable thing, was that his whole life had revolved around this woman—and yet he had never understood her, never suspected that she was concealing anything, never imagined, never even dreamed, that another man's image was before her eyes when she had— loyally—responded to his embraces.

Step by step he had moved towards a crisis. The most senseless thing happened: he was overcome by a sort of bitterness against the dead woman. He got so intensely involved in the affair that Dagny herself finally disappeared—he no longer knew what she had really been like, or what he was really complaining about. He then tried to summon her back, to make her come to life again. In vain. She escaped his memory. In the end he found it impossible to imagine what the woman he had loved had been like. And at the same time he hadn't the faintest idea which of their mutual friends she had been in love with. For month after month he wrestled with the problem: he knew that it was pointless, unhealthy, nonsensical; nevertheless he could not stop himself. He had to know once and for all whether his wife had finally been unfaithful to him or not. The correspondence broke off suddenly—didn't that suggest that something had occurred that Dagny preferred not to tell her sister about? Of course she must have been overcome by passion in the end! Of course the man had not been worthy of all she had written about him: no doubt he had been a far less profound person than the dream figure of her imagination! Only one issue was possible—the most shameful, the nastiest. As usual.

All at once he had discovered who the man was.

One evening he was sitting in the house of an old friend of his. The conversation turned upon a mutual friend, a writer, Lorens Jörgensen, a man in his thirties. His books were mentioned. He had never read them. His last novel was brought out, and was left lying open. He glanced casually through it.

He came across the words, "lightly, swiftly, tenderly."

He felt as though he had received a blow. He asked if he might borrow the book. He read it through the same evening, but found nothing. None of the characters in the novel bore any resemblance to his wife. It was only the words, "lightly, swiftly, tenderly," that fitted in.

He pondered a great deal over the various possibilities. Chance? Hardly. He *must* have read her words. Why, then, so absolutely without any further connection? If the two had been joined in such a powerful experience, why was there nothing of it in the book? Did the author want to hide himself away?

He waited a few days and thought the matter over carefully. He read two or three of Jörgensen's preceding books—nowhere was there even a trace of his wife, though there were plenty of other love affairs in them.

He finally decided to go and see the man.

CHAPTER NINE

He had got up again—why should he go on plaguing himself by reliving these scenes, these feverish memories of humiliation and anguish?

But he had to have certainty, once and for all. For once and for all he must get this thing right: either he must master it, or else. . . .

He had awakened early, it was a spring morning. Jörgensen lived out in the zoo park, in a white, single-storeyed house not far from the restaurant. He had once said hello to him outside the house, but had never been inside.

He had wandered out; it had seemed only a short distance, so active were his thoughts. And now he remembered a strange thing: when he had reached the canal running round the gardens he had actually heard a horn, not loud but very tender. . . . Was that the horn that now sounded in his dreams? What peculiar laws governed memory? In what mysterious connections was his ego involved? Had he really not the faintest idea what was happening to him? Was he simply a pawn, moved about by an unknown hand?

He was standing in front of Jörgensen's house. The time must be about ten o'clock. It was not warm, but a clear spring day, with a fresh breeze blowing. He suddenly noticed how fresh the leaves were, how green the lawns, how blue the sky. "Lightly, swiftly, tenderly. . . ." Yes, there could be no doubt that it *was* Jörgensen. He stood there for a while, gazing at the elegant bright white house on its low foundations nestling amongst oaks and maple trees. It was at peace. As he turned round, a double canoe slid silently by, driven forward by brown arms. This only seemed to emphasize the silence. It was the stillness before the storm.

He felt a slight touch of giddiness. He was facing a great mystery, and the mystery was to be found in this bright white house, under these gently moving blue clouds, in this unencumbered air. Suddenly it seemed to him that the familiar words described the absolute essence of everything before his eyes. Dagny *must* have seen it too. She must have been here, many times, and absorbed all this and projected it onto her lover. For of course she had been his mistress! He was conscious of his own dullness, felt awkward and clumsy: he had nothing of all this airiness, superiority, freedom. But however had she been able to bring herself to acquiesce? (There was no doubt that this was the man who had conquered her!)

Suddenly he saw her face before him as it had been when she had died. And the word she had spoken came back into his mind: "Forgive—" What could there have been for him to forgive, except this? The memory of it no longer upset him: he had already grown quite stony. For years he had been unable to think of that dead, suffering countenance without shuddering; now he remained unmoved. The truth was all he wanted! He must know the truth, to be able to go on living. Whatever horrors it might hold, it must be brought to light! He couldn't live on tenterhooks any longer!

He had no idea how long he had been standing there, and was just about to take a few paces towards the entrance— the house lay there utterly at peace—when he suddenly heard a clear, pleasant voice behind him. Did Jörgensen really speak like that? He never seemed to have noticed his voice before.

"Edvard! What are you looking at? Admiring my house?"

He turned round. Yes, of course, Jörgensen went riding every morning. He saw him, some distance away, in jodhpurs and a white shirt, his jacket over his arm, hatless, fair hair slightly ruffled by the breeze.

He stared at the man as he came towards him.

He had often seen him, he was his friend, he was familiar with most of his ways. But never in his life had he seen him like this: "light, swift, tender." He was not exactly graceful; he was of strong but average build: possibly his walk had more of a swing than was usual, and this gave him an air of well-being and self-confidence—perhaps other people did not walk along quite so nonchalantly. His face was not young, or handsome—rather too heavy, with its broad forehead. The fair hair—yes, that perhaps had something young and light about it: he remembered that he had been struck before by the contrast between the high forehead with its deep wrinkles and the youthful hair. There were really two people. The forehead, the body, the chin, were one man. The hair, the walk, the demeanour, were the other. Perhaps he had been able to be a poet because of the tension between these two human beings who together made up his total self: one could imagine that one took after his mother, the other after his father.

The most astonishing thing about him, however, was his voice. Kansdorf had literally never heard it before. If anyone had asked him to describe Jörgensen's voice he would have simply said,

"Quite ordinary—deep—not particularly striking."

But now that he heard it aright, wasn't it a quite remarkably elastic voice, didn't it absolutely hurl its words out?

Jörgensen had reached him. He had to take his outstretched

hand. He could now no longer scrutinize him. He was looking into a laughing, fresh face quite free from deceit or mistrust.

"Yes," he said, "I came out for a walk. You live very grandly."

Jörgensen nodded and looked proudly towards the low white house.

"One could hardly live better," he said. "At least in a big city. Won't you come in and have some tea with me? Do you drink tea in the mornings?"

How should he answer? In any case he *wanted* to get inside. He wanted to see what was there, be in the atmosphere in which his wife had felt so happy, where she had loved this man.

They went into a hall, where the books began—apparently the unbound ones were kept down here—and then proceeded into a large living room with bookshelves all round the walls and an open hearth. Not a single dark colour—everything in pastel shades—light, light! Of course it must have been here! This was the man.

Jörgensen rang a bell and a young girl came in. As he asked for another cup and a little more tea, Kansdorf looked at the girl and all of a sudden it was clear to him that the two were living together. How did he know? He could tell from the familiarity, the ease, the closeness between them. He could tell from the man's look. He could see it in the pleasure with which the girl returned his look.

He sat down. Jörgensen was talking. Kansdorf wasn't listening: now and again he took in a few words. The tea was brought in, Jörgensen put it in the pot—the moment the water began to boil over the flame he poured it out steadily into the English stone teapot, warmed in advance. His movements were light and resolute. As he tipped the teapot and the tea came pouring out he held his head a little to one side like a boy, a lock of his hair fell forward.

It *was* he!

That he should never have noticed this side of his personality before! All he remembered about him was earnest arguments, a thundering deep voice and a furrowed brow.

Jörgensen pushed his cup away, then leaned back in the low, yellow-upholstered sofa, drew up one leg, put his clasped hands round his knee and said:

"Do you know, today I've just had an idea for a novel. It's a marvellous feeling!"

Kansdorf looked up.

"I understand," he said. "Or rather, I don't understand at all. I can understand how a poem comes into being—I imagine it as an unusually strong and lasting feeling, persisting right through the whole technical side of the making of the poem. I can't do that myself, but I can understand it. But a novel! How in the world can anyone sit down and imagine all the characters in a novel all together?"

Jörgensen leaned his head back.

"Yes, how can anyone do that?" he said with a laugh. "I don't understand it either. But it happens—now and again. Do you know, when you've written the first hundred pages and finished the skeleton, the characters begin to live of their own accord. But to get them moving before you've got to know them! There is nothing more exhausting than forcing yourself to describe characters you don't know. It's only after you've been writing for a few weeks that you can really begin —and then you have to throw everything overboard and begin all over again. And even then you never get what you had originally intended. Other characters suddenly start popping up, you know! And any that have anything to do with real life, any that you have, so to speak, secretly photographed —die! But the ones that have been entirely imagined live. I don't know how it happens."

"You never stick to real life, then?" said Kansdorf, and his voice trembled a little, involuntarily.

"I *have* done so," answered Jörgensen, "but I've given up trying to. It never really comes off."

Kansdorf seized his cup and emptied it. Now he felt the full powerful aroma of the tea, and everything seemed to become clear as he said:

"Recently I came across a splendid sentence—or rather phrase—in one of your books."

Jörgensen leaned forward—his movements *were* graceful, there was no denying it—and stretched out a hand for the glass of marmalade with its silver lid.

"What was it?" he asked politely, obviously quite uninterested.

"Well, in your last book occur the words, 'lightly, swiftly, tenderly'. . . ."

Jörgensen nodded, helped himself to the marmalade, spilt a little of it on the tablecloth, made a quick grimace, removed it—lightly and swiftly—with his teaspoon, and put the glass of marmalade back again.

"That's right. Well, so you think that's good?"

Kansdorf gave him a sharp look. You're very clever, he thought. Incredibly clever.

"Yes," he said. "I think it's very fine: the words have a kind of melody, and they suggest a certain sort of line to me, if I may put it so. You seem to me to have given a quite remarkable impression of delicacy with them. . . . And I too can appreciate that sort of thing."

Jörgensen nodded again. He returned Kansdorf's look—was that perhaps an unconscious confession?

"Look here," he said, barely interested, it seemed, "I thought you were more at home on metaphysical ground—so to speak."

"Why should you think that?"

Jörgensen looked at him gravely, his face took on an expression—evasive, perhaps, but not unfriendly, and he gave a quick shrug of the shoulders:

"Perhaps I'm mistaken. But the thing I had noticed about you—and it had made a great impression on me—was a certain earnestness, a sort of listening-in to yourself, which I interpreted—quite wrongly perhaps—as melancholy, a sort of daydreaming tendency—slightly German. Do you understand what I mean?"

"Perhaps I really have something of the sort in me," said Kansdorf, who was finding it increasingly difficult to get to the point. (How would he be able to choose his words when it came to the actual moment?) "But I'm not by any means without a sense of the other side of things. That was true of Dagny too. . . ."

Now it was out. He was looking at Jörgensen so hard that his eyes watered. But he saw enough: Jörgensen made no sort of reaction at all. Oh yes, he was a hard, smooth, tough, clever type! He understood what Kansdorf was getting at, all right! He knew why he had come. And now he was wondering—smoothly, like an eel!—how to get out of his grip. He was not going to succeed!

"Do you think so?" he said, too casually. "Yes, perhaps you're right. You know, I was very fond of her. You must miss her dreadfully!"

Never had Kansdorf seen a franker, more friendly look. Could any man be such a monstrous liar?

Things were not going as easily as he had expected.

"Yes," he said, and his voice became a little too precise. "I know that quite remarkably well, for she often used to use precisely those words—'lightly, swiftly, tenderly.'"

Jörgensen's forehead wrinkled into furrows as he raised his eyebrows in surprise.

"Really?" he returned. "What's that you say? Those words

occur in my very last novel! It came out a year after her death, didn't it? Cigarette?"

Kansdorf stiffened. He was coming nearer to the point!

"No, I'm certainly not making a mistake," he answered.

He took the cigarette without realizing what he was doing. After he had lit it he noticed that he put the match out with unnecessary vigour.

"She used those words remarkably often. And as a matter of fact the reason I came here was to get the whole business cleared up—"

He looked through the cloud of smoke at his friend, who had lit a cigarette too, and now, letting it droop from the corner of his mouth, was leaning back with his hands clasped round his knee again.

"Yes, it is remarkable," he said. "Do you know, I find it difficult to explain. I met her so very rarely."

"I thought," said Kansdorf, his excitement rising and no longer master of his train of thought, "I thought that perhaps she had got the impression here in this house, with you—I mean, your house, the whole atmosphere—all this—"

For the first time signs of disturbance appeared on Jörgensen's face.

"I don't know what you mean," he said, still with his cigarette in his mouth. "In the first place the words were invented by me and not by her. And in the second place she never came here. I thought you knew that."

What was he to say? He couldn't prove anything to the contrary. Perhaps it was true?

"That's quite right," he said desperately. "I'm talking nonsense. But you will appreciate that I was bound to be a little taken aback when a little while ago I came across an expression in one of your novels—a most unusual expression —which I knew that my wife was in the habit of using."

At this point Jörgensen took his cigarette out of his mouth, straightened his knee, and stood up.

He folded his arms across his chest.

"But, my dear fellow," he said, "using? Using how? In what connection?"

Kansdorf looked up. He noticed how powerful the figure facing him was, with the sunlight striking on him through the window. He felt inferior, humiliated. He too stood up.

"You know," he said. "You know quite well. And now all I want to ask you is: how long did your affair with my wife last?"

Jörgensen did not move. He clenched his teeth together.

As though before a fight, thought Kansdorf.

Then Jörgensen walked over to the bookshelves and turned round, leaning his back against the books.

"I can see," he said, "that this is becoming serious. I can promise you one thing in advance: I swear to you on my oath that every word I say in the matter will be absolutely true. Are you prepared to believe that?"

Kansdorf shrugged his shoulders.

Jörgensen went on:

"I see you have a fixed idea in your mind. But it is untrue! I never had anything to do with your wife! As to those words of mine—before I put them into the novel, they were in a poem I wrote while she was alive, and I may have quoted them once when she happened to be present."

He went to the writing desk, burrowed about amongst some papers for a while, and finally pulled out a sheet.

"It's not particularly good," he said, "but I once wrote this: as a matter of fact it was published."

He began to read, and Kansdorf gazed at him fixedly. Now for the first time he could see what he was like. He saw the point of "light, swift, tender." He raised his hand. His voice was gentle, firm, light; he held the little poem in his hand in the same way. There was an expression of youthful satisfaction on his face as he read the poem out:

A faint breeze through the dead wood fluttered,
And all the leaves fell;
A horn rang out, and dying uttered
Its own death knell.
Anguish was there in the wood that day,
And melancholy.
A form flitted by on its silent way—
Lightly, swiftly, tenderly.

"There you have it," he said. "I haven't dated the poem,
but I think I'm right in saying that it is three or four years
old. It is quite meaningless, just a fleeting utterance, as
though from a violin. It was therefore written *before* your
Dagny's death. She could have read it in a magazine, she
could also have heard me read it."

"Couldn't it be that *she* said these words *to you?*" asked
Kansdorf.

Jörgensen looked at him inquiringly.

"That is not out of the question, intrinsically," he said.
"But I happen to *know* that that is not the way it was. And
I can even *prove* it. But it is not time for that yet. The important thing is this suspicion of yours which I intend to
demolish once and for all."

"How?" asked Kansdorf curtly.

"I'll have a shot at it, anyway. I swear to you that I never
touched your wife, never had the slightest interest in her, as
a woman. I admired her, as we all did, I respected her, I
thought she was beautiful and had a presence and style and so
on. At a meal in your house I once said all this, but you
probably won't remember that."

Kansdorf shook his head. But now he did remember it.

"Do you believe me, or don't you?"

Kansdorf shook his head.

"No," he said, "you're lying. You are such a clever liar
that I am all admiration. You talk of proof. But *I* have the
proof! I have it here in my hand!"

"Proof?" said Jörgensen. "Let's have it!"

Kansdorf took out five of the letters he had found.

"These letters are from my wife to her sister, who is now dead. In them she tells the whole story of your love affair."

Jörgensen shook his head.

"But that's absolute nonsense!" he said. "I never *did* love her, I was never alone with her, I never thought of her in that way. It's all the purest fantasy!"

"You are getting worked up," Kansdorf said calmly, "and I can understand that. But in these letters my wife describes in full detail how wonderful you are—"

Jörgensen did not move.

"Would you allow me to read the letters?" he said. "Or would you rather read them out to me yourself? I don't get the hang of it at all."

He left his place by the bookshelves and threw himself down on the sofa.

Kansdorf hesitated. To read his wife's hymns of praise to this man would be distasteful. To hand them over to him would be—he hardly knew why he was reluctant. But he had to decide. He took one of the letters in his hand.

"Read this one," he said. "It's a beautiful letter. And it will clear the matter up."

His hand was trembling as he held the letter out. Jörgensen seized it, read it rapidly through, turned red, raised his hand to his forehead, pushed his hair back, revealed his white teeth in a sudden grimace, stood up and said:

"You are right. She seems to have been in love with me. But I had no idea of it! Not the slightest idea! I never realized it. . . . Never did she betray it, by a single word or gesture. There never was a more faithful wife than yours."

Kansdorf took the letter back again.

"It's time this farce ended," he said curtly. "How long did the affair between the two of you last?"

Jörgensen laid one of his hands on the back of the sofa

and swung himself over it—lightly and swiftly. He wrenched open the door leading into the hall.

"Greta," he shouted.

Then he turned back to Kansdorf.

"What's coming won't be very nice," he said, "but I must prove to you that I am innocent."

Kansdorf had no idea what he intended to do.

He could feel himself beginning to lose control of himself.

The girl came running in.

"Yes?" she said. "Yes?"

She was out of breath and looked anxious as she saw Jörgensen's excited face. He seized her by the shoulders and closed the door behind her.

"Greta," he said, "I have something most unusual to ask of you. But you must help me. All you have to do is to give a truthful answer to any questions I may ask you."

She stared at him, startled.

"Yes." she said. "Of course!"

He went quickly to the desk and took up his poem.

"Just look at this," he said, handing it to her. "When did I write this poem? Who was it about? And who was it written to?"

She read the first line and looked up with a proud smile.

"It was for me," she said. "It was the first week I was here. And that must be about four years ago now."

"Exactly. And now I must ask you something else. Your answer, I promise you, will never go beyond these four walls. You must realize, my darling"—he gave her a quick kiss on the forehead—"my friend here has lost his wife and he is convinced that she and I had an affair. She was beautiful and attractive, and there is no doubt that such a thing *could* have happened. But it didn't. And so will you tell me—when did we begin to love each other?"

The girl raised her hands and half-hid her face. She looked

at Kansdorf for a long time. Then she looked towards Jörgensen again.

"The third week after I came here," she said. "And ever since—"

She smiled, shyly but proudly. She was enchanting.

Jörgensen seized her by the shoulders and again kissed her on the forehead.

"Yes. And would you say that I have ever been unfaithful to you during this time, had an affair with someone else, for a long time, a real affair?"

She shook her head until her fair hair flopped, then smiled and turned to Kansdorf.

"No, that is quite out of the question! I can guarantee that!"

Jörgensen nodded; his face was pale and grave.

"Thank you," he said, "and please forgive me for making you talk of our love like this. But you will see that it was necessary."

She nodded, stroked his cheek and went slowly out. As she opened the door she turned round, her eyes shining with admiration and devotion.

Jörgensen took out another cigarette.

"Do you believe me *now?*" he asked

Kansdorf's mind was in a whirl. The fact was not to be doubted.

He was unable to reply.

"But—" he said. "You will understand—I hope—"

Jörgensen went up to him, gave him a hearty slap on the shoulder and said:

"I understand perfectly. In your place I should probably have reacted just as you have done. Your mistake is quite understandable. In matters in which passion is involved we are all criminals anyway. I know quite well that I could seduce my best friend's wife without turning a hair. There's no power in the world that can stop that kind of conflagration. In this case, however, I am innocent—absolutely innocent! I was the object of your wife's daydreams—oh, we all have dreams like that! You do too, no doubt?"

Kansdorf shook his head.

"Well, I do, anyway. We all make an ideal out of a woman, some woman. As your wife did with me. It is beautiful, what she writes, but as something about me it seems almost ludicrous. Don't you realize that the only explanation of it is that she just didn't know me? If she had, she would have written something quite different, I can assure you!"

He stopped. Then he turned to Kansdorf once again.

"Of course this isn't helping you at all," he said. "For if you are determined to find out all you can about her, it will obviously be just as painful to you whether the whole story is true or untrue. I can only beg you, for heaven's sake, to try to stop thinking about it. If you don't, you will destroy yourself!"

Kansdorf did not move. He felt humiliated and as though stripped naked. His wife had given this man her love—and he had not even noticed it! His whole life seemed grotesque. Jörgensen was right: this new discovery did not mean relief but further humiliation.

Jörgensen, however, was already his cool self again. He lit another cigarette and said:

"Forgive me if I can no longer take the matter seriously! But you will understand. I'm a novelist. I find the story very interesting. A husband suspects his wife of having been unfaithful to him. He goes to see the person he believes to have been the lover. In a dramatic scene he is convinced that he has been mistaken, that his wife has remained faithful to him, that his friend has not even noticed her little passion. *What happens then?* That I really cannot say in advance. What happens, eh? The human animal is a remarkable creature! Will you now in fact start hurling your accusations into the kingdom of the dead? Complain because her love was not strong enough to be noticed? The possibility fascinates me, I must admit. It's a theme for a full-length novel: a drama of jealousy—between life and death!"

He laughed, but not unkindly or triumphantly—he was the artist with a new creation before his eyes, burning to take possession of it.

"I don't know," answered Kansdorf. "I have nothing more to say. You have taken a load off my mind."

"And put another in its place, do you think?" said Jörgensen, following him to the door. "Now, don't do anything silly! Let us both be thankful to your dear Dagny—you because she remained faithful to you throughout your marriage, and I because she had friendly feelings towards me for a time, which unfortunately never came to light. Can we not join in this?"

He looked almost jovially at Kansdorf and held out his hand to him.

Kansdorf had to take it.

He went out into the open air, his head whirling.

The sun was dazzling; birds sang in the bushes.

There was a knock on the door.

Clothilde came in with the breakfast tray.

"Today it's tea," she said proudly. "And toast—!"

She put the tray down.

"But how smoky it is in here!" she said. "Won't you sit in the dining room for a bit, monsieur, while I open the windows?"

He nodded and walked clumsily out of the room.

She padded after him with the tray—the thief with the heart of gold.

CHAPTER TEN

The Dominicans in the Rue François I were very fashionable, and the Sainte Croix monastery was visited regularly by the high society people living in the nearby streets—the Avenue Montaigne, the Avenue George V, the Champs Elysées, the Avenue Marceau. The chapel was always full. The resonance of the Dominicans' singing rose up from behind the grille; they sang like warriors of the Lord. When there were processions, they advanced like an army, in manly, jubilant, battle mood. They did not bother about subtleties, their bowings and genuflectings had none of the extraordinary precision of the Benedictines, but no one could doubt their strength, their sense of direction or their unshakable faith.

Occasionally there was a sermon. Today it was Father Perezcaballero's turn.

He had tried to get out of it. He felt empty and restless—without rightly knowing why. But the Prior had been adamant

"All the better," he said. "If you have nothing to offer of yourself, God will be forced to speak through you. You *must* speak. We can't really change things just because you don't feel in the mood."

Perezcaballero might have realized this in advance. He knew his Order. But how would it turn out?

106

During the last few minutes before he went up into the pulpit, he prayed. In the middle of praying he was shocked by the sense that he was sending his prayers out into a void. There was no one to hear him. Had he really been praying like this, for years? Had he been sitting here amongst his fellow priests *believing* he was praying, *believing* he was opening himself out completely and offering up his life? Hadn't it all been empty show?

The thought gave him a shock. But he pushed it away and quickly recovered his composure. God had wanted to test him, to show him that of himself he had no power at all.

As he stepped into the pulpit a great feeling of peace came over him. Such temptations were too elementary altogether, of course: they were all in the day's work, the sort of thing that everyone had to go through. And suddenly an idea came into his head: instead of speaking on his prepared subject he would talk about his own experience! It would be a daring thing to do, but he was not afraid of improvising. In any case, what subject was he better acquainted with?

The sermon was to be talked about for long afterwards.

Father Perezcaballero was established as one of the most gifted pulpit orators in Paris, but no one had ever heard anything like this before. Never had his voice sounded so moving, never had his gestures looked so graceful or attractive, never had he presented his views so penetratingly, with such classical perfection! Above all, never had he uttered his own self so completely! That so proud a man could possess such humility!

Perezcaballero himself felt his confidence increasing the more he spoke. He kept the feeling down. In the mastery of technique, he had no rival. If inspiration failed for a moment, he could always fill in the gap with some literary or rhetorical flourish—could adopt a hushed tone, a slower tempo, make an ingenious digression until he was in a position to return to his point again and arise in majestic flight.

He did as a matter of fact deal with the subject he had originally intended to discuss, but it was clear to everyone that he was talking more about himself than about St. Paul. His audience listened in astonishment as he analyzed an apostle of the Christian gospel who had found himself in dire need, utterly empty. He preached Christianity, was delighted with his own outward gifts, thought he was devoting them to the service of God. But he gradually came to see that these outward forms were all he had. He who had so often preached love was without love. He who had given so many warnings against letting Christianity become a habit, had become a victim of Christian habit himself. When he looked fairly and squarely at his own prayers, he found that they were empty—a mockery against the Lord God! When he looked into himself, he found nothing but sin and pretense. He was seized by despair, until he realized that it was only through making this discovery that he could make any progress. Man was nothing, God was everything. He had needed these times of spiritual destitution to be able to come to see himself as he really was. . . .

The congregation was spellbound. It was a dazzling performance. This recognition of the worthlessness of everything outward was presented in a form that was outwardly brilliant. This desperate confession of his own defeat and emptiness—camouflaged as a presentation of Paul the Apostle —developed into great art, dazzling rhetoric. Once again Father Perezcaballero had won the hearts of all his hearers. But this time he had done it by speaking—under the cover of a blameless objectivity—plainly and unmistakably about himself. No one could fail to recognize the personal tone.

When he had finished he went back to his seat, fell on his knees and thanked God for the new strength that had come into him. He felt sure of himself again. It was Lebrun who had put him off his stroke. He had almost given up hope. Now he was himself again. Thanks be to God.

For a long time after the sermon the congregation remained behind in the chapel discussing in hushed voices what they had heard: the air was heavy with perfume. So that was what went to the making of a great preacher!

Many of them came up to thank Father Perezcaballero. He shook hands with them all, and then retired. He would have to hurry if he was to get to the Benedictines in time to see Dom Dusolier. He was dying to tell him about his new discovery, how he had once again come to realize that God never let anyone down, that only integrity and humility were needed for Him to perform a miracle.

On the way he kept thinking: have I ever spoken more convincingly? And just when I felt most down! He felt triumphant, though not in quite the same way as he had felt earlier. There was a slight uneasiness mixed up in it now too—he connected it with Lebrun. He must try to get Dom Dusolier to say what he thought about that. What could he do for Lebrun? And was he in a position to make up for the way he had once treated Ilse? He was ready to do anything.

He got out in the Rue de la Source, nodded to the monk in the bookshop—a Turk, a convert from Islam—was admitted, had to wait for a while along with a number of aging women, and finally came upon Dom Dusolier.

Dom Dusolier had forgotten that they had appointed to meet, and there were no seats to be had: should they sit in the cloisters? But there were monks there too, talking to the people who came to them for confession. They had to take refuge in the chapter room, which was damp and gloomy. At first they could hardly see each other's faces. But they preferred not to turn the lights on. The darkness was so restful.

109

Father Perezcaballero began, rather nervously, to describe his recent experience. Dom Dusolier sat there in complete silence: was he even listening? When Father Perezcaballero stopped speaking once, the silence disturbed him. Did it signify disapproval or indifference?

Once again he analyzed his condition: he had come under an influence, he had wavered for a while but he had not lost his faith, he felt himself to be on safe ground again, he had had a clear intellectual experience of God, and this gave him support. . . .

Actually Dom Dusolier was hardly listening. He took an occasional plunge into the fine-sounding flood of nervous words, as though to take a sample—a sample of mud. Each time he came to the same conclusion. He felt no anxiety. He had expected to hear something of the sort. He did not know, however—as usual—what to say in reply. His horse's head fell to one side and he propped it up on the lean outspread fingers of his right hand, he made no attempt to pray or even to listen inwardly, instead he became emptier and emptier—his condition became more and more a kind of stupidity. As a matter of fact he was feeling dead with weariness.

At last Perezcaballero stopped, and Dom Dusolier awoke with a start. He took his hand away and gave a deep sigh. And then:

"It must have been terrible," he said.

Father Perezcaballero started. Terrible? Was he joking? He shot a quick, angry glance at his friend in the semi-darkness, but fortunately kept his retort to himself. Dom Dusolier was always slow in the uptake. Hadn't he realized that it had been a tremendous success?—not only in the outward sense, though of course it had been that too, but above all inwardly? He had bared his soul, humbled himself, come back to God.

He forced himself not to say a word. Perhaps it was part of his trial to be in the hands of a confessor who was so senile that he didn't understand what he was told.

The silence lasted for quite a while. At one point it seemed as though Dom Dusolier was about to speak again, but he failed to get beyond the preparatory stage. He sank back again; but finally, staring down at the ground with his right hand raised in a particularly ungainly, inexpressive gesture that looked almost pathological he said:

"You see—that's the remarkable thing about you. You seem to be two people. One is the well-known, much admired Father Perezcaballero, whom people love to listen to; this person has many splendid qualities—will, knowledge, discipline and all the rest. Don't think that I am blind to them! The other—is the real you."

"That's just what I said," answered Father Perezcaballero, forcing his voice to stay low.

"Yes, yes," stammered Dom Dusolier in tones of absolute horror. "No doubt—that's what you said. But you obviously don't see that the gap—if such I may call it—that yawns between these two personalities . . . is a gap that is based on a lie."

"On a lie?"

"Yes. You see, soon you will be unable to see anyone properly. You are too clever. Anything cleverer than your lecture I can't imagine. No one but God could have seen through you this time. *I* could only do so because God spoke through me."

Father Perezcaballero took a deep breath. Well, well, he was prepared. He would not lower himself by any effort at defense.

"What I mean is this," said Dom Dusolier, hesitantly, tentatively. "I mean—I think—you really have no idea what it means—to love Christ. What have you got to say to that?"

"Go on, I'm listening," said Father Perezcaballero, still fighting to keep his voice in control.

"You see, if you loved Christ you would not want to go on persisting in your lie. As in fact you do."

"If you regard my gift for speaking as a lie, well, I have just admitted that myself; so far as that's concerned, I have acknowledged my sin," said Father Perezcaballero.

"No, no," answered Dom Dusolier in an almost childish tone of voice, as though fearing to be misunderstood. "No, that is not what I mean—that is hardly more than a laughing matter. All that business of book learning and rhetoric and vocal effects is not taken very seriously either by God or by anyone else. It's simply a lot of nonsense that you will soon learn to get rid of."

He is speaking to the most admired preacher in Paris, thought Father Perezcaballero. Let him go on!

"The more serious thing is that this oratory has got inside you—like damp into an old house."

"How do you mean?"

A silence fell. Dom Dusolier had not "meant" anything. Someone else had spoken through him. He himself was most astonished when he heard himself going on:

"All those orders and decorations you got—all the distinctions for your time in the concentration camp—all you did there: what do you think of all those things yourself? Don't you catch a smell of mould? I did, the first time I heard of them."

He leaned to one side and put his right hand up to his cheek, as though to stroke away a lock of hair that was not there.

Father Perezcaballero was sitting bolt upright. His melancholy gaze swept over the room. Was *this* the method—the new method, in this case—used by the mild Benedictines? His fluent tongue was just about to loose a retort both modest and dignified when suddenly—with a sort of pain—he felt a curtain being drawn up inside him. He was so overcome with terror at this that he stood up and clutched at his heart with one of his hands.

"Sit down," said Dom Dusolier calmly. "Sit down. We have plenty of time."

But Father Perezcaballero was not listening to him. His powerful frame swayed. He sank back against the table and hid his face in his hands. What on earth was this thing that was breaking in upon him? The concentration camp? His decorations? How could Dom Dusolier possibly know?

In the papers he had been presented as a national hero who had endured torture and persecution—he had modestly denied this once or twice and tried to draw people's attention to the real heroes, but fame had clung to him. Actually he had not come out of it at all badly. He had not had an easy time in the camp, but as a matter of fact he had never been tortured. And he knew why. Not because he was a priest—but because he was gifted and had a good tongue. He had noticed very early on that it was the not-so-clever, loud-mouthed ones who came off worst: if you kept quiet and toed the line you would probably be more or less all right. If you knew how to choose your words there was not much risk of physical brutality. He was a past-master at saying the right thing, he was a good psychologist . . . how often had he not succeeded in saving his skin through a word skilfully chosen? He had saved others too, as a matter of fact. But only now did he begin to suspect a terrible secret: mould and lies had insinuated themselves precisely into his most precious possession, his greatest consolation, his behaviour in the concentration camp!

He stood up in amazement. Was this a case of some kind of suggestion? Were evil spirits after him? But all he saw before him was the old Benedictine, who after his attack was sitting there half asleep, holding his chin propped up on his long fingers and gazing at the floor.

And now memories came crowding in, through collapsing ramparts and protective walls. He had avoided suffering! He had done everything he could to avoid suffering. He who had so often preached on the subject of vicarious suffering, who knew so well how much mankind owed to all those who freely took upon themselves the burden of sacrifice—he had entirely *dodged* suffering, tactfully, smartly, like an experienced diplomat. He had not betrayed anybody, his behaviour had been unimpeachable, he had not brought any shame on his country: from the human point of view it was quite understandable that he should have done all he could to avoid useless and unnecessary pain, like everyone else. But he was a Christian! How often had he not—in the concentration camp, too—preached about Our Lord's sacrifices! He had become famous because he had managed secretly to make a movable altar and then collected French prisoners round it for two years.

On his return he had stood up in front of the Palais de Chaillot in his striped prison suit, and his voice had echoed over the packed square as he had described how the French prisoners had gathered faithfully round the sacrament in the utmost secrecy. What a triumph that had been!

He was shaken by what seemed to be shudders of cold, but was in fact shame. He felt as though he was under a bombardment—and yet there was only a tired, senile old monk sitting motionless before him. In the silence, accusations flashed at him as though from a battery of machine guns. You have never loved Me! You loved yourself! You were shrewd and adroit like the children of the world: when will you follow *My* way? You made successful literature out of your lie, you played at being a Christian, you became famous, all the women in Paris admire you: why don't you love *Me?* Do you remember the German guard who came to you, broken and desperate,

114

on one of the last days, asking you to bless him? You refused, you sent him away! Had he not for three years shown himself to be a man of great heart and humanity? You drove him away—from Christ, whom he had served more faithfully than you had! And do you remember the trial, the mass trial in the camp? You said nothing that was untrue, you were not involved in the affair yourself, but you knew that your comrades were to be shot, and you heard an inner voice saying: "Declare your solidarity with them! Offer up your own life! Take their guilt upon yourself! *Perhaps* you can save them! At least you will strengthen their courage if you march by their side!" What did you do? Talked literature, spoke of humanity. You felt the shame burning within you when you went to see them before the execution. Do you remember the look on the face of that young fellow as you blessed him? You might just as well have been lifting a stone against him: he looked right through you! And about those dead men you later made high-sounding speeches, which brought you decorations and fame. . . .

Father Perezcaballero groaned aloud. He fell on his knees before the Benedictine, who gently laid his hand on his head.

"I know," he whispered. "I know. I am nothing. Inside me there is nothing but lies."

He leaned his head against his friend's knees. Silence fell.

"*Deo gratias*," said Dom Dusolier slowly.

At that moment Father Perezcaballero could see nothing but darkness before him. Why had this had to happen? Why hadn't he changed in time? Now the game was up: he was lost! There was no salvation for people like him. He had seen this coming nearer daily, but on a lower, less distinct level of consciousness. Not only was there nothing of any value in him any longer, but everything, his whole self, was composed of lies and self-interest. And *he* had "unmasked" Father Guillon! *He* had imagined that he had a duty towards

Lebrun! *He* had, only today, given an utterly false impression of himself to others in a shameless address, feigned a humility which he did not possess!

"What am I to do?" he whispered.

"Thank God," said Dom Dusolier. "As I thank Him. Can you feel the burning pain which is His love? Now for the first time you really know that He loves you! Now for the first time you can fully appreciate what forgiveness of sin means."

That was true. Now he knew. But could he really believe that there was still love, even for him?

"Christ cannot love me," he said. "He cannot."

Dom Dusolier stood up.

"He can," he said. "No one else can. Except me—a little. But Christ can. It is just people like you He does love."

Half an hour later the two priests emerged together. Father Perezcaballero looked drawn and sad. Don Dusolier's horse face was glowing.

As he said good-bye to Father Perezcaballero at the door, his last words were:

"God bless you! You have made me happier than I have been for many years."

Then he turned rapidly away, to hide the devil's leer that suddenly rent his face.

CHAPTER ELEVEN

On Kansdorf's desk there had been lying for some considerable time a letter from the police.

If there was any institution in Paris that could vie with the
sports' stadium, it was the prefecture on the Ile de la Cité,
feared by everybody as the citadel of all that was evil, senseless
and bureaucratic. Many foreigners broke down when they
were summoned to appear there: they knew that before them
lay day after day of sarcasms, humiliations, senseless misunder-
standings, and endless standing about.

Kansdorf unfolded the summons with a certain pleasure.

He knew of nothing more exciting than a visit to this
chamber of horrors, where all the things that the French
people were as a matter of fact so exemplary at avoiding in
their daily lives were collected together and raised to the
maximum pitch of folly. It would give him the greatest
pleasure to go there. But not unarmed. He took a couple
of books he wanted to read with him, and also a new notebook
and a freshly filled fountain-pen.

"It was as I expected. I spent the whole morning standing
in two queues in the prefecture, and then when it came to
lunch time I was thrown out! Now I have come back again
and been given place number seven in a new queue. So

perhaps I shall get to the little table today. But this is not certain.

"I find all this uncommonly amusing. The prefecture is an invention that would make Kafka go white with shame. His castle is a well-run guest house compared with this sample of the French people's talent for organization!

"In the corridor stands a quite especially hardened sinner whose job it is to show people into the different rooms, where they have to join the queues of waiting humans. He is brainless and heartless, and he likes to show off these characteristics. He never washes, so he has a nasty smell. He takes bribes in full view of the public. Anyone who slips him a hundred francs can produce his shout of command: '*Un numéro!*' This is heard by another warder in uniform guarding one of the doors further inside: this fellow comes running up and hands out a *lower* number that he has been keeping back, which enables the person concerned to go past all the people waiting in the queue and be *first* at the table. No one says anything. Everyone sees what has happened. The thing is accepted as quite natural: no one has any right to feel annoyed about it. It has never occurred to any of the, say, hundred and fifty people who have been sitting waiting for days in this vast frowsy hall being snarled at by petty officials that there could be any honour or decency amongst the police. Why is this?

"I too could go up to the scoundrel and get a low number from him at the cost of a hundred francs. But I am waiting, instead. I have a chair and I am sitting on it, writing. There is a lot to see and note down here.

"What gives me the greatest pleasure is this. The oaf *knows* that everyone has to get a stamped form on the floor below and fill it in *before* they take their place in the queue. But he never *tells* them this! For day after day, month after month, he lets all these refugees from every country under the sun,

118

all these wretched, harassed creatures, stand and wait—so that when they have worked their way forward to the table he can inform them that they have waited in vain. I have watched his face when those who have been waiting break down one after the other: It is no uncommon thing for the women to go into hysterics. He doesn't look exactly pleased, it wouldn't be fair to say that. But he looks unmoved. And I ask myself why.

"Of course it would be foolish to expect the slightest sign of sympathy or humanity from him, he is a criminal who should be strung up on the nearest tree, but it *must* be in his own interest to keep the queues as short as possible. He is not acting in his own interests. That is the mysterious thing about this haunted castle. Torture and cruelty go on being committed endlessly here, bureaucratic inefficiency and vulgarity reaching depths without parallel are rampant almost on the grand scale—but to what end? Another proof that the philosophers are mistaken when they try to discover egoistic motives behind everything! This machine is driven by powers of quite a different kind. Here irrational forces are at work driving human beings to torture each other. No one gains anything when Polish workers who can't understand a word of French get into the wrong queue without their official form. Nevertheless this *has* to happen. Why? Because the system will have it so. Craziness demands it.

"I love this great dirty hall with its ghastly wooden floor, all the helpless, agonized faces, all the gross beasts in uniform. Naturally all the most unsuitable people that the French police mentality can produce are sitting pretty here. Nevertheless, the achievement is impressive. There is not a single detail that is not handled wrongly: everything is done as badly, as slowly, as senselessly, as cruelly, as heartlessly, as is humanly possible.

"No one has thought of coming to our little table yet. The

bureaucrat will be eating his gluttonous lunch, of course, or have gone for a stroll.

"The only response to a question asked by the fair-haired Norwegian painter, who will soon be committing murder here—it is his third day—is a shrug of the shoulders. No trace of sadism on the face. None at all. There is no conscious cruelty. It is just the system working itself out—stupidly, senselessly, grinding slowly and exceeding small.

"I'm not complaining. I have ink in my pen and an empty notebook to write in. For how many people is not the whole of life this kind of senseless waiting?

"Will it be granted me to write down anything of any importance while I wait? I will try. But it would be nice if people would stop pushing into me while I sit here writing so assiduously. I'll turn my chair a little towards the wall. Here, in an evil-smelling queue of human beings, in an equally evil-smelling hall, in my mackintosh which smells of damp, I sit with my coat collar open, facing a wall whose paper is peeling off and with large spots of damp on it, and I write. People think I'm mad. But I'm a human being—a human being afflicted by other human beings. I'm not complaining.

"Now I intend to do something preposterous: I intend to try to write down the indescribable. This is really an experiment for my own sake. I want to discover what the experience looks like when it is written down.

"I feel a little anxious about it. Is it not a fact that once one has tried to describe any particular experience—and the description never quite corresponds to the reality!—one can never reconstruct it afterwards as it really was? I believe that I made such and such an observation—but I simply do not know if it was not someone else who was involved. A memory comes to one, of its own accord, as the result of some attraction which one is quite unaware of. I believe I have discovered it to be a fact that once the memory has come back in this proper, spontaneous way, it never comes back again! It can only, subsequently, be forced back.

"Should I then ruin a moment by trying to cling to it?

"This, in point of fact, is what happened.

"It was after three years of marriage. We—Dagny and I— were in Copenhagen. We were what is usually described as a happily married couple, though the burning of the senses was already a thing of the past. The desire was still there, but it burned in its own fire, which was no longer ours. I suggested that we should go to the cinema. There was a perfectly idiotic American comedy on. We got in in the middle of it. At the end I got up to go, but Dagny stood by my side in the gangway for a moment in silence—the lights had just gone up— and said quietly:

" 'Look, I'd like to stay on and see the beginning.'

"I nodded and went out.

"But before I got to the door I felt my heart sound the alarm in a wild excited beating, sweat burst out on my forehead, and I stood for quite a while outside the cinema, panting in the light rain.

"For while she was saying those simple words something had happened. Something that shook me and shattered me, something that utterly destroyed all my ideas of the world and human life.

"I know that it cannot be described, and that the description I am now about to make of it is bound to be misleading both for myself and for anyone who might read it. (It's terribly uncomfortable sitting here: I've got pains in my arms and back!)

"But I can't describe this most decisive event in my life in a few perfunctory lines!

"The impression I have of the event is something like this.

"When Dagny made that ordinary remark, which did not in itself possess the slightest significance and which she could quite easily not have said, I looked at her. And the Dagny I saw was not the Dagny of 'real life.' Without realizing it she had become someone quite different. I saw that the defeats she had suffered, all of which had left their mark on her face, had vanished. She was—the person she had been when I first met her? Or simply and perfectly herself? Neither, perhaps, exactly.

"But everything clear and earthly-human, *over* her and *in* her and connected *with* her, had vanished. She was liberated, pure! She stood before me bathed in a glow of mysterious light—like no other light, quite outside real life. Or: I was looking through a window into another world where there were no compromises or defeats, no sin and conflict, and there I saw *her herself*. . . .

"I saw her as someone maidenly pure, liberated. I saw her resting in safety and relaxed. I saw her more like herself than she had ever been before. I saw her through all that might be described as chance, change, age, humiliation. . . .

"For a long time I walked alone through the streets with her luminous image gazing at me. I could not understand my experience. I tried to submit it to various psychological inter- pretations (stupid ones) —e.g.:

"I had been watching a film. The film provides a series of very powerful rapid impressions, it stifles criticism at birth, it makes us believe in all that is simplest and most uncom- plicated—for it stupefies our reason for the time being with its technique. This had happened to me in this case. The lights came on. I stood up. I looked at Dagny. I looked at her with the naive, uncritical, gullible eyes of the filmgoer. A sentimental memory came into my mind—which was set upon sentimentality, *wanted* sentimentality. And still blinded by the sudden light, I vaguely saw a Dagny who was the Dagny of the vague dreams of my youth, which had gone on existing somewhere inside me.

"Anyone who likes to believe this explanation is free to. It is as good as any other.

"But I know that it is *untrue!* I cannot as yet say with certainty how I know this. But that what I saw at that moment was real, in a deeper sense than anything I had ever experienced, I cannot doubt. I am more ready to believe that everything else in my life is illusion. That was *not* an illusion. It was a reflection of *reality itself.* For a second I was allowed to look into another world, whose existence I had never before suspected and with which I have spent my whole life since that night trying to make contact. I know that many people, great and small, in the religious field, have had similar and greater experiences. None of them has been able to describe them in such a way as to convince unbelievers of their reality. Nevertheless they do not doubt the reality of their experience. Nor do I.

"I could not bring myself to tell Dagny about it.

"The next day she was the same Dagny as ever; but *I* was no longer quite the same person. I longed to tell her all about it, to tell her that I had held a tip of truth in my hand and that the only thing left for us to do was to hold onto it tightly.

"I did not dare to—I missed the chance of a lifetime. Today I know that what was then vouchsafed to me was precisely what some call freedom and others grace. It was a quite gratuitous gift of light, lightness and liberation. I might have accepted that gift. Instead, I drove it away with my psychologism, and I let it—it was not so easy, but I am very clever at that sort of thing—fade and vanish until only a vague, queer memory of it remained.

"I don't think much of the way I have lived, and nothing I have done seems in the slightest degree admirable. There is a great deal in my life that I hate and despise. Above all, the fact that I failed then. Coldly, untrustingly—I passed by! A warm wave came towards me; I looked away and preferred my own coldness. I stood before a bright, pure truth: I chose illusion, the appearance of lies and uncertainty."

CHAPTER TWELVE

Dr. Lebrun had said the day before that he would not be going to his surgery. He had not given any reason.

In the morning he went off home in plenty of time. He shaved carefully, chose a new shirt and rummaged around amongst his ties for a long time until he found the right one. His breakfast was served to him in the library. He helped himself carefully to both kinds of jam and the honey, decided that the coffee was excellent, and allowed himself the pleasure of reading Mauriac and Guermantes in *Figaro*.

He had just got up to go when he heard footsteps. He frowned and opened the door to the dining room. As he did so, the door leading to the pantry closed. A few rapid strides and he was there. As he thought, it was his boy.

"Louis?" he exclaimed. "What are you doing at home—at this time?"

The boy came up to him. He was fourteen, dark, stocky—like his father. In his face, however, there was something of his mother's openness and vulnerability. His features had not yet matured.

"We were sent home after the first lesson," he said. "I think there's an epidemic. There were four people ill in our class."

"Epidemic? Nonsense! But by all means do as you like! You can all of you hardly learn less lounging about at home than you do at school."

He was just about to turn his back on the boy when he remembered something.

"Just a moment," he said. "Have you found your savings yet?"

The boy went red. It was a tragedy. He had been looking for the money for a fortnight. He had a money-box, and by the New Year he would have saved enough for a tent. He had broken the money-box open—and found only a few small coins inside. He was heartbroken. His mother had at first suspected him of stealing the money himself. But his misery was so genuine that after a while she had realized that she must be wrong. But how had the money disappeared, then? Someone in the house must be a thief! Were any of his friends to be suspected? Or the girl in the kitchen, Annette, who had been with them six years? Both possibilities seemed equally unlikely.

His father had kept puzzlingly quiet. He had not been angry, as Louis had perhaps expected. He had simply nodded and said that Louis must find out what had happened himself: he was old enough to get to the bottom of such a matter.

"No," said Louis. "I have looked everywhere. I have thought and thought about it. But I have no idea—"

"So you still think that the money was stolen?"

Tears came into the boy's eyes.

"Yes," he said, "someone *must* have taken it. It is so mean. Now I shan't get my tent."

His father let him go on rubbing his eyes for a while.

"So you mean that it's wicked to steal?" he asked.

The boy looked up in astonishment.

"Of course it's wicked!" he said. "To take something away from someone else! No one has the right to take for himself what does not belong to him, something that someone else has been saving up!"

Dr. Lebrun nodded.

"So that's your point of view? Well, it's quite a defensible one. Of course there are others—in politics, for instance—where the stronger party takes what he wants from the weaker one. But I take it you don't think that right?"

"No."

Louis was beginning to wonder. What was his father getting at?

"And you act according to this principle yourself?"

"Yes, of course."

The answer came so quickly that the boy gave himself no time to think.

"Good. Since you are in favour of this law yourself you will want others to observe it too. That is quite in order. That is only right."

He paused. The boy was fiddling with his coat buttons.

His father, who had been looking out of the window, now turned slowly and stiffly, from the waist upwards, towards his son. In the same indifferent voice he said:

"Can you explain something to me? *Why* then on the fourteenth of December of last year did you steal three thousand francs out of my brief-case when I happened to be in the bathroom? On a Friday, at about *a quarter to nine?*"

Louis went white and one of his hands went up to his cheek. His father's eyes had been on him for a long time, now his face and chest were turned towards him.

"And another question: *Why,* on at least five occasions when the matter has been mentioned, have you lied about it? Lied in the most barefaced way and denied the truth?"

The boy took a deep breath and opened his mouth—but no words came.

"Now then, answer me!" said his father.

Louis shook his head. He tried to speak, but his voice failed him. He sank down on one of the chairs by the dining table and burst into tears.

His father remained standing. Slowly he turned round, went up to the boy, and in one movement seized him and pulled him to his feet.

"Do you own up?"

"Yes," sobbed Louis.

"You did take the money?"

"Yes."

"Why?"

"I don't know. I wanted to buy something. I can't remember what. The other boys had money. I hadn't any."

"Because you had spent your pocket-money, eh!—do you admit that you have been lying systematically ever since?"

"Yes."

"Why?"

"I was afraid."

His father paused. It was impossible to tell whether he was angry or not.

"I can understand all that," he said. "It's the sort of thing that happens. One makes mistakes. And one is too cowardly to take the blame for them. We have all done that at one time or another. But the thing that I can't understand is how, after all that, you complain when you yourself get something stolen from you. How could you do that? Why *shouldn't* you be robbed—of all you have and possess? Why should anyone consider you when you don't even consider your father? Answer me, Louis!"

The boy stood there with drooping head. He was unable to speak; his head had slumped onto his chest and he was sobbing.

"Forgive—" he finally got out. "Forgive me!"

Dr. Lebrun laid his hand on his shoulder.

"Forgive"—what a word! However could he forgive? What authority had he, what qualities, that gave him the right to forgive? Wasn't this boy, in spite of his thieving, utterly pure,

compared with himself? And yet he could come to him, looking to him for protection—in a sort of spontaneous trust.
And the moment he forgave the boy, he would be set up again,
set free. What a strange world, in which there was a higher
power which could forgive, which could take responsibility
and guilt from our shoulders and make possible a new beginning! That was what the Lord God did, according to the
Christians. But what if the Lord God's authority was as feeble
as his own? There was a great deal to suggest that it was!

"Of course I forgive you," he said, doing his best to keep all
emotion from his voice.

And then he went on to utter words which he himself
found astonishing, and which he did not really understand:

"That's what you have a father for, isn't it?"

The boy looked up in astonishment. Between the tears a
glimmer of light began to appear. The transformation was
beginning. . . .

Was he a god, to raise up human beings and grant them
forgiveness of their sins?

"And by the way, I rather think you'll be having a tent,"
he said.

The boy merely stared, not daring to say a word.

"And therefore you'd better have your money back."

He went awkwardly towards his desk and pulled open the
drawer. He took out an envelope and emptied its contents of
ringing coins onto the desk.

"It wasn't so easy getting the money out, I can tell you. It
took me two hours. You happened to be at the cinema at the
time. Here it is, anyway."

He hadn't turned round. He could hear Louis sobbing. The
next moment the boy was at his side, he was given a fleeting
kiss and a hug that nearly sent him toppling. Then the boy
released him and rushed out.

He turned round awkwardly.

"But, my boy," he cried. "The money! You're forgetting we've found the money!"

But Louis did not reappear.

He would soon be back.

He raised his arms and was just about to let himself laugh, then controlled himself.

Why should he ruin such a splendid sentimental scene by laughing? He really was an odious old monster!

He wrote "Belongs to Louis" on the envelope, put the money back into it, fastened it up and threw it onto the desk.

Then he moved slowly towards the front door.

A few hours later Dr. Lebrun was getting out of the train at Versailles. He debated whether to take a taxi, then decided to go on foot. It was cold, the ground was frozen hard. It only took a quarter of an hour to get to the convent school. He was on his way to see Michèle.

Michèle was fifteen. She had been going to the school for four years. Hardly anyone knew of her existence there except her teachers. At first, doubtless, they had suspected that the girl he wanted them to take in was an illegitimate daughter of his own. He could easily have proved to them that this was not the case. Michèle was the daughter of a certain Jacques Letellier, a man he had once been very friendly with, but who had subsequently become his enemy.

Jacques Letellier was a painter. He had had a whole string of affairs with women. He had been divorced three times, and then went on living with one woman after another. Lebrun bought some of his pictures, and also lent him money—which he never got back. This was a subsidiary matter: he had never expected anything else. One summer, however, something that he had not expected happened. While he was away Letellier had come into his house and said he had the doctor's permission to borrow the ten pictures which the doctor had bought from him over the years, for an exhibition he was giving. The paintings were handed to him—he was well known in the house; no one had any idea that all was not as it should be. The exhibition was simply a pretext. Letellier sold the pictures, and when Lebrun tackled him about it he had the cheek to say:

"My dear fellow, I needed the money. And you had been lucky to have had the pictures for so long, in my opinion. You must let others have a little pleasure too, don't you think? Besides, I'll paint some new pictures for you, much better ones."

Lebrun had looked into the weak, talented, effeminate face, ruined by alcohol. He had hit it and walked away. He didn't want to have anything more to do with him.

When he got home he looked out the few remaining drawings and sketches of Letellier's and sent them back to him with a note:

"Perhaps you would like to sell these pictures too. I should be glad if you will. And then go to hell!"

So the relationship ended. During the war, however, a message came one day from Letellier, saying that he was ill and could be visited at an address which the messenger, with evident misgiving, passed on to Lebrun.

Letellier was a member of the Resistance, was in fact one of its leaders outside Paris. He had been captured but after severe ill treatment had managed to escape. Now, as a result of his experiences, he was ill. He needed a doctor.

Feeling no sympathy and fearing new tricks, Lebrun went to see him. He found Letellier in a garage, in an icy room, lying on an improvised bed. He had a high temperature. He was a dying man. The Germans had done their job thoroughly —he had been absolutely beaten up, his kidneys smashed, his ribs broken. Besides this he was riddled with consumption.

Silently, Lebrun set to work to examine him. As he did so he looked into his former friend's face. It had changed. The flabbiness had gone. He was a new man.

"You've no need to tell me anything," said Letellier. "I *know* how it is with me. I had another reason for asking you to come."

"What was it, then?" asked Lebrun.

"You know me," said Letellier, his eyes burning and flickering feverishly. "You know what kind of a life I have led. There has never been any discipline in it—until—well, I was give a last chance, and I took it. And now I'm lying here. I'm not asking you to forgive me for what I did to you. What does forgiving mean anyway? But just because you know all about my ghastly life I should like to ask you something."

"What is it?"

"I have a daughter—Michèle. . . . Could you adopt her?"

He died a week later. At the last moment, on the day following his death, his hide-out was discovered and his friends were arrested. Lebrun too was questioned, but lied his way out. Amongst other things he mentioned how Letellier had taken him in: as he poured out cognac for the Germans, he had them roaring with laughter over the story of the pictures. Did they imagine that he would help a cheat like that? Oh no, he had made his bed and he could lie on it!

They believed him and went away.

From that time onwards he was left alone by the Gestapo.

But he took charge of the girl. She was living in the studio and had her meals with the caretaker. She was neglected, homeless, neurotic. He installed her in the institute run by the Dominican nuns at Versailles. And he went to see her regularly. Her mother had been dead for years.

Lebrun liked the school. There was a remarkable bishop there who had worked in Russia and obviously been tortured there. He had a special liking for the little girls and the older nuns; to the young nuns, however, especially the pretty ones, he found it difficult to speak. His face would darken and he would make a gesture of abhorrence whenever he had to pass one of them in the corridor. Perhaps he was a little mad. He had a horror of the human body in its full bloom. But whenever he met a wrinkled old nun he would smile. And when he came upon a young girl who did not as yet know the meaning of desire he would, for a moment—no longer—lay his thin, shaking fingers against her chin. The very old and the very young were people after his own heart. Between them came the blood—humiliation. It horrified him.

Lebrun had to wait as usual in the little waiting room with its plush sofa and its terrible photographs of bishops on the walls. It always smelt rather damp and musty. After a while the Prioress and the housekeeper came in with Michèle.

As he talked to the older of the two nuns he surreptitiously watched the younger one. She was laughing and joking with Michèle. Lebrun decided that she was the most beautiful woman he had ever seen. And he thought: the only women in France who have beautiful, healthy faces are nuns! Their colour is natural, and when their features move they don't ruin any hard make-up.

He watched the young nun's face for so long that he began to be afraid that the Prioress would notice, so he finally turned back and faced her rather plump but pure and smiling features. Her face was relaxed, the effect it gave was one of utter peace and strength. A strange power, that these women served! How could anyone maintain that they sacrificed their "real" life by giving up the chance of becoming mothers in the physical sense? They sacrificed nothing. They travelled along a sensible, cool byeway, avoiding humiliation. Hence the peace in their faces.

Meanwhile he had had to take another look at the young nun, Mother Pia. What a perfect face! How clearly meant to express passion, intelligence, fire! It could easily have appeared under great lights on a film screen and become the rage. Its possessor was still talking quietly to Michèle; but then she slowly turned and looked towards Lebrun, and through the long, half-lowered eyelashes the full force of her personality streamed across at him.

That look, as though purified by the dark lashes, that aristocratic, faintly melancholy face—he felt himself blushing. O what joy, after having to look at all the flabby or brazen or stiff, dead women's faces, to be able to look into a face that reflected a soul! He was only half listening to what was being said. It was about a donation—would he make a contribution? They wanted to take in another girl who had no parents but were unable to because of the money. He answered absentmindedly and really looked rather strange. He had in fact made a discovery.

While the young nun was explaining, with lowered eyes, how much money they needed and how pitiable this particular case was, he noticed a tiny peculiarity about her face. Even the most splendid marble bust can have a small fault, a crack in it, a spot. Mother Pia had three little downy hairs on her chin. He saw them, and a whole picture with them. Each morning she was conscious of this little blemish. She knew that but for that she would be a perfect beauty. Were nuns allowed to use mirrors? Her veil was so straight and dignified that she must surely look at herself in the mirror occasionally? Mother Pia knew that she was beautiful, and the devil whispered in her ear each morning:

"So easy to be rid of them, and you would be the most beautiful woman in the world!"

He smiled at the idleness of his thoughts, and pulled himself together to listen to what they were saying. He found out what it was about, agreed, signed a form which the nun produced with amazing rapidity, and therewith immediately pledged himself for five years. The nuns assured him that

God would reward him. He bowed. He was very highly thought of in the convent. They asked him whether he would like to accompany them into the chapel, which had just had some new coloured windows installed.

He followed them. As they did, he knelt down. Behind the altar he heard the novices singing. Probably they were thanking God for the fact that he had come. With unmoving face he laughed inwardly. Two pure women were thanking God for him! If only they knew that all this was only a whim, that he was in fact an odious old horror—and intended to remain so. . . .

After he had said good-bye to them and given Michèle a last kiss—she had told him delightedly that she wanted to be a nun and he had given his friendly approval, but the nuns said that it was too early to decide yet—he wandered off to the park and went in through the Trianon gates. He came across painted, gabbling women with thin, silk-clad legs and short skirts, heard their shrill voices—he was back in the world of human beings.

Even here there was a lot to put up with!

He banged his walking-stick hard on the frozen ground and wandered on between the leafless trees.

PART TWO

"Lightly, swiftly, tenderly . . . ."

CHAPTER THIRTEEN

All of a sudden, Kansdorf had found himself involved in a series of events that forced him to adopt an attitude and make decisions. This was, for him, an unusual and estranging experience. It meant the introduction of precisely that which his utterly isolated and hidden existence in the company of books in a lonely Paris lodging was supposed to be a protection against.

He now had a twenty-year-old Russian girl in his house—Katharina Seidel. Clothilde was quite beside herself, and it was not going to be easy to win her around: she was convinced that the girl was his mistress. He himself had no idea what he should begin to do with her.

He had been sitting in the prefecture enjoying the general craziness and senselessness of it. In the queue in front of him he saw a young girl who obviously had no papers of any kind; moreover, she didn't seem to have the faintest idea what the bad-tempered official was getting at.

Then his interest was aroused. When she turned her head round he saw that she was beautiful; a narrow delicate face, with large sad eyes, and a slim—in fact thin—figure.

By now the official had talked himself up into a high old rage. Kansdorf was amazed at the language he used. The bystanders listened stolidly: most of them were accustomed to such scenes. One was grinning.

The girl stood quite still, perhaps she straightened her head slightly. She did not answer.

Kansdorf followed the scene in amazement.

When the official finally brutally shot his hand out and pushed the girl out of the queue, he left his place and went up to them. He put his arm round the girl's shoulders.

"Excuse me," he said angrily to the official. "That's no way for a Frenchman to treat a lady."

The official glared in astonishment. He seemed to be working up to another explosion.

At the same moment, however, the girl turned towards Kansdorf, and he saw a faint smile on her face.

"No, no," she said quietly. "Just let him go on talking."

Kansdorf left the queue and led the girl to the window.

"I couldn't bear to see you being treated like that," he said. "You do see that, don't you? I hope you didn't understand all the words he used."

Again the girl smiled.

"Oh yes, I did," she replied. "I understood them. But why are you angry about it? The poor man is only in a state of nerves. He is overtired. He doesn't really know what he's saying. I feel rather sorry for him."

Kansdorf looked at her in amazement. She was calm, unconcerned, unconstrained.

They went together towards the exit. Behind them could be heard the shrill voice of the official. When Kansdorf turned round, he saw a corpulent middle-aged woman at the table burst into a fit of hysterical weeping. That he could understand. But where did the young girl at his side get her calmness from?

He asked her a few questions and realized what the official's outburst had been about. The girl had been standing in the wrong queue.

"I can well believe it," she said. "I've been standing here for two days. No one really seemed to know."

"Two days!" Kansdorf exclaimed, taking her into a café. "And you're not absolutely all-in?"

They had sat down at one of the tables.

"No," she said, "I hardly every get tired."

Kansdorf ordered tea.

"How do manage it?" he asked. "I nearly always feel tired."

"Oh, it's quite simple," the girl answered. "I just pray."

He looked up quickly. She had said the words in a perfectly natural voice.

"And what—do you pray about—or for?" he asked dubiously.

"Oh, there are a lot of people I pray for. Just now I was praying for the poor women in the queue—they looked so unhappy. Most people haven't the faintest idea how to set about praying. And yet it's so easy."

He looked at her. A young girl, simply dressed. A foreigner, probably Russian. To judge by her face, she must know quite a lot about trouble and suffering. Despite that, she radiated peace: it was as though the world and its annoyances did not exist for her. He suddenly felt a longing to know more about her. Who was she?

Quite right; she was a Russian. Her case seemed to be well-nigh hopeless. She wanted a residence permit, but there was hardly any chance of her obtaining one. She was one of a group of refugees who had suffered a sequence of disasters. To begin with, at the outbreak of the war they had been interned by the French themselves and, strange to say, very badly treated. Then they had fallen into the hands of the Germans, who had split the group up. Many of them were put into German concentration camps and perished as Jews, others

139

died under torture. Katharina's parents had been killed—she was partly Jewish. Later, she had applied for a visa to America, where she had relatives, but she hadn't used it and it had lapsed and couldn't be renewed. Meanwhile her French *permis de séjour* had run out too. So that she now had no right to live anywhere.

But why on earth hadn't she gone to America? Why had she stayed in France?

She looked at him calmly.

"Because Abbé Auclair didn't wish me to."

"And why didn't he want you to?"

"He felt—that it wasn't right. He felt that I should help him with his work."

"What kind of work does he do?"

"Oh, he is a great man, a saint."

"Really! But what has that to do with your not taking your only chance of getting across to your relatives?"

"He needs me. He can tell from my name that I have work to do."

"From your *name?*"

"So he says. He is a great scholar. He says the will of God can be known through people's names."

Kansdorf was taken aback. A Catholic priest! But a charlatan, surely? What on earth could his real motive be for keeping the girl with him? He decided to go home with her.

They had to take the Métro to Corentin and then go out to Clamart by bus. The presbytery was near the church, but Abbé Auclair didn't live there: he rented a couple of single rooms from an old lady in the neighbourhood. The girl lived in the same house. They climbed up the stairs; there was nobody in. The girl's room was small and clean, but freezing. When they entered the priest's room they found it in a state of disorder, with the chairs and table all loaded with books.

"I'm never allowed to tidy up here," said the girl. "Abbé

Auclair insists on doing it himself, he won't have anyone else helping him."

"He obviously doesn't do it himself, either," Kansdorf replied. "Can that be God's will?"

"He has so much to do," Katharina answered. "He has his troop—twelve patrols, with twelve in each of them. . . ."

"Troop?"

"Yes, a troop of little boys. He is raising an army that is to go out and conquer the world. Oh, he does such a lot of work with the youngsters. He gets the worst ones off the streets and then licks them into shape. He works, and holds parades, and—"

Kansdorf couldn't bear to hear any more.

"Where is he now, do you think? I should very much like to have a word with him. I can't be of any assistance to you until I get a full explanation from him."

"I don't know where he is. Perhaps he is in the church. There's going to be a party for all the boys this evening—there are several hundred coming. Nobody is allowed in there yet, it's all being kept a secret, and the boys find that terribly interesting."

Hundreds of boys alone in the church with a mad priest!

"What does the parish priest say to all this, though?"

"Oh, he doesn't say anything now. At first he was really wild. But then Abbé Auclair went to the Bishop. And the Bishop understood."

"The Bishop understood? We'd better go into the church and see what's going on for ourselves. If he'll let us in, of course."

It was quite right: when they got inside the church they found a priest there, in the middle of a whirl of activity. He was busy laying out hymn books and putting up decorations for a kind of church show. He didn't seem in the least surprised to see Katharina with Kansdorf.

"No good?" he said. "I knew it. I told you so yesterday, didn't I? And this is Monsieur—?"

"Kansdorf."

"Kansdorf! Aha, I knew you'd be coming, but I didn't think you'd be so thin. Would you be good enough to take these cards and put them out, one on every other seat, right along the row, please! And you, Katharina, can sweep up a bit here under the front benches. The dustpan is in the cupboard near the sacristy."

And he actually got them both working. What else could they do? Kansdorf could hardly talk to him until he had finished what he was doing, and so the best thing to do, ultimately, was to give him a hand. So he went round putting out the cards. They contained a number of extracts made up into two very simple-minded hymns.

What kind of a man was this?

He had a round, healthy face, with black eyes that never stopped moving. He spoke in a loud, deep, clear voice, and had a certain compelling power which Kansdorf noticed at once. He might quite easily be a most effective preacher. It was understandable that little boys would like listening to him. He had a short, rather thin black beard, and moved with rapid, often surprising movements—there was something playful and mercurial about his whole being.

Such a man could not possibly be a fake. He must have quite different reasons for having the girl with him.

When Kansdorf had finished he went up to the priest; he was standing at the sacristy door contemplating his work with his arms folded across his chest and a look of satisfaction on his face.

"Isn't it looking splendid?" he said. "Don't you think it will be a marvellous evening? Just imagine it: the whole church filled with hundreds of mannerless louts, and not one of them more than twelve years old! Real little sinners—

thieves, liars, young gangsters, a few of them wanted by the police—oh, I know them so well!"

"And—you're trying to bring them up to be decent people?"

He looked at Kansdorf, his face beaming.

"To be decent people? Not in the least! Decent people are the ghastliest types I know!"

"What are they going to be, then, may I ask?"

"Prophets, and warriors of the Lord! Just that: prophets, and warriors of the Lord! Just consider for a moment: in ten years' time half of them will probably have fallen away—yes, I've taken that into account: half of them will have gone. It only needs a girl to come along waggling her hips and this kind of little sinner forgets all about Christ and the Cross. It would be the same with all of us. Of the rest, however, the majority will not only hold on but they will win over at least one other schoolboy each—one a year. And even if you reckon that at least half of these new ones disappear in their turn, still each of the remaining ones will bring in at least one more schoolboy a year again. My dear man, in fifteen years the number will be colossal! I'm very conservative in my estimate and I'm making great allowances for unforeseen occurrences. But in fifteen years' time we shall have the entire youth of France on our side! I know that, in any case, not only by my statistical reckonings: I can *see* it."

He was fascinating. Kansdorf forgot all about his criticism: he felt almost inspired himself as he listened to the brisk, powerful voice, he was delighted to be looking into such a frank, open face, lit continually by a smile—you could never tell when one smile was coming to an end and another beginning.

"But Katharina?" he asked. "What has she to do with this business?" (Incidentally, where was she? Ah, there she was,

143

sitting in the front row with her hands folded!) "She hasn't even got a residence permit!"

"That doesn't matter. She is my first girl. By the end of the year I shall have five hundred more. Shan't I, Katharina?"

He nodded towards her and she returned his look enthusiastically. It looked like love to Kansdorf.

"But she'll be thrown out!"

"No she won't!"

"She *will* be thrown out, I know it for a fact! She has absolutely no chance of staying on French soil."

The priest laughed, and waved his hand in denial.

"I'm not the slightest bit interested in these earthly ordinances. No mere policeman can take the girl away from a work that God has given her to do, you can see that for yourself! But now I must go."

He went to the entrance, Kansdorf and Katharina following.

At the door he turned to Kansdorf.

"What did you say your name was?"

"Kansdorf."

"Kansdorf. Aha, I might almost have known as much! K is Our Lord, that's the challenge. N is *numen*. In the middle comes 'nsd'—that means something that saws up and cuts and destroys. You know about the Gospel and God's omnipotence, but you cut it all up, for some reason or other. Are you an intellectual? Or a philosopher? You must give it up!"

"Have I to stop thinking?"

"No, but you must stop thinking *wrongly*. There is something more important than thinking: obedience!"

"Obedience?"

"Certainly. Obeying the things that one knows to be right. And that, you know, is something I can *see*."

Kansdorf was getting annoyed, and also a bit apprehensive. The man might not be a charlatan, but his nonsense of

144

letters and sounds was certainly charlatanism. Yet in its silly way, his analysis of himself was in fact true.

He wanted to stay with him a bit longer, but was packed off. If Kansdorf would like to come to his lecture the next day, however, he would be welcome. But he mustn't bring anyone else with him; he wanted to select his audience, he was only addressing an élite.

"Why do you think that I belong to the élite?"

"Oh, I don't mean an intellectual élite. You are not specially gifted, so far as I can see. Fairly normal. But I can tell from your name that you possess something very unusual. You have the challenge within you, you can hear it, you have looked into the kingdom of God but not dared to take the first step towards it."

He said this with a wonderful sincerity; his jet-black eyes sparkled, but it was a friendly sparkle. Once again he was right! How could he know that Kansdorf had once, long ago, really looked into the real world? That very day he had been sitting in the prefecture trying to write down what he could remember of it—unsuccessfully, as it had turned out. He was beginning to find the priest disturbing.

Kansdorf tried to detain him, but he tore himself away.

"I'll see you at my lecture. Bring a pen with you and take notes. It will be the first time you've ever heard the truth—and nothing but the truth! I never say anything but the truth!"

He slapped Kansdorf good-bye on the shoulder, took hold of Katharina's hand in an oddly childlike fashion—she only had time to nod to the Swede—and led her rapidly away. Kansdorf watched them go—he was talking away, beard wagging, hands gesticulating, immediately absorbed in his plans.

Kansdorf went back to the stop and eventually arrived home. He felt churned up. The priest was a fool and at the same time a visionary. He must meet him again. Was he one of those simple pious, uncomplicated people who, with all their foolishness, are nearer to God than the rest of us, who, with our self-created idea of reality, try in vain to capture the truth? He must certainly meet him again.

Kansdorf sat so deep in thought over his lunch that Clothilde noticed it.

"Isn't monsieur eating anything?" she said. "The soup has gone quite cold. And it was so hot when I put it on the table."

She stood before him with her hands hanging by her sides, a powerful figure blooming with health, red in the face from the kitchen fire.

"I'm sitting thinking," he said. "It is simply a question of whether I am—thinking correctly. . . ."

She stared at him in astonishment, started on another question, thought better of it, and went out into the kitchen.

CHAPTER FOURTEEN

In his student days Jules Lebrun had made his great formulation: there could be no greater triumph in life than the capture and physical conquest of a highly spiritual and intellectual woman. To assert oneself intellectually, to prove oneself her equal in clearness and quickness of mind, spirit, knowledge and refinement. And then to conquer her and subjugate her.

But he soon realized that he had no great power, either intellectually or amorously. He had frequently observed that the girls' eyes tended to look past him and come to rest on his companions. When he had been younger he had cursed his appearance: why had he had to be burdened with his ridiculous body, his short neck, his broad, squashed face? He had to be satisfied with the women the other fellows didn't want. And he had to pay for his experiences. But even when he was in the arms of these girls he would dream of the proud, superior woman whom he would one day subjugate even with his body.

She never seemed to want to appear, however. He was not too mortified about it. He had other things to think about. But for a long time he was unable to forget one painful episode.

One evening, at a students' discussion meeting in the main

lecture hall in the Sorbonne, he had happened to sit next to a girl whose self-possession and self-confidence had made a great impression on him. She didn't seem to have anyone with her. He pushed a note over to her: "Isn't it dreadfully boring here? Shall we go and have a drink somewhere?" She gave him a pleasant smile but wrote back: "In a while. I have put my name down to speak. But afterwards!" After a while it came to her turn, and he was quite dazzled: she spoke energetically, confidently, and lucidly, and demolished two or three of the previous speakers with a sort of sadistic disdain. Whereupon a young Dominican got up and emitted a brief riposte that went like an arrow to its target. His words scored a bull's-eye. Even Lebrun had only one feeling at that moment, and that was that what the fellow had said was final. The audience, who had been irritated by the girl's self-confidence, applauded at once. Perhaps she went a little pale. But when the applause died away she was ready with her answer, straight to the point again, brilliant, full of matter. She dealt with the objections—perhaps there was an element of sophistry but even so. . . . And then it was her turn to bask in the applause.

Lebrun was enchanted. He accompanied her proudly from the hall. Now, he thought. Now or never. This is the woman of my dreams.

That very evening he fell in love with her. And the next day he went to see her. She explained that she was busy. But some other time. . . . He felt the rebuff but accepted it gracefully and tried again later. To be given the same reply. He came back a third time. He was standing in the vestibule of her hotel as she came down the stairs and he could hear her talking to the man who was with her:

"Hurry! He may be coming. He is unbearable, he looks like a frog. And he has no ideas of his own at all. . . ."

Lebrun just had time to dodge into the telephone box to

avoid being seen. There could be no doubt that she had been talking about him. And she was the person he had been hoping to conquer, to win! He felt the wound for years. In those words he had heard his formula's death warrant.

Cynicism frosted his whole being as frost encrusts the earth. Now the only thing that mattered was self-protection. Attack was out of the question—now it was a case of defence, the struggle for existence!

This scar was still burning in his soul when he fell in love with Ilse Lemat, the fair-haired, far from intellectual Swiss student. He had given up the idea of studying for the priesthood a long while before and had switched to medicine: it seemed more attractive to cut up human bodies than to meddle about with human souls. He noticed that the impressive Perezcaballero was interested in the girl, and felt like giving way. He would never be able to stand up against such a fellow. However, he made a desperate effort and put everything into one last try. And one evening, to his great surprise, he succeeded in getting the girl. The game was won. It was no great triumph, but a triumph nevertheless. He had gone in for a fight, even if an unimportant one, and emerged victorious. When later Perezcaballero became a theological student and a monk, he smiled: he knew why.

The marriage turned out an unexpectedly happy one. Ilse was a very level-headed girl and seemed quite content with her lot. She had no conflicts. Only a short time ago he had discovered that she was interested in another man—a friend of theirs. She had confessed at once—not that there had been anything to confess. But she had been so carried away by her confusion that she had told him something that until then she had always kept to herself: that she had originally loved not him but Perezcaballero, that she had gone to Perezcaballero and begged him to take her back, but that he had refused. Lebrun had never suspected that there might have been anything dubious about his victory. He had had no difficulty in getting the whole truth out of Ilse. Why hadn't Perezcaballero wanted her back? Because she had already given herself to him, Lebrun? A woman who had yielded to his passion was no longer worth having, in fact!

The matter did not vastly upset him. His main feeling was one of pity for his wife.

And then this proud monk had turned up at his house. Lebrun had sent him one of his articles and added a few words saying that it would be nice to see him again. He had no ulterior motive; it was simply that he could not stop probing the faintly nagging tooth.

He rarely thought of other women. Once or twice there was a *malheur*—but never anything sensational. There is a whole class of women who regularly fall in love with their doctors, and this happened in his case too. Occasionally he would succumb—always, however, with a feeling of disgust afterwards.

Until a day came when a new patient turned up and enslaved him irrevocably. It must have been about two years ago now. She was the actress, Agnès Lutri.

Everyone knew Agnès Lutri. She had her own theatre, and it was a very popular one: the only theatre apart from the Odeon of any importance on the left bank of the Seine. She could produce the classics with an absolute minimum of decor, using players who were quite unknown. But she could also put on star performances featuring the most important actors in Paris, many of whom were her friends. These would then—without any publicity—appear in her revues, which were quite unlike anybody else's and might be written either by young students or well-known authors. She never had to pay her writers anything: the honour of having a lyric or sketch included in her programme was sufficient reward in itself. She was an original, versatile woman who did what she wanted to do.

At first he could not understand why she should have come to him. He examined her and found that she had all the usual actress's complaints—nervous tension, too much working at night, nerves, indigestion, complicated love affairs. . . .

He dutifully accepted her; as a matter of fact, he was rather proud to have her as one of his patients. He asked for a most modest fee—she never had any money—and in the end he fell in love with her. This was before he had learned about his wife's secret.

To his surprise he found his passion increasing. At his age? After all he had been through? It was ridiculous. But in spite of his cynicism he was unable to do anything about it: the thing grew on him. In spite of attempts to preserve his self-control and a proper sense of his own dignity, he was soon acting like any idiotic boy. He hung a signed photograph of her in his surgery and stood another up at home on the piano. He went to see her at the theatre several times a week, visited her in her box, sent her flowers. . . . He was accepted in her circle as a mild joke. He protected himself by joining in the joke, acting the stolid ignoramus caught up amongst brilliant theatre folk. Agnès herself was grateful to him for his help, but that was all. He could discover no sort of personal interest. Nevertheless, he persisted. One day his chance would come.

It didn't.

Instead, he suffered a further humiliation, which he was too blind to save himself from in time.

He had asked to be allowed to give a late supper to the cast after the first night of a new show. He had done his best—hired a whole restaurant floor, chosen the various dishes and wines with the utmost care, found out what Agnès Lutri's special tastes were, ordered her favourite flowers, bought her what was for him a most expensive present to wear. . . .

The evening had been a great success. Everybody praised the way he had arranged things. Everybody felt happy. At last he had found a way out of the narrow circle of his life and created his own atmosphere, something really worthy of himself. He made a speech and there was a burst of applause—whereupon, greatly daring—and to the accompaniment of much laughter and jocularity—he kissed her. His triumph seemed complete.

If he had not been so blinded by success, he might have paid a little more attention to odd winks and whispers. He might have caught the expression on Agnès Lutri's face. Above all he might have noticed Georges Lecompte, the singer, who was sitting opposite him. If he had been perfectly himself, he would have seen quite clearly, from Lecompte's face and hers, that she was his mistress. Instead, he went on forcing his attentions upon her, to the point of trying to get a seat in her car. She froze—and with one scornful, superior gesture of her gloved hand dismissed him. At the same moment Georges Lecompte climbed into the car.

There were many witnesses of this episode. Several members of the party were standing round the car laughing and they saw every detail of it. Lebrun staggered back. Quite suddenly the truth was clear to him. He made two quick decisions: that he must punish the woman, and he must save what face he could with the onlookers.

He invited everyone to come home with him, put champagne and pâté de foie gras on the table, showed the best of good spirits throughout the rest of the night. As face-saving, it was not much but at least it was a distraction.

When the guests had departed he took his strongest sleeping powder and slept nearly the whole of the next day. And

152

then followed a time when he was entirely ruled by his obsession, in that one matter quite beyond reason.

He had made his resolve. He would take up the challenge —but he would conduct it in his own peculiar way. He knew that Agnès Lutri had a weakness for certain drugs. Once or twice he had discreetly helped her to obtain them. He now went to see her—she had not been to his surgery since the night of the party—behaved as though nothing had happened, was good-humoured, jovial, gallant. She told him she was unhappy about what had happened. He looked at her with wide, uncomprehending eyes.

What had happened? he asked. She didn't imagine that he seriously. . . ? Didn't she understand, then, that it had simply been fooling?

"Agnès," he said, "don't let's have another word about all that nonsense. I'm only concerned about one thing, and that's your health."

She looked up inquiringly. She was forty, rather plump, but still desirable with her blonde hair, her large eyes and her smooth marble skin.

"But you are quite satisfied about that, aren't you?" she said.

"Well, yes," he replied. "More or less. But I have not been quite honest with you. Now, I think, I'd better be."

He went on to describe a more or less imaginary complaint, ending by saying that if she was to go on with her artistic work she would have to risk taking certain powerful stimulants. But she could only do this under his supervision. Did she understand?

She listened carefully. Was that all? It was splendid of him. She had so often pleaded with him for a little cocaine! Had he forgotten that? All the better. She tried to hide her delight.

She was so afraid, she said. She didn't want to run any risk. But she had complete confidence in him. If he assured her that

—for the sake of her art—she should take such a risk, of course she would do so.

So he bound her. The way now lay open to him, and before long, after careful treatment, he had made her a slave to cocaine. And to himself, its dispenser. Later he was to look back on the whole episode incredulously. But for the moment it filled his horizon.

He began to work on her in another way. He knew quite well that she was still living with Georges Lecompte. He discussed the matter with her as though it was an understood thing. When he mentioned him, he always spoke most respectfully, with admiration indeed.

At the same time he could see that Lecompte's position was not by any means as secure as it had been. She was beginning to grow a little tired of him. If he had launched into a direct attack on the man, she would have warmly defended him. But he didn't. He had collected a good deal of material about Lecompte, but he didn't make use of it. He gave not the slightest inkling that he knew anything about Lecompte's other affairs, for instance. When she herself asked him anxiously whether he had heard anything, he answered that he knew nothing at all.

When he discovered that Georges Lecompte was making use of her financially, he made a note of the fact but did not refer to it. Instead, he gave her money himself—the theatre was run in far too bohemian a fashion to pay its way. Each week he bound her ever more tightly with three strong ties —drugs, money and sympathy.

Soon he would be able to cash in on all this.

But first Lecompte's head must fall. And fall it did— right into Lebrun's waiting hands.

He managed to arrange things so that the truth about Lecompte's affairs not only came to light, but appeared in the newspapers. He got an evening paper to publish the story, and took care to see that a copy of the paper came into Agnès's hands. He saw her rage and despair. When she handed him the paper, he read the article through in her presence, slowly, looking grave.

Could it really be true? He doubted it. You couldn't believe everything you read in the papers. Wasn't it possible—didn't she think—that the whole thing had been invented, by some rival?

In her rage, she told him how much Lecompte had borrowed from her. He knew how much it was, approximately, but he behaved as though the figure gave him a shock. He realized, he said, that things had become critical. He must help her straighten her affairs out. He would like nothing better than to be able to help her materially—in her own sphere he had nothing to offer, of course, but he had some experience of practical affairs. People like him were there for that kind of thing. He would be delighted if she would tell him her difficulties.

At the same time he explained that she must now take the drugs regularly—under his strict supervision—unless she wanted to have a complete breakdown. He would see that she reduced the dose when the time came.

And now he was strolling through the Trianon gardens, banging his stick on the bare branches, his mind filled with the curious two-year story. He thought:

She asked me to go and see her at eight o'clock. She asked me herself. I didn't force myself upon her. She will make the first moves herself. I shall be passive, amazed, happy, until—!

But *I* shall have the last word!

He gave a bare branch as thick as his arm a resounding blow, and it fell with a crash to the ground, but his stick broke too. With a powerful heave he threw the stump away, in spite of its silver handle. Stooping with the exertion, he

155

stood there, his right hand resting on his knee. He shrieked out his laughter, and his short left arm jerked out.

Two terrified dogs rushed away into the distance. The park-keeper in his splendid uniform watched the passer-by in surprise, and hoped he was not ill.

But Dr. Lebrun straightened himself and moved slowly to the exit, his body swaying heavily.

Now for a good lunch. Then a little walk. Then a long bath—not too hot. Then an hour's sleep. Perhaps a glance at the newspapers.

And then a slow stroll up to Agnès Lutri's house, at 20, Rue de Tournon. . . .

CHAPTER FIFTEEN

Kansdorf:

It's strange.

For a long time—for years—I could never wake up without feeling that consciousness itself meant pain, punishment. I was invariably overcome by an immeasurable sense of disgust as soon as consciousness became active and the ineradicable memories returned, the mill of associations resumed its endless grinding and thought began to probe all the smarting wounds again. On how many mornings have I lain in this little room and tried to *duck down under* the images, *under* the stream of consciousness which seemed to be streaming through me, to dive. I realized that this stream was my own self, but I wanted to cut my innermost being off from it. I never managed to. After a short struggle I was always swamped by all the painful, humiliating things. I had to force myself either to read a book, or to get up and occupy myself with something mechanical—to develop some new line of thought which would not lead to anything sensitive or painful. But there was no book that didn't sooner or later lead me back to myself! However much I tried to keep myself out of the picture, a spark would flash, contact would be made, and I would have to put the book down. Then Clothilde would hear me walking up and down for hour after hour.

It seems to me that our existence within time, in fact time itself, is the result of a sin, a form of punishment. I can't give any logical grounds for this, I just feel from my own repeated experience that it is so. From sleep, which means peace and death, we are whipped back into this prison by the pitiless sun and our body, as soon as its dull senses begin to recover their urge for movement. There are people who say that they *like* being in this prison! That isn't so with me and never was. Can I remember a single day in my life when I felt anything like that spontaneous happiness untrammelled by thought, which so many people say they experience? Happiness—in this rotating, strictly ordered system? Happiness—imprisoned in these concepts of time and space, this un-freedom? One can thank God for everything else: for the Redemption; for the fact that, perhaps through trial, He has opened our eyes and purified us; and for so much else. But how or why can one ever feel thankful for being a human being? That would be like the prisoner thanking the prison officer with tears in his eyes for allowing him to go on for year after year, picking oakum in his striped clothes!

But all that is over! Now I face something new! What do I care about the past, now that this new thing has come surging over me? I have been set in motion, and I believe I have glimpsed a new truth—which is that one can never experience anything true so long as one remains passive, stands still and cogitates. I can see more clearly when I myself move and act.

As a matter of fact there is nothing paradoxical in this. A human being sits still either to meditate or to brood. He looks into himself. What he sees fills him with melancholy. He concludes from this that the whole destiny of mankind is melancholy. But this picture which the passive, meditative human being sees of himself is not the true picture, for the real human being is the one who is in movement, active, involved in the life of society along with other human beings. It is a sick, amputated self I see when I look into myself! How could I ever have dared to connect my conception of the real essence of human life with this paltry half picture? I cannot come to a true knowledge of my self through analysis or self-inspection, since everything I grasp in this way can only be a part of my true being. On the other hand I can *experience* a deeper truth through acting, through movement.

Strange to relate, only when I cannot see, but act, can I— see! If I simply try to see, then I cannot see anything.

But I am no longer in a position to brood. I have been drawn into a flood of events, I have been thrown into contact with other human beings, I have in fact made a choice, have acted, plunged in and stamped my will on a sequence of events. How did I manage it? I can't say. But through my dry feeble veins blood more richly oxygenated is suddenly running.

What was it that injected the oxygen?

Movement, activity, responsibility.

The next day Kansdorf went back to Abbé Auclair's church.

It was full, and swarming with little boys belonging to his troop. There was a sense of brimming life in the small space; Auclair himself was going around joking with everybody. In a chair at the side of the altar sat the parish priest, a tall, thin, close-shaven man; he didn't seem to be regarding the affair unfavourably. When the performance began, everyone went quiet. The play, performed by the boys themselves, was moving. The choir was excellent: Auclair had turned these dead-end kids, whose minds and language had been formed on the pavements and in the public houses of the big city, into sheer voices ringing out in celestial harmony. Celestial? they were no longer the voices of humans bowed down by care and suffering, but clear, pure voices coming from some sphere above or beyond the human prison. The singing flowed into

Kansdorf like a refreshing spring, like morning light or the rustling of trees in a wood.

When it was all over Kansdorf went off to find Auclair. He was standing by the door mustering his troops man by man. He knew them all, and he was giving them greetings for the people at home or shouting messages to them. He gave an impression of being both relaxed and concentrated, quiet and communicative. He had a remarkable power, this young priest.

He nodded and made a sign to Kansdorf, to indicate that he would be with him shortly. And he was. He invited him up to his room, which looked just as untidy as ever. He made a cup of bad tea, and then filled it with old pieces of bread. Kansdorf had to wait for them to soften. Auclair himself ate nothing.

"I always fast on days like this. The soul is livelier, freer, lighter, when you fast. Haven't you ever tried it? Do! You'll never again be able to get along without it!"

Kansdorf asked him a whole series of questions, which he answered in a most friendly fashion. He explained his plans for conquering the world. When Kansdorf pointed out that a bomb could wipe out the whole block in a second, and all his followers with it, that he had to remember that he might fall ill or lose all his boys, he laughed amiably and shook his head:

"You are quite sensible, in a worldly sort of way. But you don't take God into account. What does it matter to me if *one* of my instruments is knocked out of my hand, when I know that I have someone almighty behind me? Almighty: do you realize what that means?"

He looked through a few books, then pulled up a chair, sat down, leaned forward, looked Kansdorf in the eye, and suddenly said:

"I knew you'd be coming. I know that we shall be having

a good deal to do with each other. You will find a job for yourself in what I'm doing. At the moment I just can't see what it is to be. But it will become clear."

Kansdorf shook his head. He said that he had only come along in order to try to help the girl.

"Of course," he said, "we always have our own motives for doing what we do. Always. That's the way God leads us on. It's only very rarely that He lets us see His motives. You had to meet the girl to be able to come here. It's always like that. God controls what happens—and us too."

He sat silent for a while. Then he went on:

"I'm a farmer's son from Brittany, I've only recently become a priest. My mother and father and brothers are pagans, and they laugh at me. I tried to do what God wanted me to do. A few years ago something strange happened, that's to say, something not at all strange but quite normal, really. God told me to go to Rome, without any money and without a visa. I had to go there in a straight line."

"In a straight line?"

"Yes, without going round anything. At first I thought it was more of a symbolical sort of order; but it appeared that I was meant to take it literally. I set off. Barefoot. When I came to the Swiss border I was arrested and had to wait a couple of months until the Bishop managed to arrange for me to go on —without a visa! Everybody thought I was mad. Most people think that."

He smiled slightly, without a trace of resentment, without a trace, either, of self-dramatization. It was as though he had stated something obvious. He went on:

"I can never really understand how priests can be satisfied to go on living, simply being respected by their fellow men and regarded as quite normal, without its putting their backs up! Our Lord said that his disciples would be persecuted. As soon as I talk or act as though Christianity were something normal, likable, reasonable, then I *must* have made a mistake and be on the wrong track. I can only be sure of myself when I am treated as Our Lord Himself was treated—like a fool. In the eyes of the world our teaching *must* seem to be madness, otherwise it can't be right.

"So, then, I went on; nothing gave me greater confidence than being arrested and treated as not quite right in the head. I was on the right road. But you will want to hear what happened next. I went on and on and finally got right up into the Alps. It was no easy matter making straight for Rome, but I did my best. Now and again I stopped and did a bit of work to get some money; then I pushed on. And then one fine day came, it was in June, when I found myself standing at the top of a steep mountain-side, and I could go no further."

"Not by going straight on, anyway," Kansdorf interjected.

"That's right," he said, unsmilingly. "But of course I had to go straight on. Do you know what I did?"

Kansdorf shrugged his shoulders.

"I prayed to God, and He didn't answer. I felt He was so disgusted with me for being such a ninny and not being able to follow a clear order from Him that He had taken away His support from me. I *knew* what I had to do."

"You mean—"

"I jumped down, of course. I went rolling down like a ball. I gave myself a few nasty bumps, and I even think I must have lost consciousness for a while. . . ."

Was he talking nonsense? Was he imagining it all?

He pulled up one of his trouser legs and showed a number of fearsome-looking scars.

"See, this is where I got cut by the ice!"

He pointed to his neck.

"And here's where I was hit by a boulder: it could easily have knocked my head off. Oh, there was blood everywhere!

But I went on to Rome in the same clothes, and I didn't even wash them."

"But. . . . How did you get on after that?"

"I picked myself up, gave thanks to God, and then I found there was a precipice in front of me. At that moment a little white rat came running over the snow—I have never seen such a rat in the Alps before. I realized this was a sign, and followed it to the left and came down into a snow valley. Then I came upon a fork in the road: just then an eagle suddenly flew less than a hundred feet above my head, down the road to the right. I followed it and went on."

"And you managed to get to Rome like that?"

"Yes, of course. It took some time but I managed it. The journey lasted—including being arrested and tried five times —nearly six months. In Lugano the French consul tried to give me a visa, but I wouldn't have it. He tried to get me arrested and sent back home. But then he let it slide. I was allowed to go on. And in Rome they arrested me again."

"Who did?"

"The Pharisees, of course, my own fellow countrymen, priests even. They were ashamed of me, they set a doctor on me and the poor chap came to the conclusion that I was ready for the madhouse! Just think of it—not to realize that anyone who follows the voice of God is *bound* to look a fool in the eyes of the world! He didn't know that, poor chap!"

He leaned back in his chair and burst into a loud boyish laugh. His jet-black eyes sparkled more than ever.

"And then?"

"Well, there I was, among the idiots—not God's idiots like myself, but these poor defectives. Oh, I loved them. They used to give me the most awful beatings-up, and use the most awful language. I thanked God for those days. I was there for rather more than a year. I never felt better."

He leaned forward and said confidentially:

"I'll tell you something: those crazy creatures are far more normal than normal people! They are nearer to God. They are no more mad than philosophers who imagine that whatever they can see in the cracked, dirty mirror of reason is reality! They were splendid people. Many of them were saints. There was one unfortunate fellow there: the devil made him hit me every morning. He absolutely ruined my shoulder—you see, it's a bit lopsided, it didn't knit together as quickly as it should. Oh, you should have seen that fellow!—over six feet tall, with a beard down to his chest; he never spoke without screaming and he always had to bang something at the same time. But when he did bang anything his eyes were wild with despair, 'I can't help it! I can't help it!' he would shout. Whenever he maltreated me I used to say to myself, 'You are suffering for someone else; some other poor wretch is missing this torment because of you! Stick it out!' And I stuck it out. Oh, vicarious suffering, that is our secret! I often think I should give my whole life up to God—I mean my eternal life —to redeem the poor lacerated creatures I come across here in this *magna meretrix,* Paris. For this city is a great harlot— you realize that, of course? Oh yes, that's exactly what she is."

"And how did you get back home?"

"I was sent home with papers that said I was mad. But before I set off I went to see the Holy Father. I showed him my papers and said that I was glad to be looked upon as a fool for Our Lord's sake. The Pope read the papers, looked at me for a long time, then leaned forward and blessed me. Oh, he understood me, the Holy Father did!

"I was never happier than when I was brought back by my keeper. When I got here my colleagues wanted to put me into a home or something of the sort. So again I was sent into a madhouse. But I was released from there—as normal. That worried me. If I was beginning to be normal, passive, harmless—then I must have betrayed Our Lord. And then I got this job and began to work seriously with my boys. You must realize that twenty-five per cent of these youngsters had sexual troubles—or have! They belong to the army of Satan, all right. If they had grown up as they were, they would all have become his gallant soldiers. Oh, I know the kind they are— liars, drinkers, sexually queer, wild, cruel. They go from girls to revolutionary meetings. Others goad them, and then they goad others—just what the devil wants. But I took them over. I didn't try to raise another army of my own against him—my colleagues do that, but they never get the right ones. No; I took over the very people the devil had chosen for himself. And now they are mine! Now we'll get on with the fight!"

He laughed out loud like a boy. Torn by conflicting feelings, Kansdorf stared at him. Was he a genius, one of the people who turn the world upside down? Or was he really an idiot?

That was the end of his story.

"And now," he said, "we must have a few words about the girl. She has been sent to me by God. Her parents are dead— died in Mauthausen. She is the only one left; there is a great work awaiting her. . . ."

CHAPTER SIXTEEN

A quarter bottle of dry champagne to keep him company in the baths—an excellent idea!

Dr. Lebrun had weighed himself and discovered that he had put on another pound. That didn't matter—he could still beat any youngster off the course, because he was intelligent. He had given a rapid look at himself in the mirror: terrible, absolutely terrible! But women are remarkable creatures: they are magnificently prepared to overlook physical deficiencies as soon as they imagine they have found a noble, sympathetic soul. . . .

He took a little stroll, looking casually into the windows of the bookshops and lounging carelessly along. He met one of his patients and calmly walked past him. He tried two or three cafés—and finally he got a real Pernod put in front of him. They were beginning to appear again: it was simply a case of knowing the right places.

The afternoon passed more quickly than he had imagined possible. To get through the last few hours he went into a news cinema and let the images flicker past his eyes. He slept for a while, and when he awoke found that it was just time for him to go, if he was going to walk. He had twenty-five minutes to get to the Rue de Tournon. That was where she lived, of course—in the intellectual quarter: where else would she live?

Dr. Lebrun walked slowly down the avenue through the Tuileries gardens, followed the embankment as far as the Rue de Seine, stood in front of the antique shops, had time to let his shoes be given a last polish, and two minutes before the stroke of eight was standing at the front door.

It was less than two years since he had walked up and down here so often—tortured, ill with desire, possessed. All his reasoning powers, all his critical apparatus, had been unable to rid him of the poison. He laughed grimly. He was not as miserable as that now. Now he could experience a different pleasure from that of passion or intoxication—the pleasure of stripping off veils and revealing the truth. No other pleasure really counted for him, he felt. If any single passion had lasted throughout his life, it was the longing to unveil the truth, to see things as they really are and to say so, to get rid of illusions and tissues of lies. It was no great task. He did not in fact by so doing solve any problems; he certainly never imagined that it made himself or anyone else any happier. But it was hygienic.

He went slowly up the stairs, his footsteps soundless on the soft carpet. He was enjoying every movement. You unfortunate ugly devil, he was saying to himself, you misshapen apology for a Aesculapius, now, slowly but surely, you are approaching your victory and no one can snatch it from you! And you have brought off this victory all by yourself—without any help from anybody—done it entirely out of your own head! You are free from passion, you are not crazy, your head is clear and you know what you're doing; there is nothing to stop you enjoying this moment to the full!

When he got to the second landing he stood still. Could it really—? What if—?

He stood quite still. He heard the porter's voice coming up from his lodge.

Could it really be true that nothing unexpected was going to happen to interfere with—?

He went suddenly solemn. Had he been so simple-minded as to imagine himself once again beyond the slightest possibility of failure? Of course he couldn't see all the links, in a complicated chain of cause and effect, and control them! Something could easily have happened. Something could still happen. The woman in the room above was an irrational type, she didn't think with her brain like him but with her guts, her diaphragm, her bile duct. There was no need for any logical, comprehensible reason, for her suddenly to decide to do something quite senseless. She might have just fallen in love with a taxi-driver or a caretaker, or the old pump in the yard. Why not? Anything was possible. She might have seen through him—though that was unlikely. She might suddenly have decided to react in quite the opposite way from yesterday—without any reason. Perhaps at this very moment she was regretting that she had asked him to come. Perhaps she detested him. Perhaps she would meet him with crocodile tears in her eyes, and talk about being ill and so, unfortunately. . . . Anything was possible, so far as she was concerned.

He was still standing there quite still. There was a distinct possibility. But it was a slight one. If anything could be regarded as humanly certain it was his coming victory. There was, of course, a risk of failure; but it was a very minor one.

There was no doubt, however, that he had to be prepared— *in case* anything of the sort should occur. He must think up an excuse in advance. He had to be able to change round quickly and easily, had to be able to tell himself that none of this was of the slightest importance to him, that he had already achieved his aim, that the affair had not been intended to turn out in just one way, that it could quite as well end differently. . . .

He took off his hat and coat in the hall, was led into the

168

drawing room, advanced to meet her, and saw at once that all his anxiety had been unnecessary. It was right not to have arrived too promptly; that would have made him look too impatient. He saw her "striding forward to meet him." This was serious! The make-up, the whole get-up! And the perfume —and the hands, carefully manicured and a shade too white —and the smile, the professional, practised smile—and the hip movement as she walked away to get him a drink—oh, the whole battery was out and no mistake! This didn't signify indifference!

They were to eat at once. He knew that her question would soon be coming. He could see this from the way her face was shaking, and her hand, as he kissed it. She wanted the cocaine.

In fact he had gradually been reducing the dose. He had told her so quite frankly. But what he had not told her was that even the grains he was giving her had been thinned down to such an extent that in the last few months they had been practically innocuous. Nevertheless they had done their work. He had seen for himself how subject she was to his influence. He could have given her sugar pills and she would have shouted for joy. He could have given her chalk, and set her nerves at rest.

He was proud of this point. Even in the course of this intrigue he had ended by behaving perfectly properly from the professional point of view. If he had given her the habit, he had broken her of it, slowly, without her noticing it. He couldn't have managed it better if he had been interested in her as a patient. The only difference was that he had at the same time bound her to his own person by a strong bond of auto-suggestion. She could no longer live properly without him. He had become indispensable to her.

There was another point. He had taken over her business affairs, he had poured money into her theatre, he had undoubtedly helped her. But with regard to the money—he had had it back! The lawyer he had entrusted with it had got the whole theatre onto a firm footing. It was safe now.

So he had acted in his own interests on the business side, and he had done his duty as a doctor. And yet, despite all this, this wonderful, warm-blooded, widely admired woman was now in his hands. Now, at this very moment. This was no commonplace revenge, this was special. He could have hugged himself to think how special it was.

She clinked glasses with him. Then she said:

"I must say, you are very hard on me."

"Hard? Not with you, my dear, surely?"

"Yes you are. You know how tired I am. Surely you understand me? I really need some sort of stimulation. I think I deserve it. I am under your supervision, after all."

He looked at her closely. Women were incredible. This experienced coquette, this practised seductress—she stood there like every woman since Eve and with an imperceptible movement of her shoulder let her shoulder strap slowly slip down, so that he should be seduced by the naked white flesh. He had to force himself not to laugh out loud. Was she really unaware what elementary wiles she was using? Did she seriously believe that he wanted to take a bite at that white shoulder?

He went up to her and kissed her, following the accustomed ritual.

"Agnès," he said, "you've been great. You've done what I told you to do, even when I've been hard on you. You mustn't think I'm not pleased with you."

Now she was listening. It was like playing on a responsive instrument.

"Well, where did I put it, then? Ah, here we are! Virtue shall be rewarded."

He took a packet out of his pocket.

She snatched it out of his hand.

"Real pearls!" he said.

He saw her start—was she really only getting a piece of jewellery, when she was expecting something so different?

"Oh no, you can't take me in—"

She was still not quite sure. She had to open it. She saw the powder, saw that there was quite a lot of it, more than she had had in all the past six months. She came to him with the calm, dignified, profoundly soulful, motherly air which actresses who are no longer so young love to put on—there was strength in her age, and her eyes were cloudy as she first of all pressed his hand and then kissed him.

It doesn't matter that you're lying, he thought, as he returned her kiss with interest. But you're a bit too old, a bit too stout, my dear! And to think that a couple of years ago I had such nights of anguish on your account!

"You are wonderful," he said. "You are so incredibly young —so fresh, so spontaneous, so vital! Like a young girl!"

She smiled—she liked that. But her thoughts were already elsewhere.

Now would come the next lie. He could see them coming. Everything was going according to plan.

She looked round slightly, pretended to be concerned.

"Darling, why are they keeping us waiting? Excuse me a moment, I'll go and see."

Yes, I'll excuse you for a moment, he thought. Many, many moments, if you like. You must go and see at once! Swallow the whole lot if you like, it's quite harmless. I'll excuse you because you are proving my theory so absolutely up to the hilt.

He lit a cigarette and sipped his drink. Was there still any danger? Could anything happen? Should he be prepared for the worst? Hardly. He could be perfectly easy.

When she came back her eyes were bright. She had taken the powder, gulped it down eagerly—the way she gulped down life. Now she felt the excitement coming. Oh, she was grateful to him, so grateful.

A few more volleys, he thought.

"You know," he said, "you women are incredible. You're not like us men."

"How do you mean?" she said, raising her glass.

In that light, and with her eyes so bright, she *was* beautiful. From a distance she must have looked absolutely marvellous.

"Well, you know, we men judge women by their beauty. I love you, you know that. But do you think I'd love you if you weren't as beautiful as you are? I don't know. To my shame I must admit I'm not so sure about that. But you women, you're above all that. You look for deeper things. If only you knew how wonderful it seems to me, that you can love me!"

He was delighted to be able to risk such commonplace tactics. There was no need now for anything subtle. The cash was there, so to speak, on the table; all he had to do was to pocket it.

She stood awaiting the expected stimulus. And gratitude for it combined with gratitude to the loyal soul who had backed her up and helped her so much—the man she could rely on.

"There's no need for you to belittle yourself," she said, slowly nodding her head, as though divulging a great secret. "A man isn't beautiful in the same way as a woman is. But it's not only a man's mind, or his will power, or his intelligence, that we admire. It's his strength too. My friend, I love you because you have such strength."

He had to swallow hard to stomach this answer. This woman was an outstanding performer in high French tragedy. Her Phèdre was famous, likewise her Antigone. She was said to be almost incomparable in her interpretations of involved and subtle ramifications of the soul. She had fathomed

172

its deepest recesses and could present them in flesh and blood on the stage. The most sophisticated Parisian critics had been moved and shattered by her artistry.

And now. The plays of the younger Dumas, Scribe, Augier, were psychological masterpieces compared with the act she was now taking part in!

"It's simply that you're greater as human beings than we men are," he said.

He could quite easily venture another commonplace without any fear of the consequences. Anything was permissible today.

"And there's nothing like being human," he said with great solemnity.

No, the bust of Racine did not fall off the mantelpiece. No look of anger shot out from the signed portrait of Coquelin hanging on the wall. He heard no shout of laughter from the print of Molière over the door leading to the dining room.

And she herself stood there listening, and waiting with quivering nostrils for the longed-for stimulus.

"How right you are," she said, with a heartfelt look. "How right!"

This was the voice which had captivated the whole metropolis!

The blood went to his head, and his heart throbbed delightedly. This was exceeding his wildest expectations.

At the same moment the maid appeared in the dining room doorway and they betook themselves to their solitary supper.

He hoped she had ordered champagne! Yes, that was all right. He took good care to see that she drank properly. Now she would be unable to distinguish one stimulant from the other. That would come soon enough. But by then he would have disappeared.

The meal went off in the accustomed fashion. She was her smart, voluble self. He played on her simplest instincts, rousing her interest by asking her questions about her triumphs in the theatre and getting her to talk about them.

She felt at ease, gay, happy. He could almost see in her the kind of person she must have been as a young girl. She must certainly have been enchanting in those days. Behind all her technique, behind all that had been hidden by the years, there could still be seen traces of freshness, unaffected vitality, genuine originality. At moments, especially when she was talking about her earlier triumphs, her face became dazzling with its grace and beauty—and he suddenly realized that it is not so much the body as the soul that ages.

The contempt he had felt for her vanished. For the last few minutes of the meal he sat there, genuinely interested, indeed moved, listening to her as she laughed and chattered away. She was relaxed: without a trace of malice she imitated the way he screamed with laughter and flapped his arms.

And in a little while, after the coffee and liqueurs, he had reached his goal. Strangely, he felt rather tired, he didn't feel the joy he had expected to feel. They looked at her etchings—including the ones in her bedroom. She began to talk about him, when he was going to get divorced—he had told her that he had not been living with his wife for quite a long time!—and he answered gravely.

In no way did he take the initiative, either in word or in deed. It was she who took hold of his hand, she who asked him whether he thought it out of the question that they should get married. They belonged to each other now, surely. No one understood her better than he did. He had absolutely saved her, as a human being—and her theatre too. He modestly protested. It was almost exactly a year since the incident when she had sent him packing out of her car. He could still see the gesture of her hand: it had been like a blow in the face. Now his hatred had all gone. For a moment he thought, you might just as well please her; you might just as well take her body, now that she is prepared to give it you. Why struggle against it?

Then he pulled himself together. The game must be played out to the end. He had a duty to perform, a humiliation to repay.

And as she began to take her clothes off and he saw that much desired body, which had once intoxicated and excited him so much and cost him so many sleepless nights, he stiffened into contempt of the whole human race. He made not the slightest attempt to help her, despite her efforts to encourage him. She pouted like a little girl, slightly hurt. He kissed her. The younger Dumas, he thought. With a feeling of revulsion he seized her fiercely and noticed that she took this as a sign of passion. Had she entirely lost all sense of human feeling?

He caught sight of a torn packet lying on her writing-desk, and went over to it and picked it up.

"Yes, love," she said. "There's not much left! But that was your idea, wasn't it?"

"Yes, that's right," he said. "Next time you can have more!"

Slowly he approached the bed.

She smiled expectantly.

You are buying me, he thought. If it weren't for my cocaine you wouldn't have me in the house. Now I am to have you as the reward of my services and my honour as a medical man.

He was suddenly like a man growing sober after long drunkenness.

The moment had come he had been preparing for so long. A hundred times he had lived through the scene. "A man can love a woman madly," he would say, "when she is very beautiful." She would listen delightedly. "But you are no longer very beautiful," he would go on. "You *were* beautiful. That's the difference." She would be startled and angered. But before she had properly grasped his meaning he would go on: "A man can also love a woman madly because, simply by being what she is, she has poisoned him, got him into her power and penetrated into his innermost being." Then she would smile delightedly again. "But in *your* case this isn't so," he would say, throwing the ball back at her again. She would look at him, thunderstruck. "When you were living with Georges Lecompte you had me in your power like that, but in those days I wasn't responsible for my actions. Now I am." At this point she would stammer a question at him. He would continue calmly: "But strange to say a man can also love a woman madly even though he hates her. Oh, don't look so surprised! A man can be bound to a woman by other things than passion; by sorrow, pain—by hatred, in fact. I used to think that was how it was with you and me. But even that doesn't quite fit the case now. I don't hate you at all—though I used to." Now surely she would understand? "What silly fancies are these you've got in your head?" she would ask. "Why don't you come to me?" Then he would answer, calmly: "Because I—quite simply, and without any sort of passion—despise you, Agnès. And I despise you because you are prepared to buy me, because I only count as a lover to you because I can get you cocaine. You made a laughingstock of me once. Now it's your turn." That would be the end of it.

"Why don't you come to me?" she said softly, almost sadly.

He was now wholly sober. No, he couldn't do it. He felt tired. His whole grand scheme looked imbecile.

But he couldn't simply go away, without more ado. He either had to go right through with the thing, or else—

He went up to her. "I feel so sorry for you," he said.

She looked up in astonishment and put her arm round his neck.

"Why do you feel sorry for me?" she said. "Why, Jules?"

Because you don't understand, he thought. Because you are a little human being, like the rest of us. Pathetic, like the rest of us. Because you're just—like me. Because we are both pitiable and commonplace. Because we are both human beings.

"Why, Jules?" she asked again. "Why do you feel sorry for me?"

He looked at her.

"Because you have to be satisfied with a person like me," he said.

She smiled and kissed him.

He stood up and looked at her.

"You almost frightened me," she said tenderly, putting the light out.

"Never . . ." he said.

CHAPTER SEVENTEEN

Lebrun had rung up.

No, said Kansdorf, he didn't want to go and see the European all-in wrestling championship. He had lost his enthusiasm for it!

For years he had been bent over himself as over a thick, stagnant pool, feeling mists and anxiety arise without rightly knowing the reason why. He had whipped himself up into watching the shows in the sports' stadium or studying metaphysical systems. But now that he had got going he no longer felt any need to delve into himself, and in point of fact even the past seemed to be losing its hold over him. Memory had always stood in his way like a sort of curse: how he had beaten around to escape from it, but always in vain! Now, however, the past with all its evil was sinking away into utter stillness, the pain no longer smarted so much, and more recently his dreams had begun to lose their sense of anguish and their images of dread.

Clothilde was angry about Katharina. She was quite incapable of seeing the matter in Kansdorf's terms. He ought to keep his affairs out of the house, she did not want a woman over her. When he pointed out how unlikely it was that a tired old man like him would want to live with a mere child, all she did was to make a face. She knew all about tired old men. She had asked Katharina point-blank, and refused to believe the plain answer she had got.

What could Kansdorf be up to with the girl?

In the course of the long conversation he had had with Abbé Auclair after the special children's service the Abbé too had talked about Katharina. The three "a's" in her name, if Kansdorf remembered aright, were supposed to signify three Aves, and these meant a very clear vocation. The "r" and the "I" had something to do with *Rex Judaeorum*, and "K" naturally stood for "Christ." Kansdorf had been unable to go on listening to such nonsense any longer, and had abruptly brought the conversation to a close. Auclair laughed. He quite understood that the Swede should prefer the "correct" etymology, the one followed by the men of learning. He could go on doing so if he liked. But *his* learning was of a higher kind: he held the key to all mysteries in his hand. He could read people's souls. He had no desire to be understood immediately. But no one would ever succeed in shaking his faith. He had been put on the right road by a white mouse and an eagle, and after that there was not much chance of his going wrong in the matter of what constituted true heavenly knowledge!

Katharina was a saint, or was going to become one. She was predestined for mighty works, all she had to do was to go ahead and perform them. The fact that she had no parents, no papers, no visa, was a clear sign of her vocation. Greatness was always unexpected, and always aroused opposition. He had great plans for her. She was *virgo*, the highest kind of womanhood. She was Mary the Mother of God's favourite daughter. He spoke beautifully, inspiringly, about her—the fellow had a purity that was really quite out of this world. But all the same, he was a fool.

Kansdorf was finally given a printed invitation to his public lectures, which were to begin the following day. He went along. A number of people had turned up, but there was no sign of the priest. Time passed, and after an hour's wait even the patient French crowd began to grumble. Finally the curtains parted and instead of Abbé Auclair the old parish priest came onto the platform.

He was very pale. He bowed to the audience and announced in the most obscure and devious way possible that the talks had had to be cancelled because of certain circumstances which he could not as yet fully explain. Abbé Auclair had been taken ill—though not exactly in a physical sense. He therefore begged those present to forgive him for having to disappoint them, and told them that they would be given their money back at the door.

In the hall excited voices arose. Apparently Abbé Auclair had supporters.

"It's a plot!" shouted one stentorian voice.

And right at the back of the hall an oldish man stood up and said loudly and clearly:

"Ladies and gentlemen, what we feared has come to pass. Obviously our friend and teacher has upset the Pharisees again with his zeal for truth. They will say that he is queer in the head, as they have done more than once before. But, ladies and gentlemen, can this man be queer in the head when he has remade our whole parish, changed hundreds of young gangsters into decent, well-behaved Christian young men, and reawakened in us all a respect for purity and the Christian spirit?"

The uproar in the hall increased. The parish priest tried in vain to make himself heard. Kansdorf heard him assure them that he too had a great respect for Abbé Auclair's personal achievements. But the Church had spoken, and against her word there was and could be no appeal.

At last the audience broke up. Kansdorf managed to push his way through to the priest and take him on one side. He was extremely excited.

"Where is Abbé Auclair?"

"He is under medical care," said the priest, mopping the perspiration from his brow. "Why ever did I put up with him here? He is absolutely crazy!"

"How do you know that this time?"

"Through the draft of his speech, of course! I sent it to the Bishop, and he came to see me within the hour, in his car. He absolutely refused to allow Abbé Auclair to appear in public. We sent for him, and the Bishop told him the whole speech was not only nonsense, but almost blasphemous nonsense! The idea of trying to create a higher knowledge than the Church's based on ridiculous word meanings and combinations of letters was a dangerous one, he said, and he would have to put a stop to it officially. And I was given the job of passing the news on to the crowd."

"And how did Abbé Auclair take all this?"

"In an exemplary fashion. He is of course in himself a splendid person, a man of the utmost integrity and humility. He bowed and replied that he was an obedient son of the Church and would of course give up his talks and not publish the book he had been thinking of writing on the subject."

"And then?"

"The Bishop ordered him to go at once into a sort of rest house, a place for nerve cases—not exactly a mental home— which is quite near here. It is run by nuns. He has already been in there once anyway, they know all about him."

"But, Father, how could you allow such an obvious madman to go on working in your parish?"

"Well, but don't you realize—he has done wonders! In his crazy way he is a religious genius! He has cured the sick, mended broken marriages—it's thanks to him that so many people come to confession and Holy Communion! And just think what he has done for those boys of his! They were a curse throughout the whole district. He took an interest in each one of them individually, and he has made human beings of them! It is a tremendous achievement. I can't think what's going to become of them now. What on earth will we do? If only he were sane!"

Kansdorf left him and went straight to Katharina. He expected to find her in despair. He knew how fond she was of the abbé.

"I felt I must come and see you," he said. "The whole thing is really too dreadful."

"Dreadful?" she said with a smile. "Why dreadful?"

"But surely you've heard! They've stopped his entire work!"

She laughed.

"I have given thanks to God. I have never felt so happy."

"Happy? What on earth do you mean?"

She looked at him delightedly.

"Perhaps he will be a martyr," she said softly. "Isn't it wonderful? I always imagined he would be allowed to go on with that great work of his. No one else could do it. But now it looks as though God wants him for something even greater —to suffer and become a martyr. I know that he himself is giving thanks to God for it."

Kansdorf stared at her.

"But then what will become of—his work?"

"We shall have to leave that to God! There is nothing more effective than suffering and prayer! Do you think the Church will be kept going simply by her active members, her organizations and societies? No, she will be kept going by suffering— by Our Lord's suffering and the sufferings of His followers!"

He gazed in astonishment at her uncaring, blissful smile.

"The only snag is, I shall now be without a roof over my head," she said. "Another priest will be coming here."

"And where will you go?"

"I don't know. I shall soon find somewhere."

He thought for a moment.

"If you like," he said, "you can come and stay with me. I have my own apartment and I can let you have a room. Until we find something else."

He thought she might have qualms about this; but she looked straight back at him.

"Thanks," she said, "I knew something would turn up. Oh, what a wonderful day this is!"

He helped her to pack—it didn't take long.

Then they took a taxi to the Rue du Bac.

Katharina never talked about her mother and father or her own childhood. All Kansdorf had discovered was that both her parents and her nearest relatives had been killed. She herself had escaped this fate in a quite incredible fashion. Twice on the way to the gas chamber she had managed to get away. In a field near the gas chamber she had discovered a large pile of sticks. Amongst other refuse there was a heap of cardboard boxes, half sodden by the rain. She had hidden under these. During the night, when everything was over, she crawled back, and found the camp crowded with another batch of women and children. When it came to their turn to be put to death—they were all Jews—she tried the same trick again and it succeeded: for some strange reason her absence was not noticed on this occasion either, despite the careful counting. Again—after an interval of two days this time—she crawled back to the camp. A girl recently arrived had just died there, her body was disposed of secretly and Katharina took her place. When death threatened her for the third time—the Americans arrived, and she was liberated.

This girl, who not long ago had been enduring horrors quite beyond his imagination, now went around in his flat, light of foot, obviously happy. She possessed some secret that lay outside his ken. Was it a gift that was only granted to the elect, or could he too obtain it?

CHAPTER EIGHTEEN

Kansdorf:

How am I to describe Katharina?

One remarkable thing about her is the seeming fragility of her face. It isn't white, like spotless marble. When I look at her forehead it reminds me much more of delicate porcelain. A fragile shell of the choicest material, enclosing something very precious.

She has adopted the French mannerisms to perfection—the high shrug of the shoulders, palms of the hands turned outwards, to signify an ironic "I don't know," all the various degrees of lip- and eyebrow-movements. These speak just as comprehensible a language as the mouth, full of implied provisos and ironic reservations but also of unexpectedly gentle requests, or protestations of sympathy too affectionate to be expressed by word of mouth. She has mastered all these —her face is not smooth and expressionless like most women's. The thing that I find most striking and moving about her is her vulnerability. Yet, her happiness is real happiness.

I sometimes find it hard to look a woman in the face without feeling uncomfortable and I have often wondered about the reason for this. For a long time I thought it was because I didn't want to admit to an impulse I feel, a sort of desire to weigh up the person concerned physically, as though I am afraid of being caught taking too deep an interest in her. This won't do, however, if only because even intellectual women regard such a lowering of the level as a form of flattery. A scientific treatise could be written on the mental and physical contact between two people who have reached intellectual maturity and who live in close physical harmony with each other, this harmony—and this is the strange thing—at times using the *same* forms of expression for both sensual and intellectual agreement. I don't mean a movement of the hips; or the line of an arm suddenly raised in an enchanting curve— to tidy the hair, for instance; or the shimmering of a shoulder, or a sudden forward movement of the body revealing the outline of the breast—I don't mean physically attractive movements like that. I mean such things as the eye brightening as a thought suddenly bursts upon the mind and clamours for verbal expression; or the whole face expressing a sudden mood of awe or melancholy or silent sympathy. At moments like these, if you watch closely, you can perceive a different kind of harmony, deeper and doubly significant: the intellectual companionship is suddenly, without any perceptible hiatus, given an added sensual undertone that at once finds its response. And this kind of contact goes on unconsciously, without any effort, without any regard for aesthetic or psychological laws. The human countenance has its own rules of beauty, and it manifests them—I seem to have noticed this particularly in the case of Mediterranean types and Slavs —on a higher cultural plane.

I can meet Katharina's eye without embarrassment. Why? Because I can face her without being personally involved in any way—perhaps for the first time in my life. She has great suffering behind her; her fragility and remoteness are the after-effects of the time she had to spend in the concentration camp. She fills me with a sense of awe. Occasionally I notice what a wonderful figure she has; I can well imagine that even the erect way she carries herself, the noble line of her back, helps towards the general impression I have of her as an untouched, unapproachable soul. There is hardly any physical feeling in this dual impression—at most the merest trace. I look longingly into her clear, wide eyes and there I see a gravity that persists as the shadow of earlier suffering. Her eyes are young, intelligent, but not particularly warm and by no means yielding. When I see them focused upon me, a faint, bubbling feeling of delight rises up in me—at last I am looking at someone possessing dignity and content.

I don't know what colour her eyes are. Perhaps I can't see them properly. Even when she is looking at me, she seems to be gazing inwards, into the landscape of the soul. Under those wise eyes are engraved lines of grief, as though in delicate porcelain.

Integrity—why should that word come into my mind? Because she looks so young and direct and responsible.

At times there are other expressions which never cease to enchant me—sometimes I think they manifest her essential being, at others that they are signs of a sudden release, her soul's excursion into foreign lands. And she can look proud. Her head will move, slightly but quite perceptibly, as though she is tossing back a lock of hair. This movement is like a faint undertone, in a melody that is otherwise all melancholy, humility and truth. All this—the gesture of freedom, the tossing back of the lock of hair that is not there, the serious expression engraved by suffering—makes up a picture of what I can only describe as—courage.

Through the years, I have found a great deal to astonish me in the women I have come across—though I must confess that I can't look back on any vast experience. In nearly all of them I have felt a kind of spiritual death. They can react —with a show of great enthusiasm, even—but it always seems to be merely on the basis of impulse. I can, so to speak, play on them with my answers—admiring, or ironic, or scornful— and watch their immediate reactions. But what I really love— and have only found in exceptional cases, and in women with whom I have had no closer contacts than merely watching their faces secretly in trains or restaurants—is something different: a countenance that registers its emotions according to an inner impulse of its own, a beautiful, dominating, womanly countenance whose eyes light up, or which gives out a regal smile, in that brief second *before* the thought becomes an answer. These moments when only the face speaks, when I look into eyes made larger by slightly raised eyebrows, or am drawn towards them and lose myself in them, with no idea what is going on in the soul of the woman concerned— these moments are my greatest secret. Perhaps there is no one apart from myself who enjoys refinements such as these, perhaps to most people these observations, and these delight- ful experiences of mine, will seem utter foolishness. That doesn't matter to me in the slightest. I'm no Don Juan. I am on the whole quite an average sort of person whom women seldom look at. Women and I, however—we have our little secret, and, it may be, not even the greatest connoisseurs, the masters of seduction, share it. Oh, I love the sort of thing that is only faintly suggested, and mysterious—the thing that is driven away by the spoken word and killed by vulgar touch- ing, by any desire to be up and doing. In my solitary way I am familiar with works of art comparable with the greatest of all time, though hardly anyone else knows about them. Perhaps there are very few people like us who have been initiated, who can *see*. Our works of art flare up into life for a second and then disappear never to be seen again, they can- not even be resuscitated in memory, so delicately are they made, so rich and varied in their shades of meaning, so ex- ceptional in their delicacy: all they leave behind in the soul

187

is a sweet sound, which I love above all things else. The faces of real women are works of art of this kind. A virtuoso pianist may battle to improvise a shimmering cascade, or a wave of melancholy, or a choppy sea of disgust with life, but he remains a novice compared with a beautiful woman who without any sort of technical device, through the faintest suggestion of melancholy in her remoteness, of irony in her affection, of scepticism in her belief, suddenly suffuses the lovely play of her features with a rich, I might almost say fragrant spiritual content—crystal clear, irresistible, rich in shades of meaning.

Great lyric poetry has a few echoes and suggestions which can give spiritual riches of this kind. Otherwise, only in music of the highest genius have I ever felt anything to be compared with that greatest of all human works of art—a beautiful, vital, dramatically moving feminine countenance.

I have wandered far from my subject. I love to watch the way Katharina's features move, so closely following the movements of the mind behind her forehead, with its finely drawn net of veins forming a sort of secret signature of pain. We do not talk about anything important. She is so young, she has been involved in such frightful things, there are sensitive spots everywhere that have to be avoided—but my whole being is refreshed now that I find that I can emerge from my solitude, now that my words rouse an echo, now that I am able to experience the truth of the saying that a man who is alone is not really a proper human being at all, that human beings only become human when they come into contact with a "thou."

A mysterious, healthy, *other* human being has come trustingly into my life, like an unearned blessing. Who is actually guiding my fate now? How have I managed to escape from that dead determinism, according to which trifling causes produce an endless succession of grim, melancholy effects, and which was making every year seem greyer than its predecessor, until finally not even the warmth of the returning spring could shake the dust off my weary soul? For all too long I have felt old and exhausted, and yet I have hardly reached middle age. I was like a bear in a cage, powerless. I felt only a dull curiosity as to what form the next horror would take—when I was dead.

Outside it is still cold and rainy, and there is never any sun. Despite this, I feel the pulse and the glow of life, and now and again I am suddenly seized by hope and a longing to do something, I feel some sort of process at work inside me, I feel the pressure of that strong but gentle hand which, despite my resistance, despite years and years of self-defence and cowardly flight, has been all along endeavouring to awaken my well-nigh deadened soul to life and health—to reality.

CHAPTER NINETEEN

Dr. Lebrun could now pause occasionally in his work and, to the nurse's amazement, laugh in quite a new way, without any waving of arms, without the usual scream. He would simply smile slightly to himself.

What on earth was he thinking about?

He was amazed at it himself.

What had happened between Agnès Lutri and himself had not led to anything important; he had explained to her that it need not be taken as anything more than its single self. He found it rather amusing, in retrospect. The long scheming—and in the moment of victory, he had been taken unawares by his own good nature. And he had let himself be seduced by her. . . .

Again his thoughts were miles away, and he was smiling to himself.

He must be in love, thought the nurse. That's the only reason for that kind of behaviour. . . .

He had noticed that his son Louis had changed too during the last few weeks. He seemed to have been liberated, set free. He had bought his tent and had put it up in the drawing room to try it out. He had drawn closer than ever before to his father and chattered away to him in the most friendly fashion, without any sort of shyness whatsoever.

I make an excellent teacher, thought Dr. Lebrun. But my method is really a very queer one. I play about with my son's money-box!

Even Louis had noticed the difference in the way his father laughed.

"Why do you keep on laughing all the time, Father? Is there something funny?"

"Yes, when I think about it it's really rather funny."

"Can I know about it?"

"No, that wouldn't do. Not yet. But I'll tell you about it one day. . . ."

One day, however, Dr. Lebrun noticed that the boy had changed again. Further developments? Another conflict? He said nothing. The boy must come out with it himself. But he kept an eye on him.

Several days went by, and nothing happened. Then one evening, when Ilse was out, Louis came, seriously and resolutely, into the library.

Dr. Lebrun looked up from his book. The boy had grown up. He would soon be a young man. Then all that fuss about sex and girls would begin. The poor chap had no idea what he was in for!

"Well, what do you want?" he asked, to help him out.

Louis carefully closed the door. Then he planted himself in front of his father and began to speak. His voice was at first very uncertain and occasionally petered out, but then it steadied into a kind of hoarse gravity. He was very overwrought, that was obvious.

"Well, there's something I wanted to talk to you about, Father," he said. "But it's rather serious."

His father lowered his book.

"Then that's all the more reason why we should discuss it. What's on your mind?"

It would be something to do with sex, of course. Perhaps he should have discussed the matter with him personally and not simply left it to the good, easily understandable literature he had given him on the subject.

Louis stood there, his lips pressed tightly together. He was not a good-looking boy. He had his father's broad face and clumsy body—there was nothing of the Apollo in his appearance. But he had a gravity that gave him a kind of beauty. It was to be hoped that he would be able to go on looking at everything in this serious way!

Let us see whether we can solve these difficulties together, he was about to say; you are not the only person who has gone through a difficult time before growing up into manhood. But before he could say a word, the boy had taken the plunge.

"Father," he said, rapidly, nervously, "I know that one shouldn't listen to other people's conversations. I know that."

What was this? Had he been listening to something? What had he picked up? Dr. Lebrun put his book down and took his pipe out of his mouth.

"It was a pure accident. I didn't want to listen, really. But once I'd begun I couldn't stop myself. And so I actually heard everything."

His father gave him a searching look. What particular conversation had he heard? Could it be about Agnès Lutri? That would be the very devil! It wouldn't be at all easy to explain that affair—to an immature boy, anyway! He would have to watch out, if that was what he had to talk about.

"What did you hear, then?" he asked.

The boy gazed gravely at his father, with an expression of mute affection, indeed sympathy, on his face.

"Something that hurt me, Father," he said. "You know what I mean?"

Something that hurt him. The only thing that hurts me is

my gout, thought Dr. Lebrun, but he did not say so. Perhaps it was best to be wary.

"Out with it!" he said. "Don't be afraid! There can't be anything wrong in two good friends like us having a frank talk together."

The boy swallowed hard.

"I heard. . . . A few days ago I heard nearly everything you and Mother said. Here in this room. I was in the house; you didn't know. I just wanted to get my football and go off again. We had been given a holiday. But suddenly I heard Mother crying. And then—well. . . ."

Dr. Lebrun's lips tightened. So that was it. This was a new business. One no sooner got rid of one trouble than another one had to crop up! Living was like standing on the walls of a beleaguered citadel, expecting attacks from every side: there was always something going wrong!

It was true, he and Ilse had had a showdown. She had come to him entirely of her own accord and started off again about the business with Perezcaballero. She wanted him to understand. She had really, on that long ago day, made up her mind to leave him and go back to Perezcaballero. It was not from love but from despair that she had married him. She had known that this was bound to hurt him: she had been desperate about it herself. But she had been so young at the time. And surely he must have noticed that she had changed since then? That she loved him? She didn't want to live with anyone else—even though she had once been overcome by silly sentimentality. She knew that he had always been faithful to her, couldn't have been a better husband. That was why she was so utterly miserable. Couldn't he forgive and forget?

She was a touching sight. He thought of his own crazy affair with Agnès Lutri, and he put his arms round her and told her that she could be quite easy in her mind. He was amazed, he said, and always had been, that anyone should ever have wanted to be married to an old horror like him. He had nothing to forgive. What *was* there for him to forgive, anyway?

And then he had told her about his affair with Agnès Lutri —almost to the end. He had no desire to pose as a stainless character. But however closely he scrutinized his motives, he could not believe that it was cowardice that had made him keep quiet about the final scene. So far as he could judge, it was out of consideration for her. (He had made love to another woman out of sympathy, had rifled his son's money-box to further his education, and now here he was lying because he was so considerate—he was really a rather marvellous character! Did they have a special department in hell for eccentrics like him?)

It was good to have got things clear. In the end they had been able to have a good laugh together about the whole business. He had got out a bottle of wine, and they had become the best of friends again—as they had always been.

And so the boy had heard all this. Then it really had been a stroke of luck not to have gone into any details about what his sympathy for Agnès Lutri had led to!

"Oh, I see," he said, "you heard that talk we had, did you? Well, it's quite true you should never eavesdrop, just as you should never read other people's letters, perhaps because you can never really appreciate all the circumstances. You don't know the facts, and you get quite a wrong picture, however carefully you may listen. Do you see?"

The boy was obviously not listening. He was following his own train of thought.

"I wanted to say that I quite understand you, Father," he said, manfully.

Up went his father's eyebrows.

"You understand me?" he said. "That's good. Let's hear what you understand!"

"I mean—you must see, Father, that Mother deceived you!"

194

he said. "Even I can see that. She was in love with someone else, and because she couldn't have him she took you instead, Father. Do people do that?"

Yes, people do do that, thought his father, fortunately managing to suppress a smile. Quite often, as a matter of fact. People do much worse things. . . .

"I don't understand how you can stay in the house, Father," said Louis. "I've been thinking it over such a lot. All through the night sometimes."

"Really? All through the night?"

"Yes. Well, I did go to sleep in the end. When it was getting near morning."

"That was a good thing."

Again he had to make an effort to suppress a laugh. How jolly everything had become lately! To him, the old pessimist and fanatic for the truth! What in fact was happening to him?

"And," said Louis, pale and solemn, "if you were to decide, Father, that you had to leave, on the grounds of principle— which I should quite understand—then—"

"Then—?"

"Well, all I wanted to say was—*I'd go with you, Father! Not with Mother!*"

The last words were enunciated in the best high tragedy style, head held high.

"Not with Mother." This raised a problem.

Dr. Lebrun thought he heard someone come into the hall, but he paid no further attention.

It looked as though the boy might be becoming estranged from his mother, and that could be rather nasty. It would have to be stopped at once.

He became the professional medical man, devoting his whole attention to the case in hand.

"I'm much obliged to you," he said. "Sit down. You must learn a little bit more about this business."

"What sort of a rotter is this Perezcaballero?" the boy asked, sitting down.

"He's not a rotter at all, he is a very respectable friar," said his father.

"Respectable?" The boy made a face.

"Yes, I think so. In our younger days we were good friends —pals. You know, when a man falls in love with a woman he can't really assume that someone else is a rotter if he does the same thing—falls in love with her too: can he? And he wasn't a priest in those days!"

"That's what I thought," the boy muttered.

It was quite clear what he would be like when he grew up. Yes, he'd be a credit to him, thought his father.

"But you didn't quite understand that conversation," he said. "I don't see things the way you do. You can't know what I was like at that age, can you? I was a very unpleasant young fellow—yes, really! I didn't have happy parents like you."

He gave his son a searching look, but could see no change in his expression.

"I came from a far from happy home. And that warped me. And there's one thing you must know: your mother fell in love with Perezcaballero first, and that is quite understandable —he was streets above me in those days. And perhaps he still is today."

"I don't believe it," muttered the boy.

His father smiled.

Nor do I, he thought.

"Well, he was, anyway. And the only really nasty thing about the whole business, you know, is the fact that I knew your mother loved the other fellow and yet nevertheless—took her for myself."

"And you were quite right!" the boy said. "People should fight for a woman when they love her! Shouldn't they? That's what people have always done!"

196

You've been reading Victor Hugo, thought his father. Well done, young fellow!

"Yes, perhaps," he said. "But people usually think they should show some consideration for others."

"In love no one ever shows any consideration for others!" the boy said with a superior smile. "People fight and fight until they've won the person they love."

"That's not the way I look at things. For even if I wasn't under any obligation to take a back seat because another man had fallen in love with the same girl as I had—still, I should have had some regard for the girl's feelings. And they didn't go my way in those days. But I didn't."

"And yet you won her!" said the boy. "How did you do it?" His eyes were shining.

"I'll tell you about that one day when you're a bit older," said his father. Again there was this jocund feeling in his heart. "If you should happen to need the advice."

"But Mother *didn't* love you, Father!" said the boy, growing serious again. "I heard her say—"

Was there someone listening out there again? What a house—it was like a family out of Eugène Scribe!

He got up.

"No, she didn't love me. How could she? She might so easily have hated me! For she lost the man she loved through me. But she didn't hate me either. Instead, she *learned* to love me—with the passage of time. And that is worth more than all the excitement at the beginning. You'll find that out one day for yourself. And now I'll tell you something. You will never be able to stop me feeling grateful to your mother. And you need never have any fear of my leaving her, she and I are far too close. Not unless an atom bomb falls on my head. And not even then!"

He said these last words very loud—much to his own surprise. It was strange. He hadn't known beforehand what he really thought about this matter. Only when he had been forced to put his thoughts into words had he discovered what they were!

The boy too had stood up.

He was embarrassed now.

"Forgive me, then, Father," he said. "I hope you aren't angry. I only meant—"

His father stumped over to him and gave him a slap on the shoulder.

"Angry? Because you were worried about me? And love me? No! But you can't take me in! I know you love your mother just as much."

Was that really so certain? There was a danger here. It was best to hammer this into his head once and for all, as something absolutely settled.

The boy was just about to answer when they heard Ilse's voice in the drawing room. Was she back already? How loudly she was speaking—she didn't usually do that! She was calling the maid.

Then she knocked at the door and put her head round it.

"Good evening," she said. "Aha, the gentlemen are having a meeting, are they? What would you say to a cup of tea?"

She smiled gaily.

"I'd like one," said Dr. Lebrun.

"I must do my homework," said Louis, uncertainly.

"Still, surely you can give your mother a kiss, even so," said his father, going off for his pipe.

It might be easier perhaps if he turned his back on him.

Apparently it went off quite well. Then—without a word— the boy left the room.

Dr. Lebrun turned round.

Ilse was standing in front of him, smiling and looking slightly emotional.

He didn't greatly care for slightly emotional looks.

198

She came up to him and kissed him on the cheek.

"Thanks, Jules," she said.

"What are you thanking me for?" he said. "For getting you a kiss from a young man?"

"No," she said.

But she immediately went on:

"Or rather, yes. You know, I happened to hear a little—"

"No, this is really a bit too much!" cried Dr. Lebrun, suddenly looking quite terrifying. "Does everybody eavesdrop on everybody else in this extraordinary family? First one person comes along and confesses that he has been listening to what he shouldn't and then someone else listens while the first person is confessing. I think you've all suddenly gone completely crazy!"

She smiled.

"I've been to see Father Perezcaballero," she said. "I *didn't* go to the cinema."

His smile vanished. What was this? Was the comedy going to turn into serious drama again?

"Really," he said, "I don't know whether that interests me very much. I'm glad I didn't do any listening in, anyway."

"But it will interest you," she said. "Very much, in fact. Quite changed, he was. He had begged me to see him. He has reached some kind of crisis and wants to get away—for a long time. He talked of trying to get to Africa."

"That would be a good thing," growled Dr. Lebrun. "Tierra del Fuego would be even better."

"He was desperate, Jules," she said. "He begged me to forgive him."

"Oh, this everlasting forgiving," retorted the doctor harshly. "What have *you* got to forgive, if I may ask?"

"Well," Ilse answered, going as red as a beetroot, "he wanted me to forgive him for—for his treating me as he did. You know what I mean—don't you?"

At this Dr. Lebrun's mouth dropped open in a gape of astonishment.

"I think I must be going crazy," he said. "Do you mean he asked you to forgive him because—?"

"Yes," she said, looking shamefacedly down at the floor, "and I think it was very nice of him. He was so frightfully depressed."

"He can be as depressed as he likes: I couldn't care less," said Dr. Lebrun harshly, his eyes blazing. He raised his arms —and his scream of laughter followed.

"I rob my son's money-box so as to make a decent chap of him. He eavesdrops on us. You do the same. I become, out of pure benevolence, a—well. . . . And now a priest comes along—"

He laughed, with lifeless eyes. "—and asks you to forgive him for *not* seducing you!" he shouted. "That's really marvellous! Life is quite incomprehensible. But rather funny— don't you think?"

He went up to his slightly confused wife and kissed her emphatically, on the mouth.

"Boobies!" he said. "Tomfoolery! All this forgiving! Well, I won't forgive you! I won't!"

"But of course you will," said Ilse.

"No," he shouted. "Never! On principle! And now I'll have that tea!"

CHAPTER TWENTY

Katharina went to see Abbé Auclair in the institution every day.

At first she had had difficulty in getting admitted. He was still regarded with the greatest mistrust. After a few weeks, however, he had won everyone over by his lovable character and gaiety. He was in fact happier than ever, delighted to be suffering for his cause. He wasn't designed to be a martyr, he explained. So great a grace was reserved for the elect, the heroes of the Faith. But *something* of what he had done must have pleased God, for He had at least allowed him to be locked up.

Katharina still went to him for confession. He was as convinced as ever that she was destined for great things.

"Believe me," he said to Kansdorf on one occasion when the latter had accompanied her to the home, "she has been chosen to be a saint." He knew it, could feel it. His eyes shone whenever he looked at the girl.

He was shocked when he discovered that Kansdorf had stopped going to confession. Why, he asked? Had Protestantism still got a hold on him, in spite of everything?

Kansdorf was not clear about this himself. It was most likely due to his general diffidence, his rootlessness.

"Don't come to me!" said Abbé Auclair ironically. "You

probably think I'm mad too. Go to someone saintly, Dom Dusolier for instance. He's a man God speaks through. Promise me you will!"

About Katharina, Abbé Auclair showed not the slightest concern. He took it as the most natural thing in the world that she should be living in his house.

"You love her," he said calmly. "We both do. Don't be afraid of loving! Nobody who loves undemandingly and in the sight of God need fear anything! You both need each other. God bless you!"

Kansdorf was touched by his friendliness, his religious simplicity, and the patient way he had accepted his fate. He had a lot to learn from Abbé Auclair.

One evening, on his return from one of these visits, he noted down the following:

"I cannot join in the hostile criticism of the Swedish church service. It seems to me excellent as it is. It is well devised, dramatic, and powerful. The fact that a 'Mass' without the *sacrifice* of the Mass has no more interest for me than a university lecture with an idealistic or religious tinge to it is not strictly relevant.

"It is a mistake to imagine that going to a Catholic Mass is as a general rule a more religious experience than going to the Protestant form of service. Visiting the parish churches here in Paris is often a really painful business. Not merely because they are often full of awful statues and the most ghastly examples of bad taste but because they are so dreadfully sophisticated. Concert hall music comes roaring down from the organ. Priests at the altar without any air or style; silly genuflections by the ministrants; annoying begging by busy-bodying old women, who pocket the money for the seat you are sitting in just at the moment of the Consecration. . . .

"Compared with much of this I find a Protestant service— impoverished, bare, but simple and decent—more appealing.

"But no one can judge a High Mass until he has heard the Gregorian chant.

"I had already come to realize the overpowering beauty of the liturgy through the Dominicans. But only when Katharina took me to the Benedictine monastery of Sainte Marie in the Rue de la Source were my eyes really opened. After my first Gregorian Mass I was absolutely shattered. No aesthetic experience I had ever had could compare with the sheer beauty of it. No music I had ever heard had given my ears such an impression of spirituality, not even Bach. I seemed for the first time to understand what posture man should adopt in the presence of God and how he should address Him.

"Those waves from the chanting choir! That mysterious flood of sound! I still shudder when I think of it—the language of my soul, which I myself had never spoken. *Once, long ago, someone spoke this language in my heart.* But it is more than that: it is the soul's native language, the one everlasting language of mankind, the only language that expresses man's real relation towards the world and history and God.

"Morning after morning I listen to this melody, this sound, transfixed, shattered. . . . Waves and powerful muted surges of sound. . . .

"Like a sea dashing endlessly against the coast, the Gregorian chant begs, implores, prays to God. These everlasting waves are like the waves of history: the whole history of the human race is mirrored in them. This is the way that man through all his centuries has rejoiced and lamented before his God.

"Anyone who has ever fallen under the intoxication of the great lyrics of the seventeeth century, with their disappointed love, their humbling of proud beauties and their shattered dreams of bliss, can only blush with shame when he hears these noble sounds. Here is utter sorrow and utter pain, not loud and vainglorious, not rhetorical with self-pity, not luxuriating in any melting self-engrossment; but a lament that is a real lament with nothing trite about it, and a joy that is real joy, not a virtuoso piece for sounding brass and organ and screaming tenor. In this anonymous sound can be heard the groaning of the whole human race. What tremendous power there is in these waves of suffering, rising up to God for century after century! The rhythm of the whole cosmos seems to beat in them, the whole world of created, fallen man is there in all his naked misery and all his naked hope. How has the true native language of the soul ever been thus transformed into bubbling cascades of music? What is the source of this aweing beauty? What has our confused and wounded heart to do with resounding organ pipes?

"I have listened in absolute amazement to the variations on the Alleluia, trying in vain to fathom their secret. Man's praises of the everlasting Love could hardly be fashioned from crashing military band music and languishing tenor solos! Here even jubilation is muted and beseeching: always behind the joy one can sense the sorrow at the knowledge that the terrible Sacrifice should have been necessary. Before that dread thing happened—the Son of God being killed for our sins—there was nothing for man to rejoice about: hence the muted tone, the purity of this elevated song. Never any raucous rejoicing: throughout all the sounds of victory one can hear the grief, the sorrow. For the victory we acclaim and praise was dearly bought. It was the greatest price on earth.

"It is essential to go and hear the Benedictines singing.

"They know all about our distress. And they not only express it as directly and frankly as we ourselves ought to: the language of their chanting is truer than our own, it opens depths in us never before disclosed: we hear modulations which we know refer to us, but which we had never before perceived. We recognize every cadence, every detail of the despair, the sadness, the jubilation; the only thing is that it

204

is all truer, deeper, and more ourselves, than we have ever been.

"It means a great deal to us when we meet someone who can share our experiences and who we feel understands us, or into whose place we can put ourselves. In this case, however, without any intermediary, and without having to put ourselves in anyone else's place, we are suddenly made one with the whole of mankind. We make contact with a wisdom which brings us closer to ourselves than we have ever been before. For the first time we realize our deep companionship with all the laments, all the misery, of past centuries. Here we are rocked by a surging tide which will break everlastingly from the ocean of time against the coasts of eternity.

"When, after many days, we become accustomed to this language—and then any other seems expressionless and unspiritual, not to be compared with it—we begin to notice the monks' movements, and discover that we are also watching a drama of exceptional beauty.

"We remember gratefully, but with a smile, the way the Dominicans move, rapidly, self-confidently, but at the same time in a busily masculine, stiffly military, ungraceful way. But here: no genuflections, no gestures, that are not full of significance, an expression of the soul toned down and polished by tradition. What is the pomp of any earthly emperor compared with such majesty? We cannot contemplate these monks' faces, or hear their calm voices, or watch their movements, their processions, their genuflections, without feeling our own earthiness and triviality. And all of a sudden we begin to long for a great and true expression of our human misery and hope: for the first time we realize that great ceremonial is truth, and that we owe the truth both to ourselves and to God.

"*Vere dignum et justum est, aequum et salutare.* . . .[1]

"Out of the cruel, aimless whirl of necessity and matter

---

[1] "It is truly meet and just, right and available to salvation. . . ."

something emerges firm and unshakable, and a mighty commanding voice announces that there is *a law* in all the flux and change:

"*Vere dignum et justum est.* . . . .

"Through all that is relative and transient this and this alone is eternally right and just. . . .

"I usually close my eyes during Mass and let myself be suffused by the truth of it.

"High above me, far, far away, I can sense Our Lady's face. I can see her as the annunciation is made to her—oh, the wisdom of her humility, the modesty of her pride, the clarity of her knowledge, the longing in her pain!

"The monks' chanting suffuses my whole being, gently yet compellingly. . . .

"I realize that there can be no drawing near to the human race, stained and spotted as it is, without sacrifice, without a kind of struggle and conquest.

"What have I made of my life?

"I used to try to understand it by using my reason, but I never grasped the truth with that deeper instrument of knowledge which it is beyond my powers to describe: a Being, pure, chaste, sensitive, utterly noble, steps of its own accord into my grim world and never tires of returning to the fray, even though I myself am its enemy and am constantly sending it away. Always it is by my side, never giving up, though blood runs from its head, groans arise from its breast, and its heart pounds heavily under all it has to bear.

"I cannot raise my eyes, I cannot bear to look up. I know that this Being is gazing down upon me, with eyes that are full of sorrow and also full of love. And although there is anguish in my heart, and essentially I want it to be otherwise, I know that the nails through its hands, the spear in its side, the thorns tearing at its head, are all—myself."

CHAPTER TWENTY-ONE

Life had become hard for Father Perezcaballero.

As before, he was living in the monastery. After his sermon he had been sought after by more people than ever. He could not give up his work in the confessional entirely, but he found it very trying. Only with difficulty could he pay attention to what was said to him. Worst of all were the many signs of devotion and admiration he received. He now knew beyond a question that he was not worthy of such trust and affection. When he was alone he would try to discover his failings. After Dom Dusolier's investigation he was quite ready to acknowledge his hypocrisies and perversities, was quite clear about his lack of charity. But it frightened him that he never seemed able to get to the bottom of it. No matter where he looked in his life, past or present, self-interest seemed to have been his leading motive. This introspection crippled him. He hardly dared to make a move: the slightest act could only increase the number of his sins. On the other hand, passivity was in itself a sin: anyone who imagined himself as a passive spectator was in fact an active contributor—to the wrong side.

He felt this process destroying his peace of mind. The only person he shared his difficulties with was Dom Dusolier. But Dom Dusolier seemed to be taking no particular interest in him now. He would merely tell him that it was quite understandable that he should be experiencing nothing but anguish and emptiness—all he could do was to wait, and make a genuine attempt to discover his failings. That was the only way to get rid of them.

The whole process soon began to affect him physically. He was unable to eat or sleep. At times at prayer or at Mass, his mind would wander miles away. His nerves often troubled him: his patience was often sorely tried by his fellow priests.

He could tell that several of them realized the condition he was in. There was no actual difference in the way they behaved towards him: they were all just as polite and friendly as before. Yet the whole atmosphere around him had changed.

One day he was listening, tired and uninterested, to one of his penitents and giving the usual answers. Then a young woman who was new to him was brought into the room. At first he listened mechanically. The girl explained that her usual confessor had been taken ill and might be ill for a long time; so she had decided to find a new spiritual adviser.

Why, he asked, had she come to the monastery?

She said she had left the matter to God and simply walked into the first place she had come across. She had not asked for any particular priest, because she didn't know any of them. Actually she would have preferred to go to the Benedictines, whom she knew quite well; she was a little afraid of the Dominicans. But she had decided to follow her original inspiration, and here she was. Perhaps it was God's will that she should overcome her fear of the Dominicans.

What had she against the Dominicans?

He saw her flush slightly. Mainly, as a matter of fact, she said, because they didn't do the chant as well as the Benedictines.

The Perezcaballero of a week ago would not have taken this without comment. A pert slip of a girl, criticizing the monastery singing, deigning to approve of one and condemning the other! And now, very decently, she was prepared to put up with a Dominican, even though it meant running the risk of having her dainty susceptibilities wounded! Now he listened patiently.

What was it she wanted to ask him? If he could help her in any way, he gladly would. He would also like to point out that everyone had the right to choose his own confessor. *That* kind of egoism was quite permissible. So if she found that she was unable to talk freely to him she must not hesitate about finding someone else.

She nodded, but replied that she would prefer to talk to the person whom God had led her to. And she embarked on her story. She had fallen very much in love with a young man, who had returned her love and was a Catholic like herself. They had wanted to get married. She had felt strongly drawn to him and had believed that together they could make a successful Christian marriage. Despite this she had refused him, a year ago. And the reason was that she had slowly come to feel that she had quite a different duty to perform and was not meant for marriage.

What was this duty?

Perhaps it sounded conceited, but she had come to believe that she was called upon to consecrate her life to Our Lord. She did not know whether this meant becoming a nun, or something else. After much hesitation she had confided the matter to her confessor, and he had encouraged her in her resolve. The young man had been heartbroken, but in the end had accepted her decision.

She stopped.

But wasn't everything all right, then?

Yes, she said. She realized that she was causing the young

man a lot of pain; but she knew too that in the end this would have a purifying effect upon him. She was praying constantly for him.

Why was she having doubts, then?

She wouldn't exactly say that she was having doubts. But she had come to see that behind her decision lay a whole series of factors which she had not previously taken into account.

What were they?

It was difficult to say what they were. She knew that she had great love for Our Lord, to whom, as she realized, she owed everything. But there might perhaps be other reasons as well. She seemed to have noticed that her motives were never perfectly pure and unselfish. When she scrutinized them closely she always found that they contained a trace of egoism—and generally more than a trace.

Perezcaballero was still asking his questions mechanically. Now he looked at her. Her face was pale and she was obviously in earnest. Inquiring into one's motives and discovering that they were not pure was a process he was familiar with. Suddenly his interest awoke.

He asked a few careful questions. What hidden motives did she think she had unearthed?

She hesitated slightly over her answer.

It seemed to her that fundamentally her one motive was pride. She was striving for the highest, something that other people didn't want, or were incapable of. For a long time she had had secret dreams of becoming a saint. Of course it was silly, she knew that herself. She had never told anyone else about it. At times this longing of hers to live entirely for Our Lord seemed to be the only true thing about her. Then at other times she found that even this contained pride: she didn't want to be just like others, she wanted to attain to perfection—and so, for instance, she had given up someone who was in love with her. Was there perhaps a lack of charity behind all this? For a long time she had taken comfort in the thought that she was simply being tempted, but times came when she could not shake off the frightful thought that everything she did was false, that in reality all her motives were evil.

His interest was now aroused in the liveliest degree. He knew all about self-reproaches. As a rule they were simply the result of brooding and a superfluity of feeling. Usually it was just a matter of loosening tensions and directing the people concerned to simpler, more immediate Christian duties. But in this case he was, perhaps, faced with something different. For there was the strange fact that this young soul took her problem deadly seriously, had obviously made one great sacrifice already, and yet was still terribly afraid that her motives might not be absolutely disinterested.

He was suddenly extraordinarily taken with the case, and with the help of a few questions he succeeded in getting the position quite clear. Perezcaballero was a clever man. He had great psychological experience. He knew how easily the moral basis of any motive can be sounded by question and answer, he knew how to apply, almost imperceptibly, little tests of honesty and integrity. He almost forgot his own unhappiness in this new task. It seemed to him that he could find nothing that was not genuine and true in her. For the first time in his life he had come upon a human being whose one desire was for integrity.

He gave her his advice. One could never be sure of one's motives but one must always start from the assumption that a certain amount of egoism was inevitable. Egoism was indeed involved in the soul's longing for redemption and purity: that kind of egoism was quite lawful and healthy. She need have no fear, but should go bravely on, though at the same time keeping a continual watch over herself. If he could be of any help to her in the future she must not hesitate to come and see him. She had to realize that God could see into her motives far more clearly than she could herself. If she prayed to God and was ready to follow His lead she could not possibly go wrong.

He devoted a whole hour to her. After she had left, he sat in silence for a while. He was told that there were other people waiting to see him. He said that he was not available. He had to be alone.

He went into the chapel and fell on his knees. Double-mindedness; secret, hidden motives: his feeling of delighted gratitude for the girl's honesty evaporated and in its stead he saw himself. He began to feel that God had sent the girl to help him. For her difficulties were identical with his own, except that he had never reached such an advanced level of honest self-awareness as she had.

His mind went back to Father Guillon. The one accusation he had made—about the misapplied funds—was true. He had made no actual accusation in the matter of the girl, but it was undoubtedly he who had caused the Prior to make further enquiry; and though nothing serious had emerged, there was at least indiscretion, and the Prior had removed Father Guillon. He had convinced himself that he was acting from the most blameless motives. But what had been his real driving force? Why had he felt that unmistakable thrill of pleasure over the Prior's decision?

He suddenly realized why. He tried to push the realization away, but in vain. Oh yes, now he understood only too well!

Father Guillon was a distinguished theologian. He had written a number of books, all of which had been well received, and they partly covered Father Perezcaballero's own particular field. Whereas he himself had been unproductive over the years, unable to finish a single work, Father Guillon

212

had become increasingly prolific. He wrote better and better every year: his books were solid works based on a fund of exceptional scholarship and they received very favourable criticism in the literary journals. He was regarded as one of the best brains in the Dominican order.

Perezcaballero realized that he had not been able to stomach all this success. For a long time he had tried to denigrate his colleague's books, both in his own eyes and in the eyes of others; in fact he had published a remarkably curt criticism of one of them, whose acid tone had caused quite a sensation. For a long time he had waited for some reaction, but it had not come; and it had irritated him even more to find that he was not even considered worth replying to.

His jealousy had, without his perceiving it, increased. Then, as he had delved deeper and deeper into Father Guillon's failure, he had been invaded by a great sense of inner release, which he had concealed under apparently objective arguments. While it depressed him to think that the power of the mission was declining, he had rejoiced inwardly over the thought that the fault might lie with Father Guillon, and when he was ordered to inquire into the affair he had proceeded with alacrity, hoping that he might be able to unmask his colleague. Guillon, without offering the slightest defence, had been sent away at a moment's notice, and now held no post of any sort.

Perezcaballero was on his knees for an hour. When he came out he was unrecognizable. His step was slow, his face grey. His first impulse was to go and see Dom Dusolier. But he didn't dare.

A few days later Father Perezcaballero asked for *correction fraternelle,* the brotherly admonition that is an established practice in the Order. He would go from one friar to another asking the same anxious question, "What do you think of me?" He knew that they were all under obligation to answer frankly. He had a feeling that he was in for a trying time. But what actually happened surpassed his worst expectations.

With very few exceptions the friars' answers were almost literally the same: "You are gifted, but arrogant. You are intelligent but have no charity. You are able but self-centred." As long as he was told this by the less gifted friars he didn't mind so much. But when he got the same answer from the best and ablest priests in the monastery, who often replied with real sorrow in their eyes, he broke down. The last friar he asked was one of the youngest. He had brought him up himself and helped him through more than one difficult period. The young man was very pale, but his answer was exactly the same as the others': "You are very gifted, but you are also extraordinarily arrogant. You think more about yourself than you do about Our Lord." Perezcaballero was on the point of humiliating himself to the extent of answering, but managed to hold back the words.

He had wanted to hear the truth. Actually there had been no need: he knew it already. He went slowly back to his cell, and threw himself on his knees in an attempt to pray. He couldn't. He felt an endless void around him. No one was listening to his prayers.

He was utterly alone.

CHAPTER TWENTY-TWO

"Do you see the mysterious thing about this church?"

"No. How should I? It's quite dark!"

"Well, look closer, then!"

"Well? Well?"

"Now!"

"I can't see a thing!"

"Don't you see, it's floating!"

"No, it isn't, my dear chap. It's like all cathedrals, lying there like a frog with its belly on the ground."

It was half past one in the morning.

Kansdorf and Lebrun, after a late supper that had included several glasses of wine, had been wandering round Paris. The air was mild, with a faint thrill of spring in it. Neither wanted to leave the other. In the end Kansdorf had led the doctor down to the embankment, explaining that there were only two places from which Notre Dame could and should be seen—from the bridge behind the apse, and from a spot on the west bank where the embankment jutted out just about opposite the tremendous rose window.

The moon was shining. The trees, dressed in their young greenery, veiled the view slightly without hiding it. The waters of the Seine went glittering by, and the mighty church floated, sailed, over the night-dark river.

Involuntarily Kansdorf lowered his voice. With excited gestures he began to explain. "You are right so far as other big churches are concerned. They really do seem to be lying awkwardly on their stomachs. Their architects knew how to deal with the inside but they hardly ever knew what to do about the outside. But Notre Dame—can't you see that it's a mighty ship, sailing ever so lightly away, into the city of sin, with all the power of God on board? Do you know any other church that floats?"

Dr. Lebrun yawned.

"No," he said, "I've not come across any floating churches, as far as I can remember. Or priests either. But perhaps there are some floating priests."

On the lower embankment a pair of lovers went by, stopped in the moonlight, swayed as though drunk with their kisses, and went on. Out on the river a row boat glided slowly downstream, its occupant resting on his oars.

"He can see what I can," said Kansdorf.

"Not a bit of it," said Lebrun. "He's looking for bodies, fresh-water bodies. They swim, if you like."

He yawned again.

Kansdorf did not answer. He was gazing enchanted at the tremendous rose window. Dark clouds slid by over the cathedral. Paris was silent: no cars, no sound of feet.

"Lebrun, you old devil!" he said. "Do you know what they did in the Middle Ages to people like you?"

"They let them go home and have a good sleep," answered Lebrun; "so that they'd have a bit of strength left in the morning to do a bit of doctoring. To people suffering from cancer and such like."

"No, no," said Kansdorf mysteriously. "Not at all. They did something quite different. When they decided that certain people were too hellishly ugly to exist they pickled them in a sort of brine."

"Brine?"

"Yes, a frightful brine. They turned to stone in it so they had to go on looking horrible for ever. And then they carried them right to the top of the cathedrals—and there they had to sit, leering out over the town, the devils! You'd better look out, Lebrun! We've still got the brine. You'd make a quite remarkably effective horror in the moonlight!"

"You think of absolutely everything."

They heard voices. A boat with its engine ticking over slipped out from under the bridge and came towards them. At the same moment a car pulled up behind them.

"The police," said Lebrun, "now they'll rope us in. That's just about the last straw!"

It was a rescue squad in shining helmets, with ropes and grappling irons.

They rushed down, hailed the launch, shouted to each other and then ran to various positions on the lower embankment.

A gleaming helmet shining brightly in the moonlight approached the two friends.

"Have you gentlemen seen a corpse?" asked a martial voice.

"Yes rather," said Lebrun, "lots."

He shrieked, flapping his arms.

"Really?"

"My friend is joking," answered Kansdorf, feeling rather apprehensive about Lebrun's somewhat bizarre sense of humour. "He's a doctor. He means that when he's practising, corpses—"

"At any rate I know *one* person who soon *will* be a corpse if he doesn't go home to bed," interrupted Lebrun. "That's this gentleman here!"

He pointed to Kansdorf.

"Take him away, constable! He keeps forcing his company

on me. Besides, he's mad. He says the church is swimming. Can you see this old church swimming, constable? I can't!"

Kansdorf whispered to Lebrun in an attempt to get him to understand that it wasn't a constable they were talking to but an officer of much higher rank.

"I don't think he is!" said Lebrun. "Anyway, people in uniform who come disturbing people and asking them questions I call constables!"

Kansdorf planted himself resolutely between his friend and the stranger.

"I suppose you're looking for a suicide?" he asked.

"If you have any difficulty in finding one, take Kansdorf," came Lebrun's voice from the background. "He'd make a very good one, I can vouch for that."

"No," replied the stranger, "we're not exactly looking for a suicide."

Kansdorf offered him a cigarette.

The face of the man in uniform, thickly moustached, glowed in the light from the match.

"Good God, it's Marshal Foch," muttered Lebrun, subsiding onto a stone bench.

"Has someone gone and thrown himself in?" Kansdorf asked politely.

"No, I don't think so."

"What's going on then?"

"Oh, nothing. We're just having a night practice. It gets boring sitting there night after night, just playing cards. And then it's good practice for the new ones."

"Incredible," mumbled Lebrun in the rear. "Here we have an expensive police force armed to the teeth the whole way down the Seine and not a single decent suicide will jump in! Obviously no sense of social responsibility. They ought to have pushed that poor couple in who went by just now under their noses, trying to kiss each other. It would have saved them a lot of disillusionment."

The stranger, having got his cigarette, had disappeared. Kansdorf sat down beside his friend.

"Aren't you a bit cracked, old chap?" he said.

"I'm all right," answered Lebrun. "But you're in love."

"In love?"

"Of course you're in love. You're forgetting you're due to die. Is the idea to get this poor Russian girl thoroughly attached to you, so that she shall be really miserable when you peg out?"

Kansdorf was not listening. He had stood up again. But now he had his back to Notre Dame.

"In case you want to go on with your swimming theory, I should just like to point out that the church is behind your back," said Lebrun, coming forward. "Still on its stomach."

"Lebrun," said Kansdorf, hesitantly, "have you ever been *inside* Saint Denis?"

"No," answered Lebrun. "I'm going home."

He got up, but Kansdorf pushed him and he sat down again heavily.

"It's a church that looks nothing from the outside. But when you get inside—you've no idea!"

"No, thank God!" murmured Lebrun, who had folded his arms and closed his eyes. "Wake me up when it's time for the first Métro!"

"Do you know St. Louis?"

"Not to speak to," groaned Lebrun, suppressing a yawn.

"You know that everything he did, or had anything to do with, has its own particular style, I suppose. You've seen the Sainte Chapelle, haven't you?"

Lebrun was asleep.

"So you'll know what a splendid shrine it is. But Saint Denis is the finest church in Christendom. You go in and you find yourself standing in an absolute forest of columns reaching up to heaven. The walls have so much filigree in them that the roof seems to be hovering over you. Not a line, not a single vista, that isn't most noble and excellent, most delicate and pure. On the ground lie all the dissolute Kings of France, gazing up at the roof—you've no need to look at them. But climb up behind the altar and look out over the church—you've never seen anything like it! You're carried away, purified, shattered! I went there with Katharina. She stood there with her hands plunged into her raincoat pockets, as she always does. She is slight and dark, you know. She slowly leaned her head back and let herself take in all the beauty and delicacy. You should have seen her: she looked enchanting! Saint Denis is the loveliest place in the Western world, you know. Can you imagine what the Gregorian plainchant sounds like there? Can you picture what it would look like if the old windows could be put back? There are hardly any of them left now. That would give you a faint idea of what Christian art really is. . . ."

Lebrun was sound asleep. Kansdorf realized that he had been speaking without an audience, but he didn't mind in the least. He was like a man intoxicated. He could hear sounds echoing and re-echoing inside him. Gleams of light were flickering in front of his eyes. His thoughts were flying, visions were racing past his eyes.

Lebrun opened his eyes.

"Is that you?" he said, standing up. "It's hard on this—"

He blinked like a goblin, swayed in the moonlight, and grimaced.

"You'd go marvellously up there, you old devil!" said Kansdorf. "But I just don't know how they'd get you up."

Lebrun nodded. After his short sleep he was tingling with cold. He suddenly felt quite sober.

"My dear chap," he said, putting his arm round Kansdorf

and pulling him along with him, "what are you really planning to do?"

"What do you mean?" asked Kansdorf.

"*Are* you going to marry her?"

"Oh, shut up about Katharina!" said Kansdorf. "She is a spirit, she hasn't got a body."

"God in heaven," answered Lebrun. "It's time you came down to earth, Kansdorf!"

"I shall be down soon enough," said Kansdorf, "if I'm to believe you. But it's a pity that despite your great talents you understand so little. The girl is a spirit, I tell you. I love her, but I don't want her. She has given herself to Our Lord, body and soul—so she's not for me. But she leads me forward and I follow; with a light touch of her hand she opens doors in me that I never knew existed. She lets light into my soul. Oh, my dear chap, if you only knew how intoxicating life can be! What bliss it is to feel oneself part of creation!"

Lebrun looked at him. He must apply the knife to this romantic boil before it was *too* late.

"You can go on thinking and dreaming what you like," he said, "and loving too—in your own way. I won't try to stop you. But *be honest,* young fellow!"

Kansdorf turned and faced him with a solemn look on his face. They were standing in the shadow of the Tuileries.

"I've never in all my life been as realistic as I am now," he said.

"You are riddled with illusions. You're crazy about a little androgynous creature and you imagine she's a spirit! You're no longer capable of wanting a woman's body and so you fancy she's a saint!"

"Lebrun," said Kansdorf, "you don't know what you're talking about. I know that love can make people blind, that passion alters one's entire scale of values. But I can see into this young girl, and she is pure. She is spirit. In loving her without desire, I love everything I've been dreaming of and searching for all my life. What do you believe that is?"

"I don't believe anything; you must do that for yourself," answered Lebrun. "But I *know* what you've been looking for, and I've already told you once what it is: a beautiful young man. This time he has appeared in the shape of a saint. Before that he looked like your wife and was dark and slender. On another occasion he haunted your dreams, blowing a kind of hunting horn. It's not hard to read you like a book!"

"I know all about these theories of yours," said Kansdorf. "But you're mistaken. I'm looking for the—Absolute. I'm tired of making compromises and being disillusioned."

"The Absolute? Thanks very much," said Lebrun, "I've never heard of a prettier piece of self-deception, over something that is really quite simple. You excel yourself. My congratulations!"

Kansdorf shrugged his shoulders, and the two friends walked slowly on. In the east the dawn was breaking.

"The funny thing about you, you old heathen," said Kansdorf, "is that if you were to practise what you preach you'd be cutting people's heads off and end up by being arrested for murder."

"Quite right," said Lebrun. "There need to be people who talk like me too."

"But why don't you practise what you preach?" Kansdorf repeated. "There's something stopping you. Why are you—forgive me if I seem to be insulting you—so kind, and thoughtful, and sensitive, in spite of the dreadful things you say? Why do you like people? Why do you spend your whole life helping them?"

"Stuff and nonsense!" mumbled Lebrun. "To get money, of course!"

Kansdorf did not answer.

"You laugh at these horn sounds I hear, and my longing

for the Absolute and perfect purity, but you can hear a voice in your own innermost being too. There are echoes in your soul which astonish you and you listen to them. Admit it!"

He was expecting another cynical retort.

But Lebrun had stopped. He was looking down at the pavement.

"Yes," he said, "it's true. I have to admit it. Not that I've the slightest idea whether it affects what I do. All I know is that—occasionally—it makes me do things that go right against my own ideas. What that means, I don't rightly know. As for your noises and visions, I laugh at them. But to tell the truth my own experience is just as strange. At times, especially when I watch myself doing something, I see a person who is not the usual Lebrun but is nevertheless more me, more my real self, than the Lebrun you know. I don't mean that he's handsome in any way: but he's not by any means as ugly as this one."

"Lebrun," said Kansdorf, moved, "there, you see!"

"No," said Lebrun, with a violent gesture, "I don't see anything. It's too dark. You're making me talk nonsense. Don't forget that things said in drink are not binding. Now I'm going home! You'll be *swimming* home, won't you? Good night, my fanciful friend. Don't forget you'll soon be dead!"

Waving his hat, he went off.

"I know," Kansdorf shouted after him, and his heart was pounding with joy, "I know that I'll be dead! But at the moment I'm alive, Lebrun!"

He stood there for a long time, motionless. In the east the sky was already a red glow.

CHAPTER TWENTY-THREE

Father Perezcaballero had left the monastery.

After his conversation with the girl he had become almost unrecognizable. Several of the friars had noticed the change. In the end he had gone to the Prior and explained his condition. The Prior had been flabbergasted by what he had told him and said that he was grossly exaggerating things. Dom Dusolier had hardly been the right person to discuss the matter with, he said. Why hadn't he kept to his own monastery? Hadn't they enough specialized knowledge and psychological insight for him? However, he was obviously going through a severe crisis and needed rest. The Prior advised him to have a few months off and in the meantime to take up his writing again.

Father Perezcaballero accepted the advice. He left the monastery and installed himself in a quiet country house outside Paris which his Order had recently had bequeathed to it by a rich benefactress. It was half hospital and half convalescent home. Perezcaballero told the sisters that he wanted perfect quiet so that he could get on with a book he was writing; and he was scrupulously obeyed. He saw no one, and his meals were brought up to him in his room.

He started work at once. He looked through his old manuscripts, sketched out a new general scheme, ordered the books he wanted from the library. But he got no further. He who had once been so active and energetic, never doubting his own gifts or the work he was called upon to do, would sit for hour after hour, sharpening pencils until the point broke. The dazzling white sheets of paper stared at him from the massive desk, the silence absolutely shrieked in his ears, he was alone and in the depths of despair.

He made desperate attempts to convince himself that he was the victim of a hysterical crisis and was making his sins out to be greater than they were. He had confessed to them. He was ashamed of them. He deeply regretted them. But then, such times of depression were normal—spiritual dryness was a trial known to every Christian—and they generally turned out to be a blessing. He had only to acknowledge once and for all that of himself he was quite powerless and then he would be filled with new strength. The whole history of Christianity showed, and it was supported by our knowledge of human nature, that this was a law of life. Why the anxiety, then? All he had to do was to thank God for working upon him! And besides this, it was nearly Easter: he knew that he was to be crucified with the Lord, but then he would arise with Him too.

With such thoughts, for a few days, he tried to deceive himself.

But then he cast them away from him in the wildest despair. His whole life was a pose. His teaching was a pose, his faith was a pose, his contrition and humility were a pose. As soon as he made a real effort to see through all these things he realized that he did not believe in his own explanations for a moment. His brain could manufacture theories all right —the sort he passed on to the unfortunate people who came to him for help. He was regarded as an expert in the direction of souls. He was in command of the whole field, he knew where the snares and temptations lay, he could see through all the double-dealing and attempts at camouflage—and he was also supposed to know where the springs of spiritual health flowed. Nonsense! He didn't know a thing! Now that he himself was *in extremis* he recognized his own helplessness. Not that he feared his powerlessness in itself, for it was a fact that man *is* helpless. No, what he feared was that even this feeling of helplessness might be an act he was putting on; that even his despair was a made-up affair; that his humility was not really humility at all.

He wandered round and round his room, unable to throw off these thoughts. He slept badly. He hardly touched his food. He had always been noted for the proud erect way he held himself: once, when he had seen Cardinal Pacelli in a film, he had seen himself in him; but now he began to grow round-shouldered, and the expression on his face had changed from untroubled self-possession to despair.

He did not neglect his religious duties; he was more severe with himself than ever. He said his office. . . .

Had his life been entirely a matter of affectation and deception? Was he absolutely in the devil's clutches? If so, however had he been able to do what he had done?

What he had done! What had he done? Spoken empty words, with a brilliant eloquence that was entirely lacking in content. How had he treated Ilse? He had wounded her viciously, for no better reason than to ensure, in his holy egoism, that his pride should not be wounded. He went back apprehensively over the various periods of his life; recalling how he had been sent on from the school in his own Basque country when the parish priest had discovered how talented he was; how he had kept away from his own simple family, because he no longer had anything in common with them; how, wherever he had gone, he had always fought hard to get the highest certificates; how he had been eaten up by ambition when he had seen his first serious writing in print and heard it praised by the experts; how depressed he had been by his subsequent intellectual sterility; how he had sought to compensate for it by becoming an outstanding shepherd of souls; how he had taken kudos from his status as a national hero; that was writhing agony.

No matter where he looked he found egoism, ambition and cold calculation. Had his entire Christianity simply been a way of buttressing his own self-importance? Had he ever cared for anyone except himself? Did he not in fact despise his fellow men?

In the depths of his misery he wrote to Ilse Lebrun and asked her if he could see her. She found him a changed man, obviously suffering from sleeplessness, weak and ill. His speech was stumbling and confused. He told her that he had come to a better understanding of the way he had behaved and realized how badly he had let her down. Could she forgive him?

She was touched, though at the same time taken aback to see him so distraught. Of course she forgave him. All she hoped was that he would soon be well. If that was the only thing he had to reproach himself with, he had no need to worry, she said.

The only thing?

He wrote to Father Guillon. When he had finished the letter he read it through and tore it into shreds. Every word rang false. He began again, but was not satisfied with this second attempt either. Was it really quite impossible for him to say a single word that was a faithful expression of the truth? In the end he wrote a short, blunt note in which he laid the guilt entirely on his own shoulders, accused himself of a total lack of charity, and asked Father Guillon to forgive him.

After he had sent the letter off he felt that he had still not told the truth. That wasn't the way he really looked at the matter either. But now it was too late to do anything about it.

The answer, when it came, shattered him. It was as cold as ice. Father Guillon remarked, curtly, that there was nothing new to him in the letter. He had seen right through Father Perezcaballero from the first. He had known that intellectual rivalry lay behind his attitude. He was glad that Father Perezcaballero had finally realized his own duplicity. He himself was quite well; he had the feeling that his sin had been forgiven; he imagined that he would soon be able to return to his writing. He wished his brother in Christ peace of mind. And so on.

It was an unexceptionable letter, fraternal, polite. But icy-cold. The words concealed utter contempt. Perezcaballero knew that kind of letter. He had written many of the same kind himself.

His desperate brooding continued. Was it true that he had become a friar simply because he had been disappointed in love? Was all his talk of a vocation lies? It seemed to him that it could hardly be otherwise. What had lain behind his vocation, in his early years, but a determination to distinguish himself? Had he ever been interested in souls? Couldn't he remember how he had to struggle against his own feelings before he could bring himself to work for his fellow men in those early days? Human beings disgusted him: he had found them unaesthetic, unlovely. With the passage of time he had got used to them and developed a certain practical skill: he had come to regard himself as a kind of doctor, who was obliged to have dealings with the sick and the deformed. But the human animal was, as a rule, a dirty and pitiable form of life.

Now he had to see himself as that kind of animal. He trembled at the thought of what he must look like in the eyes of the few people who had seen through him—Dom Dusolier, for instance; Our Lord. . . .

228

After a month of continuous depression he wrote to a certain Father Caffarel, a well-known Dominican missionary who happened to be in Paris just then. Father Caffarel came to see him. He found himself facing a bent, wasted man with an unshaven face and feverish eyes, who motioned him with a trembling hand to a chair and began to speak in a nervous, uncertain voice. He couldn't bring himself to explain everything that had happened to him, and contented himself with saying that he had been going through a severe trial. But he had now come to a decision: he would like to give up his position as a preacher and high society confessor and undertake some anonymous work—he would like to become a missionary, preferably in some remote part of the world.

Father Caffarel, who had come across this kind of thing before, asked a few searching questions. Then he gave his opinion.

Father Perezcaballero, he said, must have entirely misunderstood the missionary's function. There could be no question of escaping into a mission: it didn't provide a less arduous form of work that anyone could withdraw into if he wanted to hide or forget some sort of defeat and there lick his wounds in peace and quiet. The missions needed people who were strong and ruthless with themselves, people who presented themselves for the job quite freely and had sacrificed everything for it; they were not convalescent homes for neurotics. Father Perezcaballero must first of all try to recover his equilibrium.

Perezcaballero was transfixed when he heard these harsh words. He asked his fellow priest to allow him to confess to him. In the course of his confession his entire misery poured in a confused torrent from his lips. But even at this stage he couldn't confess a single sin without intimating by his choice of words and the tone in which he expressed them that it was an unusual, unique, interesting sin. He was desperate, a broken man, but he could not even describe how wretched he was without falling into affectation.

Caffarel drew his attention to this, and he saw the other, once so proud, burst into tears. Yes, he knew all about that, he said, but how was he to *cure* himself of it?

Caffarel would soon have to be leaving Paris. The only thing he could advise was that he should recover a strict sense of reality.

"Keep telling yourself that the spirit of Christ means a sense of reality—and charity."

Words! Theories! Schemes! Formulas!

Perezcaballero could have said all that himself. He grew desperate, became violent with Caffarel, told him that he could see through him, that it was quite clear to him that he was enjoying his triumph, that he was getting quite a kick out of seeing a fellow priest down—and he, utterly heartless as he was, was supposed to be a missionary!

Caffarel kept his temper—Perezcaballero was a sick man—and said a few friendly words in reply. Before he could go, Perezcaballero had flung himself on his knees and begged his forgiveness for saying such things.

Caffarel looked at him for a long time.

"Just think of one thing," he said: "the sense of reality. Otherwise you're finished!"

And then he left him.

When the sisters knocked on the door in the afternoon they got no answer, and the gardener had to get the long ladder and climb in through the window. Father Perezcaballero was lying on the floor senseless.

In front of him lay the crucifix that usually hung on the wall. It had been torn down and near it lay bits of plaster from the broken wall. What had happened?

Had he really—? The sister swept the bits up, put

Perezcaballero into another room, and summoned a doctor, who gave him sedatives. He sank into a coma and slept for a whole day.

When he woke up he was quiet, almost apathetic. He lay motionless, let himself be looked after, listened equably to all the advice that was given him. The only thing he said, so softly that the sisters could hardly hear him, was:

"Thanks, thanks . . . But, you see, I'm one of the damned, one of the damned. . . ."

The sister sent for Dom Dusolier, who promised to come along: at the moment he was ill, but as soon as he could he would hurry along to do what he could for his friend.

Father Perezcaballero lay in bed. His skin was jaundiced, beads of sweat stood on his forehead. His eyes were fixed on the crucifix on the wall: he had to turn his head to see it.

The sisters realized that he was suffering, and offered to change the position of the crucifix.

"Leave it, please," he said.

The window was wide open. Spring had come. The chestnut trees were in their full glory. The lilac was just in bloom and its scent came to his nostrils through the window. Birds were singing.

The invalid's lips moved. He was muttering to himself. His eyes were deeply sunken, his forehead was damp.

CHAPTER TWENTY-FOUR

One day, Kansdorf procured a car and they sped northwards to look at cathedrals—northwards across the French plain, Péguy's plain, with nightingales and thrushes in the copses, sloes on the edges of the woods, fruit-trees in full blossom. . . .

With the car roof open they travelled towards Beauvais, where the mighty cathedral rises up out of the ruins like some horrible Colossus. Stifling their sense of disappointment, they went inside. Previously they had been lost in admiration of the sky-high vaulting in St. Denis, but here they were given something very different to look at—a church built for giants, an undertaking done on a vast scale, an enormity. The average mass of crawling humanity hasn't the nerve to pray in such a monstrosity—their legs feel too short, their voices too weak. Giants ten foot high might hurl themselves groaning to the ground here, but not tiny human ants.

After silently reconnoitring the place they were in sober mood when they left it: it had seemed as soulless as a sky-scraper.

Their disappointment was depressing, and the prospect of all the ruins did nothing to enliven them. But it was out of the question to go straight back to Paris. They studied the map. There was Senlis. What did they know of Senlis? Nothing. Without any great hopes they set off. It was a blessing at any rate to be able to get away from the ruined city and its pompous church.

They parked the car in the narrow high street and before they had taken more than a few steps had left the real world far behind them. The town was enchanted.

They both felt it at once. They had no need to say anything. The whole of the little town with its slate roofs and winding alleyways was back in the Middle Ages. Down the silent streets flowed the stream of history. They wandered down to the pre-Christian arena where gladiators had fought for the entertainment of the Roman legions, while the Gauls—examples of whose unlovely, crumbling, obscene art they came upon in the museum—had had to stand outside like goggling cattle. After centuries of upheaval the arena lay there silent and unmoving. Beyond it spread the undulating plain, with its avenues of poplars standing out against a background of flashing silver copses. On the sun-warmed walls lizards squiggled.

They heard the roar of the thousands of spectators rising from their seats to greet Caesar entering his box, they heard his clipped metallic voice and saw the sun reflected from his head, bald above the commanding eyes. They followed the mighty Roman wall, today partly covered by mediaeval building but still here and there rising up in its original majesty, ten feet high and twenty feet across.

They climbed up to the Roman governor's villa and saw his phantom in the window niches, shading its black eyebrows with its hand and sweeping the enemy plain with its hawklike eyes. When they came to the cathedral they found a troop of horsemen stepping into the open square: a lithe young woman was springing from the saddle, and a thirst for action which she was destined to fulfil shone in her pure maidenly eyes, for it was Joan of Arc striding into the cathedral. They saw another troop of horsemen—St. Louis himself, fair-haired,

233

upright, light of foot, with his high forehead and his hair fluttering in the summer breeze. And when they got to the roof of the cathedral, they could see, below, a third sight. A solitary officer was striding across the square with a ringing gait to Low Mass—Marshal Foch, who had left his headquarters to come and fall on his knees in the cathedral and pray for victory.

They drew further and further away from actuality, unable to see enough of this town where the centuries seemed to melt into one another to give a complete cross-section of the history of Europe and historic figures kept cropping up at every street corner. Listening to the rustling of the tree-tops they could hear the murmur of resting Roman legionaries at full stretch in the grass; standing in front of a low mediaeval house they could see Joan of Arc sitting on her white horse, with the reins in her sunburnt hands, calling her followers to the attack. And wherever they went they had St. Louis before their eyes—head held high, firm of foot, light of heart: a Christian king with God in his soul and all his attention on his duty.

The tiled roofs under the cloudless spring sky, the ring and clang of the cathedral bells, the cawing of the rooks round the cathedral spires, more crowds of people thronging the narrow alleyways: the centuries had passed over this land like a tempest, the great ones of the world had been caught up and hurled away as though by pounding waves, and only the cathedral still stood there unscathed.

Even when darkness had fallen over the town, veiling the expanses of bricks and tiles with a soft curtain of silver and grey, they could not give up their wandering through the narrow streets. Shutters were up before the windows, and the few people they came across talked in whispers, as though not to disturb the great memories of the past. It was a dark night, the street lights were feeble, the silence was so intense that it

seemed to clang like a deep bell. Then the moon came out
from behind parting clouds, silvering the tiles on the roofs;
the squares turned into arenas, and when they came to the
cathedral they were dumbstruck to see the mighty gesture
with which the tower turned itself to the stars. For St. Louis
these things must have been an everyday experience: France's
finest cathedrals had sprung up in his footsteps. Katharina,
who, as Kansdorf had already noticed, bore a strong resemblance to the slim maidens at the portals of the cathedral at
Chartres, stood motionless, her head thrown back, taking in
all this beauty wordlessly, effortlessly, as easily as breathing.
The next moment, giving way to a sudden emotion, she sat
down on the cobbles in the market-place. He did the same.

"Edvard," she said softly.

He turned to her. Half her face was bathed in moonlight.
The cathedral tower sailed above the clouds.

"Would you like to know—?" she asked, as softly as before.

He did not dare to interrupt her. He looked at her in
surprise. What did she mean? What was there he might like
to know?

But she did not wait for him to answer. Still without looking
at him, she said, calmly—it was as though she was speaking
to the black vault of the sky:

"The Germans—made me suffer an awful lot."

Her voice was quite steady.

He did not dare to say anything. He knew what she was
referring to; he had realized that it must have been so. Her
whole face was a living witness to that kind of suffering, for
anyone who had eyes to see and was acquainted with the
language. But he had never dared to face the matter squarely.
Why should she mention it now? Why was she destroying the
evening's magic?

"I don't know much about what it feels like when everything—looks black," she said.

He understood what she meant. She wanted to destroy the last traces of self-pity in him. She knew quite well that her own experiences had been infinitely more nerve-racking, infinitely harder to bear than his own. An evil spirit had distorted his view of life, he had struggled in a senseless battle with his wife's shade until she had vanished from his memory so completely that he could no longer remember what she looked like. He had opened his soul to evil spirits, allowed them entrance to his inmost being, and let them rage to their hearts' content in his soul and body. That was why he was prematurely worn out. But she—she was free.

He realized that the young woman by his side, in this town of Senlis, so packed with memories and historical events, was God's annihilating answer to his own lack of spirit.

"Contemplate My handiwork," God was saying. "I plunge whole civilizations into ruin, but day after day I re-create them in the courageous free soul of some shattered human being. You doubted My power: see, I make all things new!"

He looked at her in silence.

"They beat my grandmother to death," she said in a hushed voice. "Grandmother was the best and finest person I have ever known. She didn't show any feeling. I was watching. They burned my parents to death. They trampled my little brother to death. And as for me—"

Her voice was so soft that he could hardly hear her. Did she know why, sitting on the ground with her hands propped behind her back and her head lifted up towards the floating moonlit spire of the cathedral, she was telling a foreigner about the worst hours of her life?

He sensed that she was acting by order. He was near to a mystery. He didn't dare move, for fear of scaring away the silently approaching secret.

It was a warm night, the moonlight had not brought any breeze, the cobbles in the market-place were still warm from

236

the sun. Age and memories played around the cathedral. All this was trying to speak to him: he had been called here, he had been guided by a gentle breeze to a town he did not know, so that in its surroundings, with beauty and the memories of great things streaming in upon him, a young woman might break through the high walls he had built up around himself and speak her heart out to him.

Faintly, like an echo, he seemed to hear the sound of the Benedictines, chanting.

"I was—very down," she said. "I wasn't really a human being at all by the time the Americans arrived. They took charge of me, got me medical help—oh, those clean sheets they gave me, their scrupulous cleanliness, their nurses, so quick and competent and sympathetic, the young doctors, with their friendly, intelligent eyes! But they couldn't do anything for me: I was a wreck, I felt that my whole life was finished. I couldn't forget all I had seen and heard. I kept thinking of my murdered grandmother."

Kansdorf listened, hardly breathing. And then! When had the miracle happened? He trembled with the longing to know more. How had she found redemption? Katharina, how does a man get free?

After a while she went on. Was he mistaken, or was that a smile dawning upon her face as she sat there, her delicate profile uplifted to the moon?

"Then I met Abbé Auclair. Don't laugh! I know what you think of him. I know what people think he is. But I know from experience what people are, so I don't mind so much what they think. Abbé Auclair says a lot of strange things. . . . and perhaps he will never come out again. But, he is a saint."

So it had been the abbé! That crazy young priest with the cheerful look and his schemes of world conquest: he had healed her! How had it happened?

"You are right," he plucked up the courage to say. "He is

queer. But I know there's no evil in him. He is one of God's sensitive instruments."

She sat silent for a while.

Then she smiled again, this time quite broadly.

"He didn't argue with me. The Americans had a young American doctor who had been brought up on psychoanalysis and he tried all his tricks out on me. He quizzed me and nagged at me, and finally gave it up as a bad job. Abbé Auclair understood everything at once. I didn't have to lie down on a couch and answer all kinds of questions. He didn't draw any diagrams. The American doctor was tall and dignified and very friendly. He was so well-meaning! Abbé Auclair was small and bustling and badly shaved. And he wasn't always very clean. Once I gave him a piece of soap that I'd got from the Americans. He put it in his pocket and hardly said thank you: he scarcely realized what it was. I expect he gave it away as soon as he left me."

She stopped speaking and smiled at the recollection. Yes, you can smile, Katharina, he thought. You are free. How does a man get free?

"All he did was to take me by the hand and lead me to the Holy Sacrament. Quite simply: he didn't say much. And one day he sat me down on one of the seats in the church, and sat down beside me—a thing he never did, usually. There were a number of his boys working there and he kept being interrupted and disturbed. But he took my hand in his and what he said to me was more or less this: Katharina, thy sins are forgiven thee. Do you know what that means?' I thought for a bit and then said I did. 'I don't believe it,' he said with a laugh, his dark eyes flashing. 'Anyway, I must talk to you about it.' Somebody interrupted him again and he had to give a few orders. Then he looked at me again and, as usually happened, he had forgotten what he had been saying. He had to think for a while. Then, growing quite solemn, he said quietly, 'Well, you see, when God forgives you your sins He gives you a new life.' I knew that. I nodded. 'And a new life means that your old life is finished with. God is all-powerful, there is nothing He cannot do. He gave you your present life, He can give you a new one—He has already done so.' I nodded, I understood that. He squeezed my hand very hard, looking not at me but up at the crucifix, and then said, in such a loud voice that I was afraid his boys would hear him: 'That means that you have become a new person, *body and soul*, Katharina! Don't ever forget that! Everything that happened before is over. That's why you should love Him. Let people say what they like and think what they like. But it is the truth, as true as it is that I have the right to speak in His name.' Then he turned to me and suddenly kissed me on the forehead—rather hurriedly and sideways on, of course— and then he jumped up waving his arms and ran about the church shouting to his boys, pulling their ears, joking with them, getting ready for his party."

"And you?" said Kansdorf. "What did you do?"

"I went on sitting there quite still," she said. "I wasn't excited or in ecstasy or anything. I felt a bit worn out, as a matter of fact. But then I stood up, walked up to the statue of Our Lady and fell on my knees. And there I realized something that I have felt ever since and always shall feel—"

"What, Katharina?"

"That what he told me is true! That God has performed a miracle in me for which I shall go on thanking Him for the rest of my life."

With a sudden movement she got up.

"I'm free," she said in a loud voice. "And I thank God for it every day."

Kansdorf sat looking at her slender figure. She had buried her hands in her capacious raincoat pockets and she was outlined against the moonlit chapter house. Slowly she leaned her head back.

He too stood up. He felt his own paltriness. He had had the temerity to flirt with his own suffering. He had fallen into temptation by despising human beings. He had enjoyed Lebrun's chatter. He had been one of the regulars at the sports' stadium.

He heard the faint rustle of the trees in the square.

Freedom, he thought. Before I die, make me—free, free!

They found a hotel for the night. Kansdorf was unable to sleep and got up several times and wandered round his room on the creaking floor. The whole of his life up to this moment seemed to have been wasted. Capriciously he had come near to the true reality, then only half-listened to what it had said. Would he be luckier this time?

"Lightly, swiftly, tenderly": the familiar theme-song of his suffering suddenly rang out in his consciousness. From long habit he bowed before the coming pain, gathered himself for the expected blow.

But it did not come.

A heavy lorry thundered past outside with a roar sufficient to waken the whole town.

When the storm had passed he looked anxiously into himself. He found that there was no fear there any more. Instead, there was a new point of light, a pinpoint.

He had felt drawn to Dagny in the first place—though he could no longer remember what she looked like—because he had seen the signs of an excellence and purity in her that he could not resist. Dagny had conceived a romantic passion for Lorens Jörgensen because he had given her a sense of spiritual reality that she could not get from her husband. *He* had perceived strange echoes within himself, even in the times of his bitterest despair, and had had a deep intuition of some woman

240

who was utterly pure and utterly free: wasn't the figure that had appeared to him so fleetingly between the trees "light, swift and tender"? And wasn't Katharina herself that figure? Hadn't she walked, a solid, actual living person, out of his dreams?

Was his mind wandering? Was he imagining similarities that didn't in fact exist? Or was he really on the track of a mystery? He could imagine Lebrun's comments on all this—well, let him comment! For he was trying to get to the truth, excitedly, eager for knowledge, longing for certainty. When he had wanted any woman, hadn't he always glimpsed in her a reflection of this dream image of his—no, of his own most inmost reality?

Why had Katharina become the centre of his life?

And how was it that during this night, in an ugly old hotel room in Senlis, he should suddenly feel all the pain and bitterness disappear, and should begin to have a sense of reconciliation with his past? Dagny too had been struggling towards the same mystery, surely; and her dream man, the poet with his little mistress, had been seeking the same reality, as his verses showed. And he himself had for a long time now been aware of signs of exactly the same truth.

They were companions in misfortune, all suffering the same misery, all striving after the same freedom: how could they possibly hate each other?

He was awakened by a knock on his door. It was time to go to Mass. He dressed quickly. When he came down into the vestibule Katharina was already there. She was always at her post: she was unencumbered and light—not like earthy women, heavy, warm, demanding.

They set off for the church. During the silence of the Mass he kept his face buried in his hands and tried to look into himself. All that was deceptive, fluid, green, had disappeared: he had found the way into his own being, he could move without restlessness or pain in his own world. There were hard, agonizing things there, true enough, but they didn't intimidate him now. In the far distance he could sense Dagny. All his bitterness had gone. He could see Lorens Jörgensen before him, and there was no feeling of revulsion. And at the Communion, when he felt the Body of Our Lord upon his tongue, he thought:

Never, never again shall I leave You, until You have blessed me! Never again shall I go back!

After the Mass he felt a slight pressure on his arm and looked up in surprise. Katharina motioned to behind the altar, smiling. He followed her.

In Our Lady's chapel she fell on her knees. He did the same. For a while he knelt in thought—or rather, without any thoughts.

For a long time he had dreamed of a chapel to Our Lady, a chapel so springlike, so pure in its lines, so chaste, that it could really be regarded as worthy of the Blessed Virgin. He had endured agonies in so many of the Paris churches. He had seen what ugly decoration philistine taste could inflict upon what should have been pure and spiritual. When he wanted to look at a statue of the Madonna in Paris he had to go to the plaster casts in the Palais Chaillet. Never, he had decided, would he find a chapel to Our Lady that was worthy of her.

Was this little town enchanted? Was it giving him absolutely everything he wanted?

The chapel to Our Lady behind the high altar in Senlis Cathedral *was* the chapel of his dreams.

He had seen more beautiful sculptures of Our Lady, he knew several masters of early Gothic who would have decorated the chapel more perfectly. Nevertheless, this was the chapel of his dreams.

He looked at Katharina. She too was gazing in front of her

242

with shining eyes and a glow of inspiration on her face. She saw! She understood!

He let himself take in all the lines of the place and as he did so felt a gentle power stealing over him, breaking down all his barriers—and gratefully, resistlessly, his whole being opened to it.

This, then, was where he had had to come!

He hid his face in his hands.

Freedom, freedom flowed over him like waves.

CHAPTER TWENTY-FIVE

Dr. Lebrun went up the steps to Kansdorf's apartment.

He was worried. His friend's condition had deteriorated. It was true that he only had a slight temperature and his head was clear; but he was hardly eating anything. It was only a question of time before he would have to be confined to his bed. He had stopped having the radium treatment: he knew that it was no use any more.

Lebrun understood him. They had discussed the matter more than once. He would do what he could to deaden the pain when it became unbearable; and then at the end he would end his agony.

He could do that without thinking twice about it.

Clothilde opened the door to him. She was scared of him, and he for his part scowled when he saw her standing in front of him. As soon as she had taken his hat and coat she promptly disappeared into the kitchen. He let her go. But after a little while he followed her. She gazed at him in alarm. But today he wasn't anything like so frightening as usual; on the contrary, he looked quite friendly.

He questioned her in detail about the way Kansdorf was eating and told her what she should give him. She nodded and jotted down a few notes.

"Is he—very ill, then?" she asked softly, taking great care not to be heard in the bedroom.

"No, not at all," answered Dr. Lebrun. "He may still live for quite a while."

"How long?"

The doctor shrugged his shoulders.

"A week; or a month. Perhaps several months. We must hope that it won't be too protracted."

"And will he have to go on lying there until—?"

"No, why should he? He's bound to die in the end in any case. So I think it's more sensible for him to do anything he likes, if it gives him pleasure! At the moment that seems to mean running into every church in Paris."

Clothilde plucked up courage and moved nearer to him.

She felt obliged to speak softly and as a consequence gesticulated vigorously to give emphasis to her words.

"He shouldn't stay so long in those freezing churches!" she said. "He catches cold. He's ruining himself. *That's* how he got his trouble in the first place! I've often told him so."

Lebrun raised his arms, but no laughter emerged. He felt profoundly pleased. She was absolutely splendid.

"You think religion's a good thing, then, Clothilde, in moderation? Not too much of it at a time, is that right?"

She looked up at him like a hen, slightly uneasy, not grasping his irony.

"I'm a regular churchgoer myself, Doctor, as you know, and I'm not one to. . . . But you mustn't go getting yourself ill, surely, just to be good? No, I'm sure you shouldn't!"

"So you think, then, Clothilde, that the God Monsieur Kansdorf prays to rewards him for his zeal by inflicting all sorts of infirmities on him?"

"I didn't say that it's God who does it!" said Clothilde, still imagining that she could win this argument. "There are other powers besides God."

"But God is all-powerful, surely? And yet, all-powerful as He is, He lets the good religious people who go and pray to Him in His churches get punished with rheumatics and high temperatures and suchlike complaints. In my view that's a very queer way of showing you're all-powerful! What do you think, Clothilde?"

She had turned her back on him and was busying herself at the fire.

"You must discuss that with a priest, Doctor. I'm only saying how it is."

Dr. Lebrun nodded.

"Yes, I've been thinking only these last few days of going to see a priest," he said.

Clothilde turned back to him, her eyes lighting up.

"Well I never! Now that's the right thing to do, Doctor! It's never too late."

"No, but it may be only just in the nick of time. You see, Clothilde, there are certain things I must try to get clear about."

"I know, I know! Yes, we all reach that stage sooner or later. But fancy you too, Doctor!"

"I have made up my mind to go and see the Cardinal himself," he said, "for the question on my mind is a difficult one."

"The Cardinal? Well, why not? He's always ready to see poor sinners—I mean, you—you too. . . ."

Lebrun was leaning over the kitchen table. He looked thoughtful and slightly embarrassed.

"You see," he said, "the thing is, I'm a wicked person and quite often I go to black-market restaurants, restaurants one shouldn't go to. It isn't right."

"No, that isn't right," said Clothilde apprehensively, turning away from him. "The black market is a nasty business. But why do you do that, Doctor? After all, you have your home and everything."

"The fact is, I get better food in the black-market restaurants," he said. "And so I break the laws and ordinances and deserve to be punished by God."

Clothilde was silent.

"But now I intend to go and see the Cardinal and say this to him: 'Your Eminence, a question, in the name of Our Lord! I have it on reliable authority that the meal that Your Eminence wolfed down along with our ambassador to Prague, the Brazilian ambassador and a number of prelates, took place in what is certainly an excellent restaurant, but it is one that is forbidden by the law: you can get masses of good things to eat there, but they are all illegal. I know this, Your Eminence, because I often go there myself. I know the head waiter, I'm a regular patron, so to speak. And now I must tell you about a dream I had. In this dream of mine, every time Your Eminence took a mouthful of food that had been procured illegally, one more soul went to perdition. Eminence— how many souls do you think went to perdition in that case?"

Clothilde had slowly turned round, openmouthed.

"You're going to say that, Doctor? You don't really mean it? It'll cause—an absolute scandal!"

"Of course it'll cause a scandal. But I'm not the first person to have caused a scandal. Didn't Christ Himself cause an absolutely dreadful scandal, in His own day? Do you think, Clothilde, that He would have gone into a restaurant that was forbidden by the state and when He knew that anyone who went into it was liable to be sent to prison?"

"But that was *Him!* That's quite a different matter! Surely you're not trying to compare yourself with our Saviour, Doctor? That's going a bit too far! Anyway, I don't believe there was a black market in those days."

"I'm not at all sure about that; it was an occupied country and under the Terror, no doubt there were plenty of things in short supply. You must realize, Clothilde: I'm very fond of good food. The meat is tender and juicy. The wine is pleasant on the palate. The sun shines through the window curtains and flashes on the silver and glass. My sense of well-being increases. The intellectual life comfortably declines. I feel earthily secure and replete. Then the waiter comes along with the liqueurs, Clothilde, good liqueurs. I know that a cloud is lowering over my head and that it will open as soon as I look up at it. So precisely for that reason I don't look up. I know what's inside it. So *I* look down."

Clothilde stood with her hands on her hips, goggling. Had this fellow gone completely crazy, sitting here at the kitchen table and talking such nonsense so calmly?

"Doctor," she said, "excuse me, but—"

He looked up.

"That doesn't matter to *me* in the slightest," he said, "for I'm not a Christian. I don't believe in God at all—at least, not in the way that the Cardinal and you, Clothilde, and the rest of you do. And so I go on in my old way. Why not? But you're a believer, and for all this stealing of yours you'll go straight to hell!"

She said nothing, but her arms went up towards the ceiling in a gesture of despair.

Lebrun had got up and moved towards the door leading into the rest of the flat. Without turning round he stood there and said slowly,

"I often think that you're a remarkable person, Clothilde."

"Of course I'm not," she said with an embarrassed giggle.

"Oh yes, you are," he said seriously, "I think you—I think you symbolize the whole of France, Clothilde. And that's something I find highly interesting."

Then he moved towards the next room. Her voice called after him.

"Did the Cardinal really go to a black-market restaurant?"

"I haven't the least idea," he answered.

Kansdorf was lying in bed. He was very weak, and unable to keep any food down. Lebrun examined him, asked the usual questions, but gave no advice.

"You go to Communion, regularly?" he asked.

"Yes," answered Kansdorf, "every morning. When I can."

"I understand. May I ask you—which has the more powerful effect, that Host, which is supposed to be the Body of Christ, or the usual Sandol tablets containing phenedrine and caffein?"

Kansdorf smiled.

"I don't know, my dear chap," he said.

"Really, you don't know!"

"No—because I usually take both."

Lebrun's face did not change.

"That seems quite sensible. I'd probably do the same myself. It also gets you out of an argument. May I ask you something else?"

Kansdorf was pale and terribly thin. But Lebrun saw that his face had changed. A sort of peace had come over it. Kansdorf had always had a tense, nervous face, in vivid contrast with his fair, youthful-looking hair. Now his face had developed a slightly hollow look, but nevertheless he looked as though he had found his balance. He *had*, obviously, found his balance. And this thanks to some kind of auto-suggestion—which he was of course quite clever enough to see through for himself.

"Go on," said Kansdorf.

"When you pray do you ask to get better?" said Lebrun.

Kansdorf did not move.

"You must realize that I know so little about these things. I'm simply asking out of curiosity."

Kansdorf turned his head and looked at his friend with a smile.

"Surely you're not going to try to make out that you never pray yourself?"

Lebrun looked down at the floor.

He coughed.

"There's praying and praying. If I'm to be quite frank, as I like to be, then I must say I'm not really in the habit of praying—because I don't know who I should pray to. But once or twice, especially when I have had to make a quick decision in the hospital about an operation or something important like that, I do seem to have found myself praying."

"You see! And *who* do you pray to, on these occasions?"

"I can't say. But if you really must know, I have actually fallen on my knees and said this, or words to this effect: 'If You exist, then stand by me now, for I certainly shan't be able to manage this business on my own!' Words to that effect. I don't know whether you'd call that a prayer or not—?"

"Certainly I would. It is a model prayer."

There was silence. Lebrun looked at the piles of books on the chairs and the table by the bed. They were mainly theology and suchlike.

"Do you pray to get better?" he asked softly.

"No," Kansdorf replied, "that's a thing I never do."

"Why not?"

"I don't know. I pray for strength to be able to accept the will of God."

Lebrun nodded.

"And you think He *wills* cancer and the destruction of our bodily organs and a painful death?"

"Perhaps."

"And you calmly accept that? Without revolting?"

"I believe that He wants me to be free, not to get better," Kansdorf said slowly. "I believe His aim is to save me from my own torpor and spiritual death. I don't know how He intends to do that. But I feel so certain that He loves me and is on my side that I could never think of criticizing how He does it."

Lebrun nodded.

"Thanks, I'm beginning to understand you. Do you think the Christians in the concentration camps took the same view? In the face of death?"

"Some of them, certainly," said Kansdorf.

Lebrun got up and began to walk up and down the room. He was in point of fact very much moved. He was very fond of this lonely man, who had always had such a frank contempt for himself, and now seemed to have developed such an unreasoning hope.

He stopped and rocked back on his heels.

"There is one other thing that I find most puzzling," he said. "If you accept pain and suffering as a kind of tactic that God adopts towards you to bring you spiritual freedom and suchlike, then how can you agree to my shortening your life, as we have so often agreed?"

Kansdorf nodded his head quickly and lifted himself up on his elbows. Despite the spring warmth he was wearing a thick woollen cardigan.

"I'm glad you've brought that up. You know—despite the way we used to joke about it, I was always grateful to you for being prepared to help me to die. If one has simply to go out for ever in a great darkness, the quicker it happens the better. I can't actually prove that there's a fallacy in that attitude. I've no arguments to put up against it. Nevertheless, I *know* that it's wrong."

Lebrun knitted his brows, looking extraordinarily grave; his head was sunk deeply into his broad shoulders.

He coughed in exasperation.

"So I shan't even be able to do *that* for you?" he said. "I shall have to sit by you and watch you suffering—without being allowed to move a finger."

"Yes," answered Kansdorf, sinking back on the pillow. "That's what I want you to do."

"But why?"

"I can't say. I only know that it's the right thing to do. Perhaps I can come nearest to what I feel if I tell you that I'm expecting something to happen to me before I die. I *must* stay awake. I *must* become a different person. And it is conceivable that—under pressure, so to speak—I shall be able to manage it. In any case I know that I've no power to change myself by being well. And so I'm prepared to accept the suffering I've been complaining about for so long: you've heard me at it! And so, too, I don't intend my life to end before God Himself wills it."

"Thanks," said Lebrun. "That gives me my answer. Allow me to add: an uncommonly crazy answer, a loathsome answer, which amongst other things assumes the existence of a God whom I have no desire to raise my hat to."

He was furious, but controlled himself when he saw Kansdorf smiling. A gentle, peaceful smile. It's remarkable, the state of lucidity and freedom he has reached, he thought. What a compelling power these old myths have, after all! They know what they're up to, those priests and monks! Or is it—Katharina?

"You must realize," said Kansdorf, "that all this seems quite queer to me too. But you will never be able to shake my conviction that someone is obstinately, continuously, working upon me."

"Do you mean me?" asked Lebrun.

Kansdorf smiled.

"Oh, yes, you too, of course," he said. "And as this Person who is working upon me gives me a sense of pure love, as He was prepared to lay down His life for me, I intend to obey Him—properly—right to the end."

He raised himself up on his elbows again.

252

"Look here, my dear chap," he said, "I like your cynicism, because it's simply your way of trying to clear the air of cant and illusion. I like the way you put things, because it shows how modest and self-deprecating you are. In you too there is a subtle, secret power at work, and you should admit it without more ado. I'm terribly keen that you should *not* take my life away from me, Lebrun! Leave it alone, please! And then, of course, you won't be breaking the law or your oath as a doctor, either. But come and see me again, as often as you can. Now I feel rather tired. . . ."

Lebrun went almost at once.

On the stairs he stopped for a while, pondering. The psychological effect of the experiences Kansdorf had had was obvious. But were they—*realities?* He was quite prepared to grant that a battle between powerful forces went on in human beings, he had seen it in his patients. He regarded any purely materialistic philosophy as a form of simpleminded superstition. But to pray! To get down on one's knees and believe that one was eating a god! To imagine that God had a Son who had sacrificed Himself for our sins, my—Jules Lebrun's—sins! Ridiculous!

He laughed softly, went down to the first floor, and stopped again.

He heard someone come into the building and ask the caretaker where Kansdorf lived. The caretaker answered, and he thought he recognized the voice as it said thank you. He went on his way downstairs. At the bottom of the narrow staircase, half in darkness, he passed a friar, who stepped to one side without looking up.

But Lebrun could see his face. It was a drawn, pale, exhausted face. The friar went slowly past him, holding heavily onto the banisters.

It was Father Perezcaballero.

CHAPTER TWENTY-SIX

Father Perezcaballero had remained in bed for a long time, like one stunned. He read nothing, saw no one. Dom Dusolier had come to see him, but had hardly said a word: he had simply sat by his bedside in silence and prayed, or, as usual, half-dozed. Perezcaballero scarcely noticed his going, but afterwards he found on the table by his bed a piece of paper on which the old man had written a few shaky words.

Perezcaballero left the paper lying there for several days before he could rouse himself sufficiently to read it.

"... *quaesumus, Domine: ad te nostras etiam rebelles compelle propitius voluntates.* ..."

"O God, direct our wills to yourself, even when they resist you. ..."

For a long time this was Perezcaballero's only prayer. Indeed, it was the most man could do, to ask God to give his rebellious will a different direction.

Physically he soon recovered and was able to get up. But he didn't look at his books. For most of the time he wandered round his room or the garden, oblivious of the fact that the spring had come. One day a letter arrived from Dom Dusolier. It was only a few lines long. The most important part was the following:

"So it is about time you became active again. The winepress has been labouring long enough, and a few drops must come forth. When I came to see you I found it hard to think straight. But I have prayed for you every day. And now I can see quite clearly what you have to do. You must go and see a certain person who is expecting you. He is a Swede. He joined the Church here in Paris some years ago, on an impulse, I fancy, and without much instruction. He has only recently, I believe, been practising his religion regularly. He often comes to our chapel here. His name is Edvard Kansdorf and he lives at 7, Rue du Bac. Give him my kind regards."

Perezcaballero had read the letter with a feeling of faint despair. This was just about the most preposterous thing one could imagine! To send him off, in his present miserable condition, to some utter stranger, a foreigner, who might easily not be prepared to see him, who wouldn't trust him, to whom he could not possibly be the slightest use. How could the old Benedictine even think of such a thing!

He sat himself down and with real difficulty wrote a reply. He explained that he felt quite useless and unable to do anything to help. He would run the risk of causing serious damage to this soul, instead of bringing him help, and so felt bound to refuse. Perhaps Dom Dusolier would find someone else, if he couldn't go himself.

He took the letter to the post the same morning.

For a few hours he wandered about restlessly in the garden. Then, much to the sisters' surprise, he rushed into the house and up to his room. He wrote a second letter on an odd scrap of paper:

"My dear friend! You have had a letter from me—or will have. Don't read it. I *will* go and see Monsieur Kansdorf tomorrow, first thing."

He telegraphed this note: it would be in Dom Dusolier's hands within the hour.

And the next morning, after Mass, he set off for Kansdorf's. It was not an easy journey. He had grown shy of meeting people. He didn't want to see anyone. Occasionally it seemed to him that some passer-by was looking at him suspiciously. In the Métro he felt queer, and the train seemed to take an unbearably long time. It was only a few yards from the stop to the Rue du Bac.

Only when he saw the Seine embankment shimmering did he realize that it was spring—the trees had been out for a long time, the air was mild, a gentle breeze fanned his face.

Tired and ill he clambered up the two flights of stairs. This *could* only be leading to a new humiliation, a new defeat. Well, he was prepared to accept it, if that was what God wanted. How long would his humiliations go on for? Was he never again to do anything useful? Was he never again to feel any sense of power or inspiration?

He was overcome by a sense of disgust at the thought of what these words had once meant to him. He stood at the door for a while before he knocked. It occurred to him that the stranger he had passed downstairs didn't seem to have moved, or else had gone away very silently. What did that mean? Perhaps his hearing was going.

He was sitting in Kansdorf's room. Kansdorf recognized him—he had often heard him at Sainte Croix and had admired the way he sang. He mentioned this, and to his astonishment saw the expression on the friar's face turn to one of distaste.

Silence fell. Neither of the two men knew what to say. Kansdorf was almost embarrassed: what could he talk to this absolute stranger about, especially such a famous theologian and preacher? What interest could his simple story have for such a man?

Perezcaballero was at his wits' end, and on the point of

256

hurrying away at every moment. But he forced himself to stay. If God wanted to humiliate him, so be it. He could do no more than confess his helplessness.

Kansdorf lay for a while with his eyes closed. Then he began to talk. He hardly gave a thought to the fact that he had a listener. He spoke his whole soul out, trying to see everything quite honestly. Lebrun's many diagnoses and observations, even his cynicism, helped him in this—helped him to avoid self-pity, exaggeration, sentimentality.

He talked about his early life, his rootlessness, his love for Dagny, the way he had worshipped her memory, his sudden discovery, how he had then gone to see the man concerned, and how Dagny had thereafter disappeared from his life, leaving not a trace behind. He couldn't even remember what she looked like. He had left Sweden and lost himself in a mass of unorganized learning and contempt for human beings. He had been left stranded in an absolute void.

Then he had heard strange sounds and signals that he had been unable to decipher. He had felt, from time to time, that he was on the track of a great mystery: a sense of infinite peace had hovered close over his head but he had been unable to ascend to it. Then Katharina had come along, a cool figure who had led him straight to the heart of the mystery. She had been leading him ever since, even though she was only a young girl.

He mentioned the thing that was secretly worrying him. He would soon be dead, and he felt that something was required of him. But what? He didn't know.

At first it had cost Father Perezcaballero a great effort to listen. What did this foreigner mean to him? Nor was his story particularly interesting. He felt a slight stirring of his old sarcastic spirit: human beings were repulsive creatures. But this reaction vanished at once. There could hardly be anyone more repulsive than himself.

257

And suddenly he forgot himself, forgot all about his own existence, saw neither the room nor himself sitting at another man's side, utterly forgot his uncertainty about what to say or do. He slipped into another human being's life. He came back to reality. Again he was standing watching the drama of lies, hypocrisy and self-pity that human beings regard as so important. He seemed to see, in this unimportant and uninteresting personal destiny, two powerful spiritual forces at odds with each other. Kansdorf had all too easily fallen a victim to them; he had failed to put up any appreciable resistance against his own deterioration. A tiny infatuation on the part of his wife, and he had become so depressed that it had turned him into an invalid. What did he know of the real difficulties of living? Instead of ruthlessly analyzing Kansdorf's life, however, he found himself gradually slipping step by step into it, feeling its pain, putting himself on its level. He experienced all the anguish this man had felt in his longing for the unattainable. He saw how for a long time he had only been able to perceive the truth as moments of coolness and purity. And yet, behind all his pitiable striving, he could see how in his helplessness he longed for truth and purity.

In the end he no longer realized that he was listening. He became the other person: he, Perezcaballero, had vanished, lost his own personality.

When Kansdorf came to the end of his story, he sat for a while with his eyes closed. Then he began to speak. He asked a few questions.

Kansdorf realized that by his side was a man familiar with the human soul, a man who didn't fumble, didn't make mistakes. His gentle hand had found the secret spot at once and touched it—tactfully, but firmly. It opened and disclosed its content. He slightly altered the perspective, and everything looked different. He revealed to Kansdorf that he had never really known how to love, that he had always been afraid to go out of himself. He sensed a certain feminine bashfulness and a possible element of perversion in this connection, but he did not mention it: those features had not really come to the fore. He dismissed everything that might suggest an interesting state of dramatic tension, and showed Kansdorf that he was a human being like everyone else—helpless, blind, unable to accept the help that was so close to him, let alone master his life on his own.

Perezcaballero was hardly aware of himself in all this, he was not watching himself, he was a medium for things to go through. He was ready to receive a new setback at any moment, prepared to discover that he was entirely on the wrong track.

Actually he was now making use of his own earlier experience. For many years he had behaved proudly and uncharitably in the world of souls, but nevertheless that was the world he had lived in. He had wide knowledge, considerable intuitive powers, he could recognize obsessions and complexes without much difficulty. He knew an extraordinary amount about the longing for purity and its counterfeits. He was well aware of the tricks the devil could get up to, to confuse people. All these abilities, which for so long had been utilized mechanically, now awoke to life. Delicate weapons, with which he had formerly only played, now came into their proper element: a firm, gentle hand seemed to be guiding them, a quicker and more certain eye could penetrate the confusion.

Kansdorf was amazed. He had never heard anything like it. A pale stranger sat with his eyes closed, hunched up by his side, asking questions in a hoarse monotone. Was this the dazzling preacher he had heard so much about? Now for the first time he was beginning to realize Perezcaballero's real worth. And for the first time he seemed to be seeing himself as he really was. The Church had possessed this kind of human wisdom all along and he had simply not taken advantage of it: he had gone around from one church to another for year after year, sad, homeless, wearing out his trouser-knees kneeling down in pews.

He couldn't bring himself to say anything, and finally Perezcaballero said:

"There are two things you still have to do, two important things—"

Kansdorf listened tensely.

"You must free yourself from Katharina. You must be able to live without her, and only by the grace she has brought you."

Kansdorf started. Free himself from Katharina? He was ready to do anything else, but not that! That was impossible. He couldn't live without Katharina: she was his one hope.

"And you must win your wife back," said Perezcaballero, in the same quiet voice.

Win Dagny back? The idea was absurd. What did he mean? He glanced quickly towards the friar, sitting there hunched up motionless. Did he realize what he was saying? Win back someone who was dead?

"How can I win my wife back?" he asked.

"I don't know," said Perezcaballero. "But God does. But that's where your sin lies, that through pride and self-pity you have broken the bond with your wife."

"But she's—dead!"

Hadn't the friar realized that?

"She is alive," answered Perezcaballero. "She is just as certainly alive as we are. And I am convinced that she has gone on suffering because she brought you trouble and is separated from you. Throughout all these years she has been calling out to you, has come close to you, has been trying to re-establish contact with you. It was she you heard—like a faint breath of wind, an echo; but you didn't want to admit it. She wanted what you did: you had the same longing—although you never understood each other. I can see that quite clearly. You must find her again, you must be united again, as you should always have remained. You must forgive her, as she has forgiven you."

If he had been able to hear his own words he would never have said them. He hardly understood what he was saying: he had never had such thoughts before. He spoke with absolute conviction, though in soft, subdued tones—his voice had grown clear, the hoarseness was beginning to disappear. He could see the whole drama quite clearly in his mind's eye. A relationship had been broken: this man had wandered round blindly, hearing calls in the distance and never recognizing the voice. And in another world the same longing, the same disquiet had been waiting. The spark had to make contact here.

Kansdorf pressed his hands to his face. Dagny, he thought. For a long while now he had felt no bitterness against her, she had simply gone completely from his mind. When he tried to imagine her face, when he tried to hear her voice, he could only see and hear Katharina's. When he tried to remember how she had walked and moved he saw Katharina with her hands in her coat pockets and her head thrown back. And he felt that it was Katharina he *wanted* to see, not Dagny.

For a long time he peered thus within himself. Useless; there was nothing but darkness. He listened. Useless; all was silent—all he could hear was a sighing noise, like telephone wires over a deserted snowy landscape. Dagny? How could he—?

Perezcaballero had begun to speak again.

"Our Lady will lead you back to your wife. You must regard Our Lady as a refuge, someone to be used, made use of: she is the Mother, she is all tenderness, she knows and understands everything."

That was true. He had in the past turned to Mary as to poetry—turned his back on reality. Slowly his condition was being revealed to him. In a few words, a friar who was a stranger to him had given new content to his life, and shown him clearly what he should do.

He heard voices outside. Katharina had come. He felt a pain at his heart. Had he to separate from her? How would he be able to live without her?

Perezcaballero got up and shook him by the hand. Then he laid both his hands on Kansdorf's head and blessed him.

"I shall come again," he said, "if you would like me to—" Kansdorf nodded.

Perezcaballero woke up. What had happened? He seemed to have come back into his own body, his own clothes. He looked round the room. He felt profoundly at peace.

"Good-bye," he said. "You've no idea what this talk has meant to *me*."

To you? thought Kansdorf. To you, an expert, you who know everything, can see through everything, understand everything! You have done nearly all the talking: I've only been listening!

"I—" said Perezcaballero, and a smile stole over his thin face—it had been so long since he had been able to smile that his face objected to it, the muscles didn't want to obey—"I— I thank you. . . ."

Kansdorf looked after him as he went slowly out.

Katharina came in.

She stopped, startled.

"Have you been asleep?" she asked.

"No," he said.

"Are you very ill?"

"Not a bit," he answered. "I feel fresh and light."

She went up to him and fell down on her knees.

"Edvard," she said, "can you imagine—something wonderful has happened to me!"

He looked into her face; her dark serious eyes were aglow with happiness.

"What has happened to you?" he asked slowly.

"I've been to see Abbé Auclair," she said. "We prayed. For a long time. And then we suddenly realized—that I ought to become a nun."

He started.

"Become a nun?" he said softly.

"Yes," she whispered. "With the Benedictines. If I can. And I know I can! God wants me to."

"What makes you think God wants you to?" said Kansdorf. "Haven't you other obligations you're forgetting?"

"No," she answered, leaning her head back and closing her eyes. "Not important ones."

"And why is this so important?" he asked. "To forsake the world—and me," he added, almost inaudibly.

"I shall never forsake you," she said. "I never forsake anyone I love."

EPILOGUE

CHAPTER TWENTY-SEVEN

Kansdorf woke up dripping with sweat. The sheets stuck to his back.

Lebrun had given him morphia, the pain had died down, he had been able to sleep. Now the respite was over; he was gradually coming back to his senses and the pain was increasing.

Katharina was out.

The shutters were drawn but he sensed that there was sunshine outside. Without opening his eyes he could see the cold blue walls, so like the walls of a mortuary. He had fallen down on the steps in front of the chapel; the monks had immediately carried him silently inside. Now he was lying in the hospital on the other side of the monastery garden. Was he imagining it, or could he really hear, faintly, the monks singing?

He lay with his eyes closed. Far away, vague figures were moving at the altar. The Host was being held up in the air, he felt himself rising up in the same movement. He was lying before the altar, the paten was gliding towards him, the next moment he would open his mouth to receive the Body of Our Lord. . . .

He shivered as though caught in a sudden icy draught. The iron curtains came down with a crash, but were immediately shattered by something blue and icy: an invisible mailed boot suddenly broke through cracking ice that fretted and tore at his nerves. He hurled himself to one side, to get away from the kicks, and yet he could feel at the same time that he was still lying still. The pain was coming on, he would soon be caught in its crippling hold again. He seemed to feel the warm, powerful body of a woman lying by his side.

He struggled to free himself from the image. The movement pulled down a wall that had been protecting him: the woman's body, covered with sweat, became a fighter in the ring, with shining limbs, groaning in an agonized attempt to struggle out of the humiliating leghold; he could hear the shrieks and screams in the sports' stadium, he himself was lying in the ring being tortured, his spine bent back as far as it would go, about to break at any moment.

Oh, what evil, damp, white power was this, overpowering him, choking him!

A heavy black head was nodding in agreement like the pendulum of a clock, its dark shadow flitting hither and thither over the room: so must it always be, so had it always been, *sicut erat in principio, et nunc, et semper, et in saecula saeculorum.* As it was in the beginning, is now and ever shall be, world without end. Amen.

It was Lebrun.

Could he nod like that, with his short neck?

A gust of wind blew the window shutter open on the left, then immediately banged it to again; he sank back and lost consciousness.

The ants were swarming out again, rushing frantically over his wet body, trying to get inside him and bite him: they grew larger, he saw two of them fighting, they had strange heads and bulging eyes and they were tearing each other's head and legs off. Their pain was his own.

Fleeting firelight flickered over him—no, he was not dead, life still coursed through him, he must still be alive to be able to feel this burning pain.

268

Where was the sound of the horn, the cool, liberating sound of the horn? Where was Katharina? Why had she gone? Didn't she realize that he couldn't live without her?

Moonlight exterminated the ants and all life; on the stony ground lay the dead limbs of the dead; *in medio campi qui erat plenus ossibus*—in the midst of a plain that was full of bones. He heard the resounding voice: "Dost thou think these bones shall live?" He was unable to answer. New life? The blue bones moved and joined themselves up to form skeletons, he heard the faint swoosh as the heads of the joints snapped into their sockets. When he surveyed the scene he saw nerves and sinews, skin and muscle growing over the bones, he realized that the miracle was about to take place, he saw the heads of the corpses being covered over with flesh and delicate white skin and he waited for the eyes to open—in a moment the landscape would come alive, a mighty army would rise up under the gentle light of the moon.

The delirium enveloped him, he closed his eyes although they were already closed, he tried to disappear behind more curtains, he felt around like an insect with innumerable arms so as to bring the iron curtains rattling down, he heard them coming, he cast one last look at the moonlit landscape with the waiting dead bodies that would never come back to life— everything went out as the curtains thundered down, he could see nothing at all for the dust and smoke, he sank down into welling greyness that hid everything, brought pain, was vague and indefinite.

The dust subsided, he lay perfectly still; without looking up he could sense the vault of the cosmos green and mouldy above him. He seemed to be lying on sharp stones—or was it a corpse? The arena was empty, he had been left alone, with his backbone broken, his arms torn off; soon the ants would be swarming over him. Oh, this night of death, in which horrors came riding over invisible black waters!

If only he could go on lying still! If he stood up, the horror would come in—all the animals he had ever hunted would hunt him; now it was his turn, nothing was forgotten. . . .

He was rushing over bogs with aching legs, stumbling through hedges, banging against the trunks and stumps of trees, drawing blood: behind him the whole wood was in an uproar—all the things he had ever murdered—foxes running behind him, woodcock falling down between the branches, and, close behind, the bloodhounds, their lean, snow-wet chests working, their baying echoing amongst the trees. He threw himself first to one side then the other, made desperate lunges, but there was not a moment's respite, always the bloodhounds were behind him, a lot of them now, baying thunderously, and birds lusting for his blood were roaring over his head—there was the great eagle he had shot when he was a young man: it had left the pedestal it had been set up on, stuffed, in the hall at home, and was now roaring along with its wings of hate beating over his head, ready to hack away at him with its steely beak.

His heart thumped to bursting point, he wouldn't be able to go on running much longer. His eyes filled with tears, he rushed straight at something in his way, tried to dodge it, was torn by thorns and more thorns until he was nearly unconscious, and in the end he collapsed, tried to burrow his way in, to take cover, to vanish. But under him, preventing him, lay the dead woman. He couldn't make out who she was—someone he had wronged, had hated, betrayed. She was no longer there, she was truly dead, but her corpse still prevented him from disappearing.

Again he was lying amongst the dead limbs on the moonlit landscape, but how was it that he was the only one alive amongst all these dead? Why live, when one was dead?

Because of Katharina. Because she had gone, but was there. Because without her. . . .

He suddenly saw Katharina.

Her face with its burning eyes and half-open mouth—towards whom was she coming, white, arms outstretched? The one she loved. He couldn't see him. She was moving towards him, the one she loved must be behind him—she couldn't see *him* at all—oh, it was dreadful to see her going past him, with her eyes shining blissfully and her arms, her white arms, stretched out before her, while he lay there unable to move. She couldn't see him, though she could have touched him with her hand. He didn't exist; he was dead—and who looks at the dead? But someone was standing behind him, someone alive and full of love—full of love for Katharina. He it was that she was going forward to meet, blind with ecstasy. He tried to turn round, but had to lie there, as though bound tightly to the damp skeleton under him, unable to make a single move. His head hurt as he tried to look round, back through himself, back through his own brain: he wanted to see this other person, fathom the secret which had succeeded in enticing Katharina away from him. But he couldn't see anything. Now Katharina was by his side, he could see her unbearably close to him, see her countenance filled with ecstasy, overflowing with love and devotion. Now he realized what the light was: the warm, powerful radiance that had overpowered Katharina, seizing her and taking possession of her, was the radiance of God, the radiance of God!

He felt the holiness and power and the lucid light behind him, and he saw Katharina glide slowly past him: he could make out every feature of her beloved face. Yes, it was the great Peace, she wanted to rest in its arms and nowhere else, nothing else existed for her. Now she was walking past him: he could see the light gleaming on her forehead, her damp lips were trembling, her eyes tightly closed. . . .

Then she had gone past him, a cold breath blew against his damaged back, pain afflicted his whole body, over him there arose the mouldy green cold vault, there was a droning in his ears as though powerful machines were at work in the heavens, he realized that these motors were inside himself too, he would burst apart, Lebrun wanted that, Lebrun had given him morphia so that he should be torn in two and go up in what was cold and grey and endless. Far behind him he could sense Katharina, played upon by heavenly light, but she gradually disappeared and soon he would be unable even to remember her—oh, he would rather lie here throughout eternity, fast-bound to the paining skeleton under him, than lose her for ever!

The engines throbbed in his temples, the cosmos trembled as though before the end. And suddenly he was free and standing, faintly giddy, upright, not himself but all pain, but knowing with dreadful clarity, in the midst of the pain that

It was all lies!

It was not true!

There was no refreshment, no peace!

There was only cold mouldy death!

He felt a pressure on his chest—he broke into pieces at the same moment as the cupola was shattered and the mouldiness crashed down upon him from all sides.

He fell, and during the endless fall he felt at his side—but faster than he—the iron curtains rattling down towards the bottom of the bottomless abyss.

CHAPTER TWENTY-EIGHT

The delirium declined. He was brought food, the pain was deadened, at times he was even able to read a book. No one was more surprised at this than he was. He didn't feel exactly joyful about it. He had felt new life flowing into him during the last few months, and now everything seemed dead again. Perezcaballero had come to see him from time to time, but he had hardly listened to him. The strong impression which the priest had made on him the first time he had met him had faded, and he now felt only distaste at the prospect of further visits. He knew what the friar would say: he should free himself from Katharina and stick to what she symbolized—Our Lord, Divine Love. The words seemed meaningless to him.

Perezcaballero realized he was eluding him. He was prepared for it: nothing seemed more natural to him than that this struggle should end in failure too. How could he mean anything to anyone who was in trouble when he himself had no real integrity to offer? But he persisted. One day he went to see Dom Dusolier, who told him that all he had to do was to go on, patiently: the outcome lay with God, not with himself. Perhaps an absolutely useless friar like himself was precisely what God needed in this case.

One day he had been sitting by Kansdorf's bed for quite a long time, trying to pray for him. When he looked up he found Kansdorf watching him with a smile on his face.

"Are you praying for me?" he asked.

"Yes," answered the friar.

"Why are you doing that?"

"Because I should like to help you."

"To do what?"

The friar didn't look up. Then, astonished at his own thought, he said:

"To make the great leap."

"What leap?"

Perezcaballero realized that the moment had come.

"Have you ever climbed up a ladder leaning against a high wall or a cliff?" he said. "Maybe you can imagine it, anyway. The ladder is narrow, it sways, and the cliff wall is slippery: you can't be sure that it will hold, and the higher you go the more difficult it becomes. However, you get to the top. But at that moment the ladder tips over. You could stretch your hand out and seize hold of a branch growing out of the cliff. But at the same time you feel that you mustn't do that. You must let yourself fall back, right down to the bottom again. You know that there is someone down there to catch you. You can't prove it, you've never seen him, but that's what you believe. And this belief of yours is stronger than the evidence of your senses. To let oneself fall in this way, trusting to an invisible helper—that's what Christianity means, that's what living like a Christian means."

He closed his eyes. Did he himself possess this courage that he was recommending to his fellow human beings? He knew that the question was irrelevant. He was not here to bring someone else down to his own unsatisfactory level, he was here as a priest, to bring a man to God. But the knowledge that he himself had not practised what he preached weighed heavily on him. He was speaking as much to himself as to the man in front of him. And once again he observed that a

274

thought only really becomes a thought—and a resolution—when it takes shape, gets spoken.

Kansdorf had closed his eyes too. The scene was before his eyes. Did the way out really exist, for him? Throwing oneself down to the ground: that was bound to mean accepting suffering and misery. Did he want that? Could his feeble, fortuitous glimpses of another world really have given him such a sense of security that he was prepared to base his life on them?

"Yes," he said softly. "Perhaps you're right, Father. But it's too late. I haven't much time left. You should have come along twenty years ago!"

"In God's eyes there is no such thing as time," said the friar, quite peaceably, much to his own surprise. "The poor thief on the cross, just before he died, went through a process that can take years and years in the case of many virtuous struggling people."

"What then?" answered Kansdorf, who felt his head swimming, "What do you want of me? What am I to do?"

"Accept your position, joyfully," answered Perezcaballero. "Your present one, and your past one; your whole life. Like most of us, you have always fled from suffering, and simply landed yourself up in worse. That is the way the natural man always behaves. But nobody can escape his suffering. It follows him like his shadow. One has to endure one's suffering and not try to dodge it!"

Was it really himself speaking? Wasn't someone else speaking, to *him*?

"I have accepted it," answered Kansdorf. "For half my life I have been trying to put up with this pain that has been sent me."

Perezcaballero nodded.

"Many people do that. Stoics do it, in their own way. Perhaps you have really been a Stoic. But that simply means pushing the pain into the background, trying to camouflage it, trying to work upon it psychologically so as not to feel it any more, trying to block all the ways leading back to the event itself. That isn't a liberation. You can see it yourself: as soon as Katharina leaves you the old wound reopens and you find it bleeding as much as ever! It *hasn't* been healed!"

Kansdorf made a violent gesture.

"What do you ask of me, then?" he said. "What should I have done? Didn't I have the right to be sad that the woman I loved fell in love with someone else and kept me in the dark about it?"

"Yes, you had the right to sorrow and to suffer," answered the friar. "Perhaps, indeed, even a duty to do so. There are two things a man has to consider when he is afflicted by suffering. One is that however severe it may be, it is insignificant compared with the punishment he really deserves for his selfishness and lack of charity. The second thing is that instead of trying to escape from his suffering he can accept it as a duty laid upon him, a gift. Our Lord humbly took all our pain upon Himself. We are called upon to imitate Him, to take upon ourselves our own share of His suffering. The only real way to freedom is to regard suffering as a duty to be performed."

"No one can do that," answered Kansdorf. "Can you expect a deceived husband to love his wife's lover, or a prisoner to love his judges? It's impossible. No one can do it."

"A lot of people can do it," answered Perezcaballero. "Christianity is precisely the history of such things, heroic deeds like that. Most people think it manly and heroic to fight against their suffering, and whenever possible to avoid it. Modern literature is concerned with practically nothing else. But how much more noble and great-hearted and 'manly' it would be to accept suffering, for Our Lord's sake! Not to go looking for it. But to accept it as a duty when it comes."

276

"The cuckold is 'nobly' to accept his wife's infidelity?" said Kansdorf. "Thank you for the information. Do you yourself believe what you are saying for a single moment?"

"We are quite free to avoid suffering if we want to," said Perezcaballero. "No one is forcing us to accept it. But Our Lord taught us—by His life as well as His words—that it is a decent, manly thing to do, to ask God for the strength to accept and endure suffering whenever it comes to us. It serves a purpose. The saints could give thanks for humiliations and pains and rejoice over them because God considered them worthy to be singled out for such trials. People like us can't do that, perhaps, but we should at least realize that we should at least suffer without moaning and self-pity."

He looked at Kansdorf and was amazed at the result his words seemed to have had. The sick man was staring at him with glowing eyes.

Finally Kansdorf said:

"For all these years, as you know, I have been a seeker. I have been seeking a truth, a meaning. I have never been given a helping hand, any kind of release, or even a lead. All I managed to do was to catch faint, obscure signs. And I tried to follow them up. It is not easy to walk in almost total darkness."

"Walking in the dark can be a great distinction," said Perezcaballero.

"Thank you, Father," he said. "But tell me one thing: can you do it yourself?"

He didn't notice that the friar turned pale at this.

"No," answered Perezcaballero. "But I know that it's the only way—for me, and for you."

He got up and came to Kansdorf's bed.

"You have lived in the dark. You have entered into a condition of irremediable desolation. That is perfectly normal, it is the end of every natural human life. But with a

277

single resolve, in as short a time as it takes to make it, you can cut through this darkness and be where you have longed to be all these years. That could happen now, before I leave this room."

Kansdorf shook his head.

"I don't believe it," he said. "I don't believe it."

Perezcaballero looked at him steadily.

"Nevertheless you know quite well," he said softly, "that some gentle, beneficent power has been working through your life. That is what led you to church, to the liturgy, to the truth. That is the power you must give way to. You will do that the moment you realize and acknowledge that it is a loving power. Then you will clearly recognize that the other power you followed, the power which told you to defend yourself, to avoid suffering in resentment and fear, is not the power of love but the power of evil. *Why* did you follow this evil spirit? Beside it there stands another, who wishes you well! You know it! You have been looking for it for years! You need to open yourself to it with everything that is healthy in you! Do so, now!"

He stood there, eyes lowered, and slowly prayed:

> *Crux mihi certa salus,*
> *Crux est quam semper adoro,*
> *Crux Domini mecum,*
> *Crux mihi refugium . . .*[1]

Kansdorf lay motionless, his eyes closed, the sweat gleaming on his forehead.

Perezcaballero bent over him and made the sign of the cross on his forehead.

"Soon it will be Good Friday, when the whole Christian

---

[1] "The Cross is my sure salvation
The Cross I always adore
The Cross of the Lord is with me
The Cross is my refuge. . . ."

world shares the sufferings of the Redeemer. Don't you realize that you belong to that great company, that you are only taking upon yourself your share of the suffering that mankind needs for its redemption? Give thanks for your pain, bless it! And look calmly through the darkness towards Easter Sunday. It is approaching, for you too!"

Kansdorf lay motionless. Had he been listening? Perhaps he had fallen asleep? Perhaps all these words had been wasted? Perezcaballero made the sign of the cross over him again and moved slowly to the door. Had he turned round he would have seen the invalid open his eyes and look after him: in them was a mingling of resentment and regret. . . .

CHAPTER TWENTY-NINE

Out in the corridor, Perezcaballero stood for a long time without moving. He had closed his eyes. Through the open window he could hear birds singing. Someone went softly past him: a nun.

He felt a surge of melancholy come over him. Who was he, to say such things to a man at death's door?

He saw it clearly: the words he had spoken were aimed just as much at himself. It was he himself who had to step into his period of suffering. It was a gift from God to himself, that he had been brought in pain and shame to the ground. He was in the winepress—not to be tortured, but to give out wine. A strong but gentle hand was working upon his soul too: he could see deep down into the hopeless waste and selfishness of his life, and yet at the same time he knew that though his thoughts had always revolved round his own beloved ego and he had ignored the voice of God, he had still remained the object of His love. The strong hand had been working indefatigably upon him, continually offering him new openings. If he had squandered them, new means must come along. He suddenly realized that he would never have made any progress without the defeat he had suffered. Nothing would have shaken him up. Further success would have reduced him to a condition of spiritual death. All at once he felt profoundly thankful.

Oh, those years when, with the attentive eye of the connoisseur, he had followed all the stages of his own religious development, comparing himself with the mystics, discovering with delight which particular stage he had reached in his trials, which particular point he had arrived at on the way to perfection! He had imagined that he was seeing the experiences of the saints repeated in himself. When he went to confession, he had felt something like awe coming towards him from the priests he confessed to: the hard inner suffering, the emptiness and fear which he had felt at times, they had seized upon—and so had he—as an infallible sign that he was one of the elect.

It had all been futile. He had lacked charity. He had been empty. He had been thinking about himself the whole time. And so everything had collapsed. Now he was standing firmly on his own two feet. He must begin again from zero. It would mean anguish and humiliation. But at the same time great security. God's love was working untiringly upon him. He had at last seen himself as he was—paltry, empty, full of self-love. And yet he felt that he was loved.

Engrossed in his thoughts, he walked slowly on. As he was about to pass through the gate he came upon Dr. Lebrun. The doctor's eyes rested on him. The friar looked different: thin, badly shaved, very different from the elegant figure of former days.

Lebrun stopped him—the fellow interested him. Was it really possible that he had at last seen through himself?

He pulled Perezcaballero into a waiting room. He said he wanted to talk to him about Kansdorf.

After a few casual introductory questions he suddenly said: "I'm not sure you're having a good influence on him."

"Nor am I," answered Perezcaballero. "That's why I try not to have any influence on him."

"Aren't all these talks and confessions simply so many attempts to influence him?"

"Yes, they are, but it's not me, it's God, who does the influencing."

Lebrun grimaced.

"I suppose there's a difference," he answered. "If only one could be sure of it."

Lebrun sat for a long time without speaking. He felt unsure of himself. At last, however, he resolutely dismissed all disturbing trains of thought and tackled the matter nearest to his heart.

"It's my opinion," he said, "that you—and the other priests —have done Kansdorf a great deal of harm. I have been a friend of his for a long time and I know the difficulties he has had. He has been destroyed by his own idealism. He is pursuing a phantom. He is one of those unfortunate people who cannot see, cannot grasp, what's there. When they meet a woman they could love they back out, they are too much afraid of humiliating themselves—and the woman concerned —by following their impulses. They want to adore her. Then other people who are not so scrupulous come along and take the woman away from them. For she always wants to be taken. Kansdorf is an absolute model of that sort of noble idealist who can never win a woman's first love. He has to be satisfied with the ones who get left over. I tried—in a very cynical way, I must admit frankly—to get him to lead a healthier sort of life. I tried to instil a little healthy realism into him. He was well on the way to it. But then you monks come along with your talk about sacrifice and this drives him into a sort of adoration of this Russian girl that is utterly remote from reality—he should either have left her or taken her. He did neither: he contented himself with her 'soul.' And you support the whole thing!"

Perezcaballero nodded.

"But don't you realize that that was bound to lead to

further conflicts? I tried to turn Kansdorf into a man, a man fit to live. You have stopped me."

Perezcaballero looked out of the window.

"I don't know whether that's true," he said. "I haven't known him long. But I should like to think that it's true."

Lebrun waved his short arms furiously.

"As a matter of fact I've no very great opinion of this being 'fit to live,' " Perezcaballero went on calmly. "I'm not so very much struck on people being masculine and virile—in your sense! A man isn't less decent because he possesses characteristics that you would call womanish. In these sex-obsessed days Our Lord would have seemed womanish, yet there has never been any more manly person than He was. The thing our friend is longing and seeking for is a whole, complete, free human being, not half a one. He found this first in his wife, but he wasn't sufficiently grown up then to appreciate it. His failure drove him to despair and into a—typically masculine—sort of self-assertion. But the longing persisted, still drawing him in his deepest self towards freedom and wholeness. He found his ideal in the young Russian girl. He was wise to hold on to her."

"You say that, yet you know as well as I do that letting her go will mean a complete breakdown for him!"

"A human breakdown doesn't worry me all that much. Most of what is in men *has to* break down."

"But he's a dying man!"

"Probably he'll die quite soon. That's nothing to be frightened about. The important thing is what he can experience *before* he dies."

"So you think he should lie there as long as he can, in torture?"

"More than that. He must *accept* his torture! He must *will* his suffering!"

"Why?"

"Because it's the only way to freedom."

Lebrun lifted his arms, goggled, stiff-necked, and emitted his short laugh. It sounded more like a shriek of contempt.

"Monkish psychology, monkish ethics!" he cried. "You bind people and upset people, you take what little chance they have of being happy away from them. And now as a special kind of penance Kansdorf has to go on lying there, tormenting himself to death. Wouldn't it be more sensible, now, to put an end to the business completely? To stop giving him morphia, for instance?"

Perezcaballero avoided the doctor's eyes.

"Did you intend to *kill* your friend?" he said slowly. "Was that your intention?"

Lebrun laughed, then at once grew serious again.

"I intended to *help* him," he answered hoarsely. "It's my job to help people. That's the only thing I'm interested in. That's why people annoy me when they get in my way and stop me!"

Perezcaballero turned his eyes upon the doctor. He could see through the rough shell, could see through to the essence, the good will—despite his toughness, he was from his own point of view only behaving reasonably. Fundamentally he was in error, of course, but compared to himself he was a decent, upstanding man.

"I think I understand you," he said. "I appreciate your motives. But you must realize that I too am on the side of life and reality. It's only that it's a different kind of life and a different kind of reality. I don't want Kansdorf to be happy in your sense, to be given the fulfilment of a certain number of futile wishes: that wouldn't bring him any real happiness. What I want—just like you—is for him to see the truth. And he can't see that unless he gets out of the state of illusion and bitterness he's in. Everything that is spiritually healthy in him wants to finish with cynicism and despair. He is at this moment in the midst of his final crisis. He must go through with it. He must learn to see himself as he really is."

"But that's precisely what I want!" cried Lebrun. "That's the whole object of my work!"

"Then we're of the same mind," said Perezcaballero. "But neither of us could influence him to any appreciable extent just now. He must try to do what he has to do all by himself. The only thing we can do for him is to pray for him. Will you pray with me that he may reach the truth before he dies?"

"I don't pray," answered Lebrun. "I see a friend of mine going under, like a wreck, though he could be a whole man. I admit that from a higher point of view that may not matter. But I am his friend and I wish him well."

"I believe you," answered the friar. "But the whole man he should become is not the pleasure-lover who has to get as much for himself as everyone else gets so as not to feel he has been cheated. The whole man is the man who feels himself to be in a right relationship with God, who *is* reality, the man who realizes that of himself he can do nothing and prays for God's strength."

"Thanks," said Lebrun. "I know all these expressions. 'My strength is made perfect in your weakness': nonsense! A nice description for impotence and being defeated by life! The philosophy of the underdog—people who are not able to face up to the demands life makes on them comforting themselves with the thought that it is really nobler to grow resigned and give up the ghost."

"Christ gave up the ghost, into His Father's hands," answered Perezcaballero. "No one was ever more thoroughly cast down, more humiliated, from the human point of view more thoroughly defeated. Even you must admit that there is no greater power than His?"

Lebrun shrugged his shoulders and walked over to the window. He loosened his tie, which seemed to have become

285

too tight for him. He was just about to turn around and reply when he caught sight of two figures in the monastery garden. One was a monk. The other was his own son Louis. He let out a sudden snarl, grabbed his hat from the table, and to Perezcaballero's great astonishment dashed hurriedly out of the room.

As soon as Lebrun had rounded the corner of the buildings and reached the monastery gate he knocked furiously on the window of the porter's lodge. He must be allowed into the garden at once, he said.

"Which of the Fathers do you want to speak to?"

"The one who is talking to my son."

"Don't you know his name?"

"No. I only just saw him, from the hospital, on the other side."

The monk gave him an inquiring look from behind the window. On his well-nigh impassive face there might even have been the suspicion of a smile. He pressed a button and the monastery door opened.

Lebrun entered in some confusion. It was the first time he had set foot in a monastery. There was nobody about. The alley leading through the cloisters was absolutely deserted. He walked out into the garden, which lay in the deep shade of mighty poplar and lime trees. At the far end a monk was strolling with a book in his hand. A different monk. Where was Louis?

Lebrun hurried right through the garden without seeing a soul. Was it possible that the monk at the entrance had been playing a trick on him? Hadn't he seemed to notice, as he came in, a faintly mocking smile on the fellow's face?

He went back to find out. A door opened and a monk emerged. Lebrun could see that he was coming out of the chapel. The monk, with a smile, held the door open, assum-

ing that the stranger wanted to go in. Lebrun felt obliged to
do so. He had a sudden feeling that he would find his boy
inside.

At first he couldn't see a thing, but soon he caught sight
of Louis kneeling with one of the monks in the very front
pew. He was seized with sudden rage: here, absolutely against
his will, something utterly unheard-of was going on—and
behind his back, too! Some perfect stranger had taken it upon
himself to interfere in his son's life, rob him of his freedom.
He was about to stride forward towards the altar, but something held him back. To his own astonishment he remained
standing there absolutely still.

He saw the figure of the kneeling boy, the short neck, the
black hair. Not a movement. Deep silence. What was going on
in this mysterious darkness? He tried to shake off the influence
of the place, for it seemed to be taking hold of him too, but
he was unable to. He felt half of him resisting, while the other
half had come to rest, yielded, wanted to stay. Deep within
him he heard a voice: "Fear not, no evil will happen to you
or your boy here!" He sat down on one of the seats and his
body slumped forward. He gripped the back of the seat in
front. He was a stranger to these feelings. His will seemed
to be giving way, as though he was losing all self-discipline and
self-control. This should really have filled him with a sense
of horror and disgust: he had always been afraid of such a
condition. But to his great surprise the exact opposite happened. He fell into a kind of security, a kind of peace, that
he had never known before. He sat quite still and closed his
eyes.

He was awakened by a slight noise and looked up. The
monk and his son had got up, they were genuflecting towards
the altar—the monk firmly and confidently, the boy a little
clumsily. Then they went out through the door into the
monastery garden. For a moment he caught sight of his son's

287

face, and was surprised: he had never seen it shining like that before. He wasn't smiling, but his eyes were glowing, he was walking slowly, delicately—he was transported, unaware of the things around him, wrapped in his own immediate experience.

Lebrun held on tightly to the back of the seat, his eyes following the boy until he disappeared. Oughtn't he to go after him and take him away?

He got up, but hadn't the will to follow them. Heavy-footed, his shoes creaking, he went up to the altar. This was where his son had knelt down, where he had met—whom? A kind of person, at least, whom his father had never found.

For a long time he stood motionless, failing to notice an old monk who had slowly come in and moved up to his side. It was Dom Dusolier. The monk looked towards the solitary man, head askew, then smiled his own peculiar smile and carefully laid his hand on his shoulder.

Lebrun turned slowly from the hips, his head unmoving on his massive shoulders, eyebrows knitted tightly together.

Dom Dusolier smiled and nodded.

"No," he said gently. "Not—not like that. I know what you're thinking. It affects us all like that at the start. But there is something much wiser—"

"What's that?" asked Lebrun abruptly.

"To kneel down," the monk said amiably. He nodded and went off, but before doing so pressed Lebrun lightly on the shoulder, as though trying with his feeble old strength to force him to his knees.

Lebrun's lips tightened.

Never, he thought. Never will I kneel down.

Dom Dusolier had disappeared behind the altar.

Lebrun remained standing motionless.

Then, heavily, he knelt, and mechanically put his hands up in front of his face.

He waited.

He saw a great frightening void.

He got up again and looked round the church: no one had seen him.

He went towards the door.

When he came up to the porter's window he saw the Turkish monk's inquiring gaze. He raised his short arms, his body shook from the waist up, and, like a distant rumble of thunder, came his laugh.

The Turk looked in astonishment at this stranger who laughed without moving his face and whose eyes looked so inexpressibly sad.

Then the door latch fell gently into place behind him, and everything was quiet again in the monastery of Sainte Marie.

CHAPTER THIRTY

Kansdorf came back to consciousness from a state of utter exhaustion. He was unable to open his eyes. Someone was busy in his room: he couldn't tell whether it was Lebrun or the sister. Despite the morphia he could feel the pain. He had been far away.

He saw Dagny on her deathbed. She had gone through all this. She had never complained. She had said only one word: "Forgive!" When he came to think about it, that was probably the only request she had ever made of him. During their marriage she had never expressed any wishes or demands: she had always simply done what was required of her, calmly and without complaint. And yet, her one request—he had refused. He had never forgiven her. On the contrary, his life had been made miserable by his implacability. What he was now experiencing was the last phase of his violent obstinacy.

It was Good Friday. He knew because the nuns had been talking about it. He had heard the singing in the morning.

He lost consciousness and sank back again into the darkness. Things were swarming around him, the darkness woke into slimy grey life. The dry ground of the moonlit landscape turned wet, became alive, at any moment it might begin to move. It was as though the boundaries between living and dead were decomposing. Even the established creation was about to be loosed, to melt into foulness and evil. Slowly a mighty work of destruction was being accomplished. The mouldiness increased and spread. A stench ascended to his nostrils: he knew that it came from himself. He had his share in this deliquescence, it was going on in him and through him: in a certain sense he had *willed* it. To his horror he realized that it was not solely disgust that he felt. There was something in him that welcomed it with joy, an ancient longing was alive in him for precisely this—for everything to decompose into chaos and rank badness.

A cold shiver ran over him.

Once again he was lying under the cold vault. Gusts of wind swept over the endless wet plain. The gusts slapped against his face and each time they did so he was hurled to one side like a falling tree and plunged into the wet and dark. Despite the dark, the air was lit by a flickering light, like the last stages of a remote battle, the last attempts of all that was bright and upright to see the thing through. It was not to succeed. The front was driven back. He himself was in the defeated zone. Here no change was possible, in this darkness everything was ultimately lost, throughout all eternity the decomposing would go on until everything was reduced to a jelly-like stinking mass.

Far away in the distance the firelight still flickered nervously, and when, without raising himself up on his elbows, he looked out into the distance he discovered that it was made up of myriads of waiting human beings; many of them were kneeling, they were all sombre with sadness and terror, some were looking away to the battle in the distance. He was one of the many, and yet not one of them. He had already been hit. He didn't have their hope. He had given way. He felt a feeling of malign pleasure that now, at last, it was all over.

He heard singing: was it coming from all the creatures kneeling there in anguish, still hoping?

> *Agios o Theos!*
> *Sanctus Deus!*
> *Agios ischyros!*
> *Sanctus fortis!*
> *Agios athanatos, eleison imas!*
> *Sanctus immortalis, miserere nobis!*[1]

Wasn't the light flickering up? Wasn't the brightness increasing? He saw the reflections of the light hurled hither and thither in the distance, which became a sea of rolling waves breaking upon a beach. How could kneeling human beings become long waves roaring forward, ebbing and flowing, striving to reach the coast? And how could waves sing? How could the roaring have become singing?

A flickering radiance, as though from a lighthouse or a powerful arc lamp, cut a segment in the darkness, he could no longer see the dead mouldy vault but instead there was a mighty monastic church; as the cone of light played hither and thither he saw the monks, head by head, man by man, faith by faith, with unwavering eyes and open mouths, singing and looking towards the flickering battle in the distance. But he himself was lying outside in the darkness. Because he himself had willed it so.

The arm of light had turned and disappeared. Would it come back again? He waited in a state of agonized impatience. Then it came gliding over the breaking waves again, nearer

---

[1] "Holy God!
   Holy God!
   Holy Strong one!
   Holy Strong one!
   Holy Immortal One, have mercy on us!
   Holy Immortal One, have mercy on us!"

to him, but this time it was weaker, it was illuminating a road, and on the road he could momentarily make out a solitary figure walking with raised arms away from him towards the flickering battle. He made a violent movement which brought the pain in his body flaring up, and saw that it was Katharina. He recognized her by the way she walked, by her upright carriage, and although she had her back to him and he had his eyes closed he could see her pale face with its deep-set eyes grown dark with longing. He knew that he didn't exist for her, that she had forgotten him, that she was only looking towards the distant point of light, now threatening to disappear.

Now everything had gone dark again, stiff with frost, wet and cold. Why didn't he too go out, like the dead pulp fermenting around him? Why had he to go on seeing?

Now the cone of light swung high over his head, it didn't illuminate anything, it shot out into the air in vain, unable to reach the vault; but under the feeble, shifting beam he sensed an endless number of people, all bowed down under the same grim curse. And the singing: why this song, exactly?

> *Pange, lingua, gloriosi*
> *Lauream certaminis*
> *Et super Crucis trophaeo*
> *Dic triumphum nobilem*
> *Qualiter Redemptor orbis*
> *Immolatus vicerit . . .*[1]

Now the pain was boring in his nerves like a twisting knife, he was hurled in and out of consciousness, hard fists were pummelling his aching body, his head banged against

[1] "Sing, my tongue, the glorious battle,
Sing the victor's crown of bay,
To the Cross, our noble trophy,
Here a fitting tribute pay,
Telling how the world's Redeemer,
Slain as victim, won the day."

293

the ground, he fell on hard rock and wet dirty pulp, he felt himself being sucked down, as though he would stick there for ever, and suddenly he was gripped in agony. If this evil power torturing him was really himself, should he then really be able to tear himself away, free himself? Oh, to be free, free! A loud noise resounded deep inside him, groaning he stretched himself up in an effort to raise himself out of all this lameness and debasement, he realized he was unable to, but slowly, nevertheless, his world changed and suddenly, through swirling fog, he was led away to. . . .

He saw a face. He was young and strong. His body belonged to him without pain. His movements were controlled, they were made without difficulty. Light-footed, he approached the face over springy grass, he could feel the sun on his back, he tried to peer into the face.

It was a woman's face, unmoving, steady-eyed. The eyes engrossed his attention: they had a look of both pain and peace. Peace flowed into him from the face. It had experienced everything, it had looked into the heart of all that was most horrible, every kind of pain had afflicted this woman, this mother, yet she was only a spectator. He saw faint quiverings in the lovely face, he saw how the mouth closed to suppress the agony she felt. But the look—there superhuman certainty; what calm peace there was in it! He fell on his knees and stared with wide-open eyes until the tears came into them and he couldn't see properly at all.

It was Katharina, and yet it was not Katharina. He tried, despite his tears, to look, but couldn't. He seemed to glimpse, as though veiled in swirling mist, another face, well known to him but long since vanished: a pale, frank, trusting face that had once been very close to him. He had seen it once in the darkened atmosphere of a cinema. He had seen it on its deathbed. He couldn't see who it was, but he knew that it was his wife, she who was dead. Chaste, refreshing, he felt the familiar coolness coming out of the mist towards him. He couldn't hear the caressing sound of the horn, even though he listened with his inner ear to catch it, but he knew that it was there, faintly echoing. He had been lifted up out of the wet vapour into a region of purity and coolness. He had been away a long time, had wanted to be away, had turned away from all that, and nevertheless was at home here: it was here that he belonged, here that he wanted to be. Was it really too late? Had he bound himself? Was he really free? He had indeed been able to move, he had gone hither and thither over feathery grasses, with a swinging gait, light and free. . . .

The mist thickened, the face had become very faint, he was unable to make his way forward and get nearer to it: the cone of light that came to help him from time to time had been sucked up by the thickening fog. He sank back, it drew him down into the depths, he felt the faint remaining strength dwindle from his limbs, soon he would be sucked back again into the wet element of deliquescence, under the mouldy cupola, the wet vault. . . .

He was gripped by great anguish. Now for the first time he really knew what misery meant. Everything he had learned before was like an idyll, like peace, like undeserved happiness, compared with this present horror. He had slipped away from the only thing that was reality and truth. He was lost. He had seen the truth and heard it, and nevertheless squandered his strength and so was now unable to hold on to it. He felt his mouth opening in a rattling, abasing shriek, a savage, horrible cry of terror which rang out over the wet swarming ground, and drowned itself in slime and dirt. No one could hear him. He was already far away from the grass and the face.

Oh, high, pure chastity! Oh, deep peace in the midst of pain! He realized that all the millions of people he had seen fleetingly in the distance were gazing at this countenance and at what it signified.

A hairy arm was raised, he saw the wet sweaty hair under the armpit and the scar of a sword wound in the muscles: with a resounding sound it drove the nail in. Again the arm was raised, now he saw the executioner's face, it was not cruel and not joyful, simply calm, professional—again the arm beat down and the hammer drove the nail deeper. He saw several strong hairy arms rise and again the hammer-blows descended upon the twitching noble limbs. He was lying right by this tortured body, yet the blows never fell on him. He didn't dare to raise his eyes from his position of humiliation, he didn't dare endure the sight of that assaulted dignity, and yet he knew that close by him the unendurable was taking place: he who had been noble and pure had fallen into the hands of thieves, he who could have destroyed the world and all its inhabitants was lying there, not defending himself. From an infinite distance he heard the echo of the blows, like the sound of a sea of pain and misery.

Again the face was there before him. At each blow of the hammer its mouth twitched. He saw that it was his wife Dagny but at the same time someone else: it was the Mother of God, pure, young, standing there watching her Son's martyrdom along with all the others.

Oh, this unfreedom! Oh, if only he could be bound like that!

Now it was his own arm flying up and down in a murderous hammer-blow. But he didn't want to! Never had he imagined that it would come to this, that he would be doing the beating, without knowing that he was striking these nails! He tried with all his might to hold his arm back—he couldn't manage it, he felt the pure eyes resting upon him, he knew that what he was doing was hellish, as hard as he could he tried but could not prevent the hammer from coming down again and striking, striking. . . .

Something broke, the faces vanished, he sank down and unconsciousness enveloped him, out of the slowly biting new onset of pain new tortures came on. . . .

He looked up. The room was bright and sunny. On the stand at the foot of his bed vases filled with flowers were arranged round the crucifix. He saw the sister nod:

"A happy Easter," she said.

Her smile was like a caress. She went softly to the door. From behind her emerged Lebrun.

"Welcome!" he said.

Kansdorf blinked. Welcome?

"Yes, welcome! You've been a long way away, as a matter of fact. Now you feel better, eh?"

Yes, he had been a long way away. He looked round the room. He raised his hand, but let it drop back on to the bed.

Lebrun had got up and now, after a careful look in the direction of the door, came nearer to him.

"You've had a bad time, my dear fellow," he said gently. "I've been sitting here all through yesterday and last night. It wasn't easy to deaden the pain."

He bent over his friend.

"I think the time has come now to—help you seriously," he said.

Kansdorf looked into the faithful-dog eyes set in the broad face.

His smile turned to a grimace.

He tried to speak, but his tongue would not do what he wanted it to do. He tried again, with the same result.

"You mustn't say anything," said Lebrun. "All you need do is to close your eyes to mean yes and shake your head to say no. Do you understand?"

Kansdorf closed his eyes and kept them closed.

He felt Lebrun bending close over him.

"Do you want me to—help you over?" he asked.

Help him over? Where to?

Kansdorf looked into himself, where the glow still flickered and the mouldy cupola might still fold over him. There was nothing he could be helped over to! Lebrun believed in an extinction, a state of calm peace. What did he know about it? There was an eternal horror, a gnawing anguish. And there was a clear peaceful light.

He looked up and moved his head from side to side.

He saw Lebrun go red.

"Do you mean that you don't *want* me to?" he said gently. "Don't you wish for—*any* help?"

Kansdorf again slowly shook his head.

Lebrun's mouth shut.

"As you wish," he said. "It's for *you* to decide. If you change your mind, let me know. I shall stay with you until the end."

He sat down on his chair again. Kansdorf looked up at the crucifix. The sun had thrown a shimmering oblong through the window onto the cold wall: it lit up one of the vases of flowers but did not reach the cross.

"Mors et vita duello conflixere mirando: dux vitae mortuus regnat vivus,"[1] he said softly and was amazed that he could speak.

He heard—inside him, or actually—the singing of the monks, the muted rejoicing, joy mingling with sadness and melancholy. He felt himself exalted by the power of the singing; suddenly he said, in a low but clear voice:

"No, dear friend. I have been running away from suffering all my life and let others suffer for me. Now the time has come for me to take my own share of it."

[1] "Death with life contended: combat strangely ended! Life's own **Champion**, slain, yet lives to reign."

He felt the swinging arm, which was his own, sink down, as though jerked back. At last! Now he would no longer go on torturing the pure One whom he loved.

He closed his eyes and was back again in Our Lady's chapel in Senlis cathedral, where it was tender and young and virginal and smelling of flowers. He was looking up hungrily at the face of the young Madonna. He recognized it again. He knew that the warning horn-sounds, the still, gentle coolness, the deep peace—everything that had stroked softly again and again over his temples and moved his senses —was the result of a power that came from her. He hadn't much time left. But he knew that he was being given a last chance. This time he would not fail.

"Lebrun," he said, "I know you understand me. Not with your ordinary day-to-day understanding. But deep inside yourself. I don't want to—harm myself any more. I don't want to run away. I want to pay the price. It is only a small one, anyway. It isn't enough. But what I have I want to give."

Lebrun nodded. He could see that his friend was wandering. He had suspected it. As long as he was clear-headed he could make sensible decisions. Now he was befogged and besides that he was under the influence of the monks. But while Lebrun's brain went on working as it always did, forming these thoughts, he saw behind them the bent figure of a boy, a short neck, black hair. He saw Louis kneeling by the side of the monk, and realized that he no longer felt angry or deceived but rather a sort of envy, an unreasoning longing. His own son, his own blood—the self-same substance as himself! And still this mystery had an irresistible fascination for him. What kind of a secret was it, that no one could ultimately resist?

He got up again and leaned over his friend; he noticed that his voice was hoarse with emotion as he said:

"Just be calm. You must do what you think right. If I can't help you, then I can't."

Crude words, mere helplessness. He had seen many people die, he had often bent over death and peered into its depths —without seeing anything.

He saw Kansdorf open his eyes and look at the crucifix.

Again this figure of the Crucified One, whose secret he could never fathom, but whose power over human beings he had so often had to acknowledge. Why did he have to stand outside, when even his own son could bend the knee?

Kansdorf's lips moved.

"The face," he said. "The face. . . ."

Lebrun bent over him. Could he see anything, or nothing? His eyes looked glassy, it was impossible to say whether he was looking outwards or inwards. The face? What face?

He looked inquiringly at his friend, and saw to his surprise that over the damp forehead, over the eyes and mouth, a smile of peace and joy lay, so faintly inscribed that it was hard to see, but still real, indubitable. Kansdorf could see something with his inner eye; he was in contact with a mystery.

Lebrun got up, and stood for a moment without moving. He heard the monks' singing coming from the chapel and went slowly to the window. The garden was bathed in sunshine, a faint breeze was blowing, the spring wafted its scent towards him.

Victimae paschali laudes immolent Christiani.
Agnus redemit oves: Christus innocens Patri
reconciliavit peccatores.[1]

[1] "To the paschal Victim, Christians, bring
Your sacrifice of praise:
The Lamb redeems the sheep;
And Christ, the sinless one,
Hath to the Father reconciled sinners."

300

For a long time he stood unmoving. Then he went slowly back to the bed.

Kansdorf's eyes were closed. The oblong of light had reached the crucifix; the glass of a picture of Catherine of Siena threw its reflected light on the damp forehead. He lay like one dead. All the tensions were over: on his mouth, almost imperceptibly, played a smile.